SNOW CITY

G. A. Kathryns

Copyright © 2017 G. A. Kathryns
All rights reserved.

ISBN: 1542858070
ISBN 13: 9781542858076
Library of Congress Control Number: 2017901517
CreateSpace Independent Publishing Platform
North Charleston, South Carolina

Her name is Echo Japonica, and she lives in Snow City. But she was not always Echo, and she did not always live in Snow City. Somewhere else, she was *someone* else, and it was to Snow City that she fled in order to escape a place and a self that had at last become intolerable.

For Snow City is a dream — Echo's dream — of a better place, an idealized place, a place of both anonymity and fulfillment. It is, for Echo, a haven of peace, a refuge, a sanctuary.

But Snow City remains, nonetheless, a dream, and dreams, being such fragile things, can so easily shade into nightmare...

Also by G. A. Kathryns:

The Borders of Life
The Wire Strung Primer
The Lap Harp Primer

In memoriam
CAYLEE MARIE ANTHONY
9 August 2005 - 16 June 2008
We're leaving a light on for you.

And deepest thanks to Ayu, Nayuki, Makoto, and the whole gang.
Please leave a light on for me.

TABLE OF CONTENTS

Prologue	xi
Chapter One	1
Chapter Two	18
Chapter Three	32
Chapter Four	44
Chapter Five	60
Chapter Six	80
Chapter Seven	95
Chapter Eight	110
Chapter Nine	126
Chapter Ten	144
Chapter Eleven	162
Chapter Twelve	179
Chapter Thirteen	196
Chapter Fourteen	212
Chapter Fifteen	228
Chapter Sixteen	244
Epilogue	257

PROLOGUE

Sometimes one has to dream very hard to keep oneself sane. And that is what I did, hiding from the world — from the terror and the bombings and the deliberately engineered famines and droughts, from the withering shreds of civility and the surging outbursts of impersonal violence — groping blindly through my shadowy, nightmare-haunted fantasies until I came upon Snow City, my dream, my creation. And it was perfect: all bright and full of color, surrounded by pristine mountains, watered by a clear river, touched with the magic of kind people and the pure air I had always longed to breathe, unsullied by the filth and despair of my physical existence.

And as the days wore on and the horror and atrocity about me increased, I turned again and again to my fantasy world, seeking shelter, seeking respite, living secretly, within my heart, an alternate, fabricated life in my little bastion of sanity and perfection.

Until one morning, I awakened to discover that what had been the real world had turned into a kind of faded delirium, and that I — somehow graced with an impossible rebirth and a new identity — was now living in Snow City.

In it.

CHAPTER ONE

My name is Echo Japonica. Rather, I should say that *now* my name is Echo Japonica. I was someone else once, but I try not to remember that, and I do my best to convince myself that I have always lived here in Snow City.

Despite its name, Snow City is not always snowy, and though winter does indeed muffle its streets and buildings and the surrounding countryside with a silent, white blanket, spring arrives with a spreading wash of cherry blossoms along the boulevards and in the parks and among the dark pines of the encircling mountains, the variegated colors as clear and immediate as if delineated by an artist's brush. In turn, just before summer and its inevitable heat, comes the rainy season, when drops as warm and heavy as ripened plums patter down of an afternoon and evening and Snow City sprouts a mushrooming rainbow of umbrellas, bobbing and weaving amid a dappling of mirror-bright puddles. Autumn is garbed in a palette of russets, reds, browns, and golds as the city swirls with leaves and color just before the air turns nippy and the first, tentative flakes of white appear.

But at present the snows have long departed, and it is in fact the rainy season, an evening shower drumming heavily against my apartment window, turning the city lights outside into prismatic starbursts, my breath fogging the cool glass as I stare into the darkness. The blurred forms of automobiles pass by in the street below, and rhythmical plashing marks the rapid tread of pedestrians hurrying toward shelter in a city that is, in truth, my own shelter, my own haven: a particle of heaven spawned from my dreams, shaped from love and fantasy and all the idealism I could cobble together in a world gone mad.

"I am Echo," I murmur, struggling to convince myself that wakefulness and a return to the unspeakable is not minutes — or the next shriek of incendiary munitions — away. "All those...other things...are behind me. I am here. I am Echo now."

Echo...*now*. Here...*now*. But now presupposes *then*, and my meditations force upon me the reality of my position: I myself am a stranger in this world. I have come here from another, more violent place, and have given myself a name and an identity and an occupation and a place to live, unconsciously tipping in a personal history and a background and even a stray relative or two. But I cannot shake my intimate knowledge of...before, and therefore at times like this, with the late-night rain at the window and the cars and people outside passing by without cognizance of me or my gaze, the fear that such knowledge makes of me a kind of infectious blight that could all too easily mar the perfection of what I have made confirms me in my determination to remain apart and unobtrusive, to allow Snow City to live its own life with its own mix of human relationships, happenstances, misunderstandings, and even, yes, occasional tragedies...but tragedies that here, in Snow City, bring not continued sorrow and regret, but rather understanding and acceptance.

Hence: Echo Japonica. Thirty-five. Unmarried. Living alone in self-imposed quarantine. Staring through a rainy window at a little piece of heaven. Unwilling ever to fully participate in the paradise that surrounds her.

But if my qualms bar me from quitting my lonely existence, the stark contrast between my life now and my life then allows me to take comfort from the mere knowledge that this place remains utterly divorced from the world of horror from which I have come. There: starving children, battered women, sad, gray men foraging for scraps amid the rubble and broken concrete of collapsed buildings. Here: shining streets, bright colors, charmingly polite schoolgirls and their stalwart male counterparts, husbands and wives who love one another, good men and good women. And running beneath it all, a trust and faith that there is nothing in the world that can or will hurt anyone.

Look, therefore, Echo, but do not touch.

And I do look. And, admittedly, I look often, and with a kind of desperation, as though filling my eyes with what is *now* can somehow cleanse my memories and perhaps even my soul of what was *then*. So, come the day, with the lonely night behind me and the more optimistic afternoon before me, I am, as is my frequent custom, outside. Sometimes I walk, wandering the streets, suppressing only with effort my instinctive urge to gape at the beauty of even the simplest things — lampposts, asphalt streets, brick storefronts, a child's blue ball — and sometimes I merely sit and watch, for even days like this, with the sky overcast and the raindrops falling warm and heavy, can be considered the purest bliss.

I am in fact sitting on a bench at a little pedestrian mall near my apartment, looking at the people, the bright shops, the reflections of the gray sky and the occasional, opportunistic rainbow in the stretches of puddle and water-glazed pavement. The rain patters down. My umbrella keeps most of the wet off, but my blouse and skirt — white and blue: favorite colors — are heavy with the humidity, as is my waist-length blonde braid. No matter: beautiful day, beautiful town, beautiful world. As full of hope as a birthday promise.

And then I see the girl.

All amber hair and big green eyes, she occupies a bench just on the other side of the broad brick walkway, well clear of the ornamental planters and landscaping that run down the center strip. Has she been there all along, then? Strange I did not notice her before. Yet there she sits, clad in a strangely out-of-season overcoat and snow boots and, curiously enough (for this is a school day), equipped with neither backpack nor book bag.

And, even more curious: school, at this hour, is in session. So why is she — anomalous dress or not — here at the mall, apparently waiting, with folded hands and downcast eyes, for someone or something?

The rain falls. Passersby, intent on their errands, step into shops, step out of shops, juggle packages, chat with one another, laugh...and take no notice of the solitary schoolgirl sitting on the bench. Alone. Waiting.

And not even, I realize, possessed of an umbrella.

Sitting. Waiting. In the rain.

Plainly, this will not do, and I forsake for the moment my self-imposed exile. Standing, then, crossing to the girl: "Begging the young lady's pardon, but might she consider sharing an umbrella while she waits?"

She lifts those enormous green eyes to me, and for an instant I wonder whether they might contain a hint of tears. But though there may be tears, there is no comprehension: my habitual, stilted turns of phrase have as usual rendered me unintelligible.

I force my tongue into something that borders on the colloquial. "Might you like to share an umbrella?"

"Umbrella?" She blinks at me. "But...why?"

"Because..." I am, for the moment, flummoxed. The answer seems so obvious. She has been sitting here for how long and she has not noticed the veritable dousing she is receiving from the cloudy sky? "...because it is...ah...raining."

She stares at me as though I am deranged. "Raining?"
"Raining. Indeed. Quite a lot of rain, in fact."
"Oh." Her big eyes lift skyward. "It *is* raining, isn't it?"

I am certainly being too forward. But I am an adult, and she is a child. And here in Snow City that presupposes an ironclad covenant of protection and help. For this child — fifteen or sixteen by the look of her, teetering on the brink of high school (or perhaps toppling well over into it) — to be left out in the rain is unconscionable.

"But...but..." She blinks at me. "I'm sorry: what time is it?"

I do not have to check my watch: the clock tower just visible over the roofs of the shops struck the half hour not so long ago. "I might be so bold as to estimate that it is a little after three-thirty."

A palpable start. "Three-thirty? OMG...school will be letting out. I have to go. I really have to go. Thanks for the offer, ma'am, but I've got to run."

School is out, and *now* she has to run?

She stands, gives me a hint of a smile, and then she is off, hair flying, unseasonable coat flapping, equally unseasonable boots splashing through the puddles.

Rain. Falling. Above: a sky painted with pillowy gray clouds.

Strange girl. Strange clothes for a summer's warm and rainy beginning. A strange sense both of time and of responsibility if she thinks she has to run to school *after* school is over. But it finally dawns on me that there was something about her even stranger than that.

She must have been sitting on that bench, in the rain, without an umbrella, for ten, fifteen, perhaps twenty minutes. Maybe even longer. But she was perfectly dry. No damp clothes. No lank hair.

Not a drop of water on her.

I watch the girl pelt away through the rain, splashing heedlessly and yet somehow remaining dry, and for some reason my thoughts beckon me toward an absurd compulsion to follow her, to find out who she is and why she runs to school with such urgency...*after* school. But I cannot follow her. Look, but do not touch. And so the girl pursues her life of unseasonable clothing, cryptic, after-school meetings, and the seeming ability to dodge raindrops...just as I now must pursue mine.

"Mine" is a pedestrian enough affair. Come evenings, five nights a week, I play guitar at a late-night coffee shop called the Blue Rose, performing a mixture of classical and pop interspersed with a bit of folk and, occasionally, some outright improvisation: an eclectic program that suits the equally eclectic tastes of my audience.

I therefore spend the latter part of the afternoon in my apartment, checking the strings of my instrument, tuning, practicing. When I finish, I have time for a shower and a light meal and then, after changing into appropriate clothing — somber black dress, stockings, pumps — I am off, gig bag slung on my shoulder and instrument case in hand, descending the apartment building's outside stairs and making for the nearby bus stop through the humid and darkening evening.

But for some reason I cannot stop thinking about the girl.

The bus pauses, picks me up, and rolls onward, tires hissing on wet asphalt. The rain has stopped for now, but the lamps and neon of passing shops and stores turn the still-puddled street into an incandescent river. Standing, one arm lapped round a pole and the neck of my guitar case, the other clutching my gig bag to my side, I contemplate the view out the windows as the quiet of my apartment recedes into the past and the bustle of the coffee shop approaches from the future. My life. My strange life. And I myself — an outsider, a sojourner among the residents of Snow City — travel, like anyone else, toward my job.

So why am I still thinking about the girl?

Is it because there was a sense of the uncanny about her, sitting there as she was, as though waiting, as though lost in some inner dream, heedless of the rain, dry in spite of it, roused from whatever inner vision possessed her only by the words of an umbrella-proffering stranger? Uncanny, yes...perhaps even impossible.

For some unknown reason I find in that thought the germ of worry and concern.

But why? Why worry? Why concern? Here in Snow City, I myself, a ghost from another world flitting through the reality of what I still find myself half-believing is a prolonged dream, am nothing more and nothing less than uncanny. In fact, an impossibility. Why, then, should I be disturbed by another impossibility?

Outside the bus windows, the lights pass, the streetlights come and go. Passengers board and depart: they belong here. This is their city, their world, and I but watch, look, observe...all as though from a distance. But though my thoughts of the girl and what she might mean dog me as I descend to the pavement at my stop, I find that the skies have cleared, and the fresh breeze that comes down from the mountains does much to dispel my darker meditations. It *is* a beautiful world, and I look forward to a reassuringly ordinary night of playing music.

I make my way along the damp sidewalks, weaving through groups of passersby headed to or coming from the movies and the theaters until I reach the coffee shop. It is already open for business, already serving patrons, and waits for the evening's entertainment I bring; but upon reaching the wide, double doors, I hesitate, not because the posters flanking the entrance with the legend *NOW APPEARING* display photographs of the slim woman with large blue eyes and a blonde braid whose physical form I have, over the last three months, learned with difficulty to identify as myself, but because of the name of the coffee shop itself.

The Blue Rose. The legendary flower of utter impossibility.

How marvelously fitting. How exquisitely ironic. But, shrugging myself out of my thoughts, I free a hand and, putting my weight into a tug on the handle of the heavy door, I step back straight into what feels like a cinder block wall. Except that it is most certainly not a wall.

"Oh, dear! A thousand pardons, I beg you!" I say instinctively.

The reply rumbles like barrels rolling down a ramp. "No prob, mama."

And when I turn around to elaborate on my apology, I find myself confronting an unnervingly well-built, ebony-skinned individual in baggy pants and a black hoodie. And sunglasses. Midnight black sunglasses.

He is indeed immense. And his iron-pumped, steroid-buffed body and black on black tattoos are dredging up memories of another world. One I would just as soon forget.

"You the guitar player?" he asks.

"Ah...yes. I have that undeserved honor, sir."

His eyes drop to the case in my hand. "Playing tonight?"

"Ah...ah...ah..." I at last get my mouth under some semblance of control. "Y-yes."

"Good." A black limousine is parked at the curb behind him, and he opens the driver's door and slides behind the wheel, his last words drifting to me from out of the dim interior: "Later, mama."

⁃※⁃

I am still rather off balance from the exchange when I enter the coffee shop. Behind me, the double doors swing to, and Luigi — owner's son and head barista — hails me from the counter with a melodious (and very artificial) Italian lilt: "*Buona sera*, Auntie Echo!"

Auntie Echo. Luigi is young, handsome, bright, witty...and, unfortunately, knows it. Though we are in no way related, he has taken it into his head to call me "Auntie Echo" as though I am some kind of spinster. He finds it funny. I find it annoying. But it is nothing more than a tease, and he has a good heart, so I am tolerant. "Good evening, Luigi," I return. "Is your father here?"

He adds a Mediterranean wave of his hand to his lilt: "Not yet. Very soon, I'm sure."

"Well, then..." I say with an uneasy glance at the front doors, "...I have a few minutes before I start, so if I may be allowed to trouble you for a cup of coffee, I would be very grateful."

"Anything for my gracious and talented Auntie Echo! Your pleasure, madam? Espresso? Latte? American dishwater?"

In the matter of coffee, it is quite obvious where Luigi's sympathies lie.

"Ah...American dishwater will be fine. It is my full intention to *play* my guitar, not reduce it to splinters."

"American dishwater coming right up!"

Luigi, to be sure, is not his real name. He was actually christened *Jake*. But upon assuming his position at the Blue Rose, he decided that so domestic an appellation was not at all proper for a barista, and therefore, when presiding at the counter, he is *Luigi*: dapper, debonair, exotic, but nonetheless (beneath it all) quite definitely Chicago Irish. And given his propensity to twig me with "Auntie Echo", I am frequently nearly overpowered by the desire to twig him right back...if I could ever think of anything appropriate to say. But even should fortune favor me with an unusually brilliant retort, I believe I would refrain from uttering it. I am not here to participate. I simply want to live, to exist within the tranquil sanity of Snow City.

But as though on cue, that thought jerks my memory back first to the figure in front of the coffee shop — hoodie, dark glasses... and, now that I think about it, the inferred presence of a concealed Glock — and then to the girl at the pedestrian mall. The girl sitting alone in the rain.

The hint of tears. The sense of waiting.

Waiting for what? Friends? But surely her friends would be at school, would they not?

What is happening in my world?

"Auntie Echo is thoughtful tonight," says Luigi, setting the coffee mug in front of me.

American though it might be, the coffee — hot, black, and strong — is hardly dishwater, and it steadies my thoughts. The girl was alone, certainly. But that does not mean that she has been abandoned. How could she be? This is, after all, Snow City.

Are these emotions and concerns I am feeling, therefore, perhaps merely a projection of my self-imposed solitude upon an ordinary schoolgirl who more than likely has a multitude of friends, a loving family, and a joyful life to which to look forward? Contrast that with my own existence...

...which I find I am reluctant to do.

"Auntie Echo? Hello? Earth to Auntie Echo!"

"Luigi," I say after another sip, "I have always perceived you to be outgoing and popular, and graced with a superabundance of good looks" —

"Oh, please!" He is all but blushing.

— "and therefore among the fair sex you doubtless find many individuals who display toward you a more than passing romantic interest."

Luigi looks blank. He is used to my language, but there are limits.

"Many girlfriends," I translate.

Blushes turn to a prideful flush. "Well...yes, of course!"

"Do you..." I lean forward confidentially. "...happen to have the acquaintance of a girl who frequents the pedestrian mall near the center of town? One who might appear to the casual observer to be at times a little strange? Odd, in fact?"

He stares at me. Then, "Oh! Yes..." Again the lilt, but I do not catch the gleam in his eye until it is too late.

"Really?"

"Yes, yes," he continues, slipping again into his Italian lilt. "She is indeed a little strange. Very peculiar in fact. Oh, yes, I know her well. She plays guitar at the Blue Rose five nights a week."

Having worried about the girl at the mall and the man in the limousine, been ridiculed and abashed by Luigi, and finished my coffee, I stow my gig bag in the back office I use for breaks, uncase and tune my guitar, and, re-entering the main room, take the chair on the small, raised stage.

As usual, the lack of anything more than indirect light all but precludes an adequate performance. I have occasional — perhaps I should say *frequent* — discussions regarding this matter with the owner of the shop. He thinks that a dim room provides just the sort of intimate atmosphere best suited to a late-night coffee shop. And, yes, candlelight flickers warmly on the tops of the neatly arranged tables, and from the shadows come whispered conversations and the murmur of lovers' confidences. To a certain extent, therefore, I agree. But I am also of the considered opinion that I should be able to see my guitar strings. Hence, the discussions. But the owner is, after all, the owner, and I therefore must defer to his wishes, though I often wonder whether I should begin to include the use of a blindfold during my practice sessions at my apartment.

But tonight I am reasonably sure that I can tell the difference between the fifth and the seventh frets, even on a classical guitar, so I fit the instrument to my body, spend a minute tuning, and sigh tolerantly as Luigi, with mock helpfulness, appears with a small stand and a lit candle. "Break a leg, Auntie," he smiles as he positions the light.

He leaves. The customers are waiting. I put my hands to the strings and launch into an easy minuet, simple to play, just the thing to limber my fingers.

My preference is to divide my evening's performance into three long sets. During this first, since the customers are mostly university students, business people, and workers, all of whom want — now that the day's classes, meetings, and labors are over — nothing more than an hour's relaxation, a cup of something hot, and perhaps a bite of something sweet, I confine myself to light pieces, mostly transcriptions of minor Renaissance lute compositions interlarded with trivialities by such Mozartian-era guitar composers as Carulli and Giuliani. Junk, perhaps, but enjoyable junk: gratifying and comfortable for both their ears and my hands.

The music flows, and as my fingers wander the strings, my thoughts are, for better or worse, free to wander back to the girl at the mall and the man in front of the coffee shop. Both seem to be anomalies in my otherwise perfect world...which, along with myself, brings (I realize with a start that almost causes me to fumble a ridiculously simple C major arpeggio) the total to *three*.

I pull myself together in time to devote my attention to the intricacies of the Fernando Sor study I customarily save for the end of the set, and then rise to acknowledge the round of polite applause that spatters up from what seems the Stygian darkness beyond the range of Luigi's now-guttering candle.

Without the music, the coffee shop falls into a gentle quiet, disturbed only by the patrons' murmured conversations, the tender whisper of the occasional stolen kiss, and the muted clink of cups and spoons. Serenity reigns. The air is filled with the aroma of coffee, steamed milk, and baked goods. At the far end of the counter, Luigi is chatting with a particularly attractive young woman while he makes a latte, and I notice that Mr. O'Dally, the owner of the shop, has arrived and is standing by the front door.

A little fat, a little balding, incessantly cheerful, he is the epitome of a shop proprietor, and as far as he knows, I have been playing guitar at the Blue Rose for years, something that I find quite unnerving, particularly when he reminisces about the time I first came to the shop and nervously inquired about a position.

I do not remember that time. I was not *here* at that time.

Regardless, he likes what I play, and he wanders over to me, softly clapping his pudgy hands. "Hot stuff, Echo. Just great."

I smile and bob my head. "Thank you. I shall continue to strive to meet your expectations."

"But...man-oh-man," he goes on, "I gotta tell ya: outside, in front of the store, there's the biggest guy I've ever seen. My God, he makes me think of a concrete telephone booth. A big *black* concrete telephone booth."

My man with the black limousine. *"Later, mama,"* he said.

"In fact," Mr. O'Dally continues, "just about *all* of them are like that."

"Ah...*all*...of them?"

"Yeah, all of 'em! Five or six at least. Scared me half to death. Not doing anything, though. Quiet as mice. Just lounging around. But..." He spreads his arms. "...*big.*"

Not only is the man still outside, but he has apparently acquired friends. Instinctively, I glance to the front windows. There they are, their manner and garb fairly screaming: *gangbangers.*

Mr. O'Dally grins at me. "Boyfriends, Echo?"

"Ah...ah...ah...well, actually...no."

"So how come you're blushing?" Laughing, Mr. O'Dally wanders off to help Luigi with the customers, leaving me to fumble my way to the back room for my break.

He...the big man...spoke to me. He asked me about my performance. There is no doubt that he and his compatriots are here because of *me*.

Twenty minutes later, I have gotten myself under reasonable control and am ready to face my next set: more complicated, livelier music now, a blend of pop, jazz, and even rock arrangements designed for a clientele that has shifted away from exhausted students and workers and toward individuals and couples from nearby bars and theaters, seeking less fluff and more verve in their musical entertainment.

The...gentlemen...continue to loiter in front of the store. I can see them through the windows when, between pieces, I glance up from my instrument, and I notice that Luigi and his father are anxiously following my gaze. And when, at the conclusion of my set, the concrete telephone booth casually swings open the heavy wooden doors as though they are made of cardboard and steps into the room with his companions, I all but flee to the comparative (but possibly illusory) safety of the back office. My world: ideals and love and fantasy.

And I am being stalked by gangsters?

I am still shaking when Luigi enters quietly with a cup of green tea. "Drink tea, Auntie," he says. "You certainly don't need more coffee right now."

I accept the cup gratefully, and he gives my head an affectionate pat as he leaves. Young he might be, and at times something of a smart-aleck, but for the moment he is more like a big brother, and when comes time for my third set, my hands are steady.

Once more I take the stage, attempting to ignore the hulking knot of muscle that hovers near the front door and refuses all tentative offers of service.

Latte? Muffin? Cappuccino?

The reply: stony silence.

Nonetheless, Luigi gives me a heartening wink and a thumbs up, and I nod my gratitude and turn my attention to my audience, which has once more undergone considerable alteration. Here now are the true night owls: deep thinkers, chess players, men and women of a philosophical bent who want music conducive to their natures. For them, I have reserved the soothing, evanescent profundities of Dowland and the sustained intricacies of Bach. But before I can begin, the front door has opened again, and I find myself holding my breath. More gangbangers? A rival faction? Are Glocks and throwdowns on tonight's program?

Yet the man who enters, sturdily but not excessively built and on the young side of middle age, carries himself with an air of authority. Yes, dark glasses again, but in this case they are accompanied by a gray suit and a gray tie of the finest cut and tailoring. His jewelry is sparse but genuine, his demeanor muted, and toward him the cluster of hulking shapes is quite obviously deferential. For an instant, his gaze swings in my direction, and though I cannot see his eyes, I feel as though a razor has just hissed past my face.

A nod to his companions, and he takes a table at the rear of the room where the shadows are darker and only the gleam of candlelight on his dark glasses betrays his presence. The others, standing, take their places around him. There is no doubt at all who is the boss. Or rather, the Boss: the capital letter might as well be emblazoned on his forehead.

And they are all waiting.

Luigi looks at his father. His father looks at Luigi. Finally, they both look at me, and I can see Mr. O'Dally mouth silently: "For God's sake, *play!*"

I play, turning immediately to Dowland. And even though the eyes of something I cannot fathom are fastened on me like twin lasers, I find shelter and protection in the music of the great lutanist, the gentle polyphony wrapping itself about me like a protective cloak. I feel the ordinary customers settle into their thoughts and their discussions and their silent battles amid the black-and-white jungles of their chessboards, and, yes, I can still sense the presence of the watchers who have materialized out of a decidedly more urban wilderness; but, rocked gently in Dowland's arms as I am, my nervousness fades, my fingers glide through the patterns laid down by the master four centuries ago, and I find I can face that presence with a certain equanimity.

Long do I linger with Dowland, but it is my custom to finish the night with Bach. Unlike his Elizabethan predecessor, the master of the Baroque does not invite so much as command, does not shelter so much as defy. Rather than enfolding and comforting, the great polyphonist sweeps the spirit up and carries it from one corner of the universe to the other, from the celestial to the fathomless depths and back again, and it is in his great "Chaconne in D minor", from the Second Partita for Solo Violin, that I have always found the most perfect expression of his spirit.

Dowland therefore bows and stands politely aside for his august colleague, and Bach takes his place beside me, eyes flashing, hand on my shoulder; and from the first chords of the piece — block harmonies butting one another aside like storm clouds portending a tempest, laying down the harmonic structure that will form the foundation and bedrock of the immense composition — I am afraid of nothing.

I bend to my music, coaxing my fingers into the complexities of the piece. The block chords shift to an angular sequence of two- and three-part polyphony, rapid-fire thirty-second and sixty-fourth note runs segue into shifting arpeggios, minor gives way to major, which in turn yields to minor. In the big room, the discussions and chess playing have stopped. The chaconne dominates all.

Finally, nearly a quarter of an hour later: a blinding burst of frenzied notes carefully shaped and controlled by the composer's genius, a restatement of the original chordal structures — magnificent, brawny, all but swaggering — and the chaconne is finished, the strings of my guitar vibrating their way into silence.

A long moment, and then the shop breathes again. The applause comes, and the chess and the discussions resume.

Instinctively, I glance toward the back of the room.

The Boss is still at his table, all but lost in obscurity. But I can see that his hands are to his face, and that his shoulders are shaking. It is unbelievable, impossible, and at first I stare, dumbfounded...but understanding at last forces itself upon me.

He is weeping.

CHAPTER TWO

Night.
Deep night. Well past midnight. I am in bed in my apartment, lying with unclosed eyes. Outside, rain patters down, but a stray shaft of moonlight, having found somewhere a rift in the clouds, slants through my window. Sleep has not come, and is, I sense, not coming anytime soon. Instead, I am thinking — cannot help but be thinking — of the people who, all unlooked for, entered my life yesterday. The girl at the pedestrian mall. And, at the coffee shop, the Boss.

The Boss. Who wept, freely and openly, like a little boy who had been beaten.

My performance finished, I could only watch from the stage as his burly associates helped him up and, with an almost maternal solicitude, guided him to the front doors. Shocked, stunned, I did not move — nor did Mr. O'Dally and Luigi — as the hulking shapes ushered their master out to the street and into the waiting limousine.

I suppose it was always my assumption that in some small way my guitar playing would add to the happiness of Snow City, providing, as the occasion might require, relaxation, cheer, or an environment conducive to thoughtful contemplation. Tears, though? I had not considered it, certainly never looked for it. Yet tears I have brought forth. And I can console myself only with the thought that there are tears of joy as well as of sadness, and I must believe that even in a perfect world that has somehow been intruded upon by the existence of gangsters, the former will in the end prove more prevalent than the latter.

Tears.

The girl at the mall, sitting alone and unnoticed. Tears in her eyes as well.

And of what kind were those?

Outside, the rain. This late, in the dark hours just before dawn, the traffic has fallen silent: for the most part, Snow City sleeps, and the only sound is the rain.

And then from the street outside: footsteps.

Running.

Drawn by instinct and intuition, I rise and go to the window. Outside, broken moonlight glimmers on rippling puddles. The city lights, stretching off and away toward the foothills of the encircling mountains, gleam and sparkle through veils of mist and precipitation.

And then I see her.

Amber hair flying, green eyes staring fixedly ahead as though into some unknown future, she races into view from around a dark turning and, like some vagrant night moth, flutters and blunders along the rain-swept street, seemingly searching for something, yet blind to its existence...or even the possibility of its existence.

The girl from the mall.

I stand, frozen, and by the time I can bring myself to move, she is lost in the night-shrouded distance. Once more I find myself gripped by the insane urge to follow her.

This time, however, I yield to it.

No time for anything else: I throw a bathrobe over my pajamas and explode out of my apartment door onto the landing. The treads of the outdoor stairway are cold and damp under my bare feet as I race down to the sidewalk, and already I am searching the empty street for a sign of her passage, listening for a fading echo of footsteps.

Nothing. Only the continuing patter of the rain. But I saw which way she went, and so I run, bareheaded and barefoot, scanning the street and sidewalks ahead of me as earnestly as she herself stared while she searched for...something.

But she has vanished.

The night grows ever later and dawn approaches as I pass empty crossings, vacant turnings, dark neighborhoods with darker houses...and now I am in a section of town I do not know, one compassed with alien storefronts and populated by shadows. The wind, chilled by the falling rain, brings a touch as of ice to my skin, and I find myself lost in Snow City, lost just as that girl is lost.

Waiting and lost. Crying and lost.

"What..." I stop at last, obscure buildings and indecipherable signs all about me. "...what is happening to my world?"

The wind whips at my sodden robe, and I shiver. And now, eyes closed, trembling with cold and fatigue both, I find myself kneeling on the pavement, head bowed, wondering what nightmares I have brought to my fantasy world. I cannot know for sure, but I fear the worst, and the cold, the pelting rain, and the frigid wind only add to my desolation.

Behind me, then: headlights. Headlights...and the deep thrumming of a big engine. A car door opens and closes, and a heavy tread of footsteps approaches.

"Hey, guitar mama," comes a rumbling voice. "What you doin' out here? You can't be kneeling in the rain. You gonna make yourself sick. What part of town you grow up in, woman?"

The gangster from the limousine. The first one. The *big* one. Without asking, he lifts me as though I were a child and carries me to the waiting car, setting me on my feet one-handed and without apparent strain as he opens the back door.

"You get yourself in there now."

"I..." From within, I catch a whiff not only of warmth, but of expensive leather and plush carpet as well. "...I am sopping wet!"

"Don't worry about it, girl. You think the Boss gonna care about a little water? Get in there now. I run you home."

Cold and distress have thoroughly addled my head. "I...I...I assure you, sir: my passing manifestations of derangement are nothing with which you need concern yourself!"

"Say what?" He pauses for a moment to sort out my Byzantine language. Finally: "Don't worry about it. You crazy, I crazy, we all crazy. The Boss...he not crazy, but anything happen to you, mama, he gonna be plenty *mad* is what he gonna be. Now get inside and warm up."

Meekly, I do as I am told. The man climbs behind the wheel, and as the limousine eases forward, he calls casually back to me through the open partition. "Towels and blankets back there. Use 'em. Get yourself bundled up: don't you be gettin' me in trouble with the Boss."

The rain streaks the windows. The tires hiss along the pavement and splash through the puddles. The windshield wipers beat out a squeaky ostinato. With a stunning lack of success, I try to keep myself from thinking about my present circumstances.

I cannot help but wonder that I am still alive.

"What you doin' out here in the rain, anyway?" comes the rumble from the driver's seat.

My concern — obsession, perhaps — forces its way through my fears and doubts. "Honored sir..." My lips are still chilled, my words an almost indistinct mumble. "...do you happen to have any acquaintance with or knowledge of a girl who sits out in the pedestrian mall near the center of town? Just sits? In the rain?"

His few moments of silent thought seem to rumble just as deeply as the words that follow. "I think I seen her every now and then," he says. "She showed up maybe three, four months ago. Can't say for sure."

In the dark passenger compartment, I settle back among the blankets and towels, trying not to think.

"Which is kinda funny," the big man continues, "because the Boss, he know everybody and everything going on in this town. An' what he know, I usually know. But we don't know about her." He half turns, casts a glance back at me. "G-shot."

It takes me a moment to understand. "Echo Japonica," I reply. "An honor to meet you, Mr. G-shot. Thank you very much for taking care of me."

"Oh, that ain't no problem. An' in any case, you best be thankin' the Boss. And don't you be givin' me no misters, either. It's just G-shot. Stands for *grapeshot*. The Boss be reading history novels 'bout sea battles when he give me that name."

"If you will kindly forgive me for saying so, grapeshot sounds perhaps a little violent."

He drives casually, one hand on the wheel, head and shoulders eased back in the seat. I cannot but feel that he should be smoking: long drags on an unfiltered cigarette. But perhaps I have simply seen too many movies of the wrong sort.

Too many movies...*there.*

"It fit me, mama," he says as we pull up in front of my apartment building. "Believe me, it fit real good."

He escorts me to my door, favors me with a comradely nod, and departs, thumping heavily down the stairs. And somehow, despite being caught firmly between shivering and fear, I manage to fall asleep in my bed, awakening late in the morning with the sun pouring in through my bedroom window and Snow City, when I at last look, appearing...very normal. Too normal for it to contain such things as gangsters or immense men named after an antique and particularly vicious form of cannon projectile.

But it was real. Altogether *too* real. And I shower, dress, and go out into the city in an effort to reassure myself that this town, with its peaceful life and happy, humane relationships, has indeed escaped the harsh encroachments of my memories.

I find nothing out of the ordinary. The shops and stores are all the same. The passersby — shopping, chatting, strolling hand in hand — are much as I have seen them before. And I, standing in the early summer rain with my umbrella, with my blouse and skirt, with my blonde braid, am on the verge of convincing myself that what I experienced last night has, *must* have, a more plausible and less ominous explanation...

...when I see her again.

Sitting on the bench at the mall, the rain falling all around her, her eyes large and green, her hair the color of fine amber. Her hands are folded in her lap, and she is waiting.

Hair, coat, jeans, boots...all dry.

I glance at the clock tower just as it chimes half past three.

She stands up...and then she is off, making her way at a quick walk along the patterned brickwork pavement. And I am following her, weaving among the puddles and the shoppers, tilting my umbrella this way and that to avoid tangling with the other umbrellas that drift singly and in waves across my path, keeping my eyes on that head of amber hair, so distinct even under such a cloudy sky, even were it not as dry as if a desert wind were ruffling through it.

School...

Given her age and the location of the nearby high school, I am reasonably sure I know where she is going. And indeed her steps take her in that direction. But in contrast to what I assumed would be increasing enthusiasm at the prospect of seeing friends and classmates, her manner evinces a growing sense of despondency, and rather than approaching the school building itself, she stops, half hidden, in an alleyway across the street, all but invisible in the muted light and haze of rain.

I halt some distance away as the teenage students begin to trickle out of the school doors and toward the street, the parking lot, and the nearby bus stop. Uncertain of what to do, I dither helplessly for a moment, then come to my senses and step under the shelter of a nearby shop awning, furling my umbrella and attempting to look somewhat less than obvious. Perhaps a casual observer will assume that I am somebody's mother.

A curious thought, indeed!

But my eyes are on the girl. She stands there, hands clasped, staring earnestly at the double doors now wide open and disgorging a flood of young people in a confused swirl of coats, hats, umbrellas, high-fives, waves, backslaps, and a hundred humming conversations. But not so confused that I cannot see the uneasy glances that dart across the street toward the alleyway, glances that look, perceive...and are quickly averted.

And I am not so distant that I cannot see the despair in the features of the girl in the alleyway. She is looking for recognition. She is looking for acknowledgement and acceptance. And she is finding only denial.

Friends? Joyful life? I feared that I was projecting my own emotions on the girl. It seems, however, that I have not been projecting at all, but rather recognizing in her a kindred spirit.

But what of her family?

As though in answer to my half-thought question, a girl, perhaps in her second year, steps out of the school's doors. By accident or by design, she has lagged behind the other students, and therefore she is for the moment isolated, standing alone at the top of the short flight of steps leading down to the walkway. But even at this distance, I can see the resemblance: brown eyes, brown hair, taller, but decidedly family.

In the alley, frantic hope. In front of the school, a prolonged, agonized stare, and then a furtive, almost guilty, turning away. The older sister (I cannot but think of her as such) descends the steps and hurries off, eyes averted, to lose herself among the other students.

I look back to the alleyway. She is gone.

She is gone, perhaps, but *he* comes again that night, arriving late in the evening, just before the start of my third set.

Tonight, however, there is no accompanying entourage of massed manflesh: the Boss arrives — conservatively, almost demurely — with only G-shot at his side, and once more takes a table at the back of the room: an obvious and considerate effort to avoid disturbing the other patrons. And as I begin my first Dowland piece — *Farewell* (one of the deepest of the great lutanist's compositions) — it occurs to me that, in their dealings with me and with the shop and the public in general, the Boss and his associates have invariably behaved with a remarkable degree of restraint and courtesy. G-shot carried me to the limousine with all the tenderness of a woman taking her first grandchild to the baptismal font, and though I sense the Boss's intense gaze, I detect in it not the faintest trace of threat.

As before, I play: Dowland, then Bach. As before, I end with the chaconne. As before...the Boss weeps.

But his tears tonight are at once more controlled and more easeful. He weeps, true, but whatever pain so afflicts him appears to have sublimed into a kind of quiet acceptance, and if his shoulders shake with emotion, it is with the sense of a heartache soothed with a balm the nature of which I cannot fathom.

Nor am I particularly surprised to find, after I have packed up for the night, that when I push out through the front doors to the street, the limousine is waiting at the curb and G-shot is standing beside it.

"If you please, ma'am," he says carefully, as though he has been coached in the precise manner of offering the invitation, "the Boss would like a word with you."

There is nothing to do but acquiesce. G-shot opens the rear door of the limousine and carefully, as though handling the relics of a saint, relieves me of my instrument case and gig bag, laying them reverently in the trunk as, with some trepidation, I enter the vehicle.

Inside is the familiar warmth, the leather and carpet, the tinted windows that veil the already dark night. And on the other side of the wide seat sits the gray-clad figure of the Boss, his eyes invisible behind his sunglasses.

"Ms. Japonica," he says as I settle in. "Very nice to meet you at last, even though I feel as though I already know you somewhat. Through your music." A slight inclination of his head by way of introduction: "Maxwell."

He does not specify whether he has given me a first or last name, though I receive the strong impression that he is most often addressed simply as *Boss*. I take refuge, therefore, in my convoluted language. "I am undeservedly honored, sir, and I might be so bold as to add that a notable someone once observed that an appreciative audience is, to a musician, worth a hundredfold its weight in rubies."

Actually, I remember no such observation at all, the reference actually being (I suddenly recall with a blush mercifully hidden in the darkness) a reference to women skilled in an interesting manipulation of a sexual nature. But the nonsense I have spouted gives me a moment to compose myself, which at this point I badly need.

G-shot slides in behind the wheel and closes his door. "Don't worry about it, Boss," he says through the open glass partition, "I can't make out what she be sayin' half the time, either."

"It's a compliment, G," returns the Boss. He touches the button that closes the partition, and just before it seals, adds simply: "Drive."

The limousine pulls away from the curb. Streetlights and store lights pass by, muted by the dark windows. Sound, too, is muted: I can barely hear the thrum of the engine, the hiss of tires on the pavement, the passing cars. The Boss and I might well be suspended in obscurity, far away from Snow City, far away from anything.

The soft glow of an interior light allows me to see him, and despite his eyes being rendered unreadable by his dark glasses, I know he is currently examining me as carefully as I am examining him. In his case, however, the action is more than likely superfluous: I am all but certain that he plumbed me down to my emotional bedrock the moment he stepped into the Blue Rose.

But perhaps not *all* the way down to bedrock. He cannot possibly know that Snow City and its world are a fabrication. *My* fabrication.

"How long have you been playing the guitar, Ms. Japonica?" he finally asks.

"Most of my life, sir," I reply, which is quite true...as far as it goes. Most of my life *here* — in fact, *all* of my life here, all three months of it — I have played the guitar.

"You're quite talented."

"I fear my talents could be, at best, described as adequate."

"And you've always played only at the Blue Rose."

Now I am on uncertain ground. To my knowledge, I have indeed played only at the coffee shop. But that knowledge, scraped together from what documentation I could find in my apartment during my frantic first days of conscious, waking life in this world, is, at best, incomplete. So: "The Blue Rose has treated me well," I say, evading the direct answer.

"Have you ever thought of playing elsewhere?"

I stare for a moment. Then, "Ah...why...no. I confess I have not." The absolute truth. The Blue Rose, Mr. O'Dally, Luigi, my audience: the environments, the situations, and the people surrounding me have all existed in a timeless permanence that up until yesterday rendered Snow City unchangeable; a stasis whose veritable demolition by such unexpected anomalies as the Boss and the girl at the mall has left me reeling.

In response to my words, the Boss's demeanor changes. From genial to intent. From casual to focused. Not predatory. Not threatening. The panther (for so he seems to me) has merely ceased napping and has lifted his head to take notice of an unusual butterfly.

He leans toward me. "*Would* you consider another position?"

A passing shower drums briefly on the roof of the car. "I should be very sorry to leave Mr. O'Dally at a disadvantage, sir," I tell him. "He has taken very good care of me, and my performances at the Blue Rose have been my only source of income for..." The circumlocution dies on my lips, and I hastily abandon it. "I should not wish to slight him or show ingratitude for his many kindnesses."

"Fair enough." The Boss shifts back in his seat. "Maybe I should say...*supplementing* with another position. One night a week. With..." For a moment, he hums tunelessly to himself. "...more than adequate compensation."

More than adequate? Every musician likes to hear such words, but: "One night...in addition to the five I already play at the Blue Rose? Six nights total then? Oh, dear, I am not at all sure." Not at all sure, indeed: for I have found that five consecutive nights of performance frequently leave me shaking and exhausted for the first part of my two days off.

"Well, all right...I can make it easier on you." The Boss's skin is almost as dark as that of the ebony G-shot, but his voice possesses not a hint of ghetto accent or slang. In his plain but elegant suit, he seems quite the gentleman. A rough-hewn, rather raffish gentleman, perhaps, but a gentleman nonetheless. "How about, maybe, one set, one evening a week," he continues. "You'd be the featured artist, of course. If you're up to it, you could play that extra set after your gig at the Blue Rose. Or you could put aside a separate night for it. Night, mind you: the club isn't open during the day."

"Ah...club?"

"Nightclub. *My* nightclub. It's on the other side of town. And I'll warn you: it's no Blue Rose. The clientele isn't anything like what you're used to."

"Oh?"

"Well...they're not interested in chessboards, for one thing." His tone leaves no doubt whatsoever that a lack of interest in chessboards is the least of the differences to be encountered.

"Um..." I am on very uncertain ground here. "I am not altogether sure that such an audience would be receptive to my repertoire."

"You sell yourself short, Ms. Japonica," he says, lounging back. "You play pop and jazz as well as classical. My troops gave me a full report. So you show up at my club, and you play a little pop and a little jazz, and..." Intent again. More than intent. "...and the chaconne."

"The chaconne?"

"*Particularly* the chaconne." His voice turns dry, businesslike. "You don't play the chaconne, I don't pay you."

"Why the chaconne, sir?" The question is, I realize too late, highly impertinent, considering that the piece reduces him to tears.

If he takes offense, he does not show it. "One of these days, I just might tell you, Ms. Japonica, but not now. You don't have to decide right away, of course. Like I said, my club would be a big change for you. And then there's your situation at the Blue Rose, though if it comes down to brass tacks, I could possibly make some kind of accommodation with Mr. O'Dally."

Accommodation? With G-shot and the other "troops" hulking in the vicinity, Mr. O'Dally could, I have no doubt, be convinced to accommodate himself into ritual disembowelment.

The Boss speaks as though having divined my thoughts. "Ms. Japonica, I think that maybe you've got some kind of misunderstanding about me. I don't — repeat, *do not* — hurt people...unless they deserve it. My team is a service organization, not a bunch of undisciplined thugs."

I cannot protest. Thugs and hurting people were most certainly *not* the furthest things from my mind, and an involuntary glance at the Boss's hands reveals scars and callused knuckles that cannot possibly have their origins in any kind of ordinary manual labor.

"Anyway..." He is at his ease again, the panther laying his immense head back on its paws, allowing the brightly colored insect to flutter along unmolested. "Give it some thought. You might enjoy a little..." A hint of a smile. "...broadening of your horizons."

"It...does give the impression of offering a rather different experience."

"Very different. But you never know: you might like it." He extracts a card from his pocket and puts it in my hand. "Take your time. You can reach me at that number. It goes straight through to my cell, no questions asked. And in general..." His voice deepens both in tone and in seriousness. "...you need anything, no matter what, you call me. Understand?"

"Ah...y-yes..." Floundering, even outright frightened, I again wrap myself in formality. "...sir. I am deeply honored by your trust and generosity."

"Just give my proposal some thought, please. And...I'll be around." With that, he touches the partition button, and the glass drops an inch or two. "Let's run this lady home, G. She looks like she's had enough for one night."

CHAPTER THREE

The Boss is perfectly correct: I have indeed had enough for one night (more than enough, in fact, for any number of nights), and after entering my apartment and safely stowing my guitar and my gig bag, I subsequently spend a half hour in the bathroom... throwing up. Then, after a hot bath and another half hour huddled and shaking under a blanket, I manage to choke down a cup of warm milk in the hope that it will settle my nerves enough for sleep.

I hope in vain: my bed proves no refuge, its sheets but the raw material for chaotic knotwork as I, terribly, terribly awake, squirm and contort myself, alternately hysterical, frightened, dismayed, and outright horrified.

What are these people doing in my world?

A bad enough thought with which to wrestle in the wee hours, but there is a worse one not far behind:

What do these people want with me ?

Well, the chaconne, for one thing. But even that knowledge offers little consolation, for:

Why the chaconne, *of all things?*

At last, exhausted equally by waking labors and nocturnal struggles, I give up on sleep, untangle myself from the sad wreck of my bedclothes, and go to the window. The night has turned cloudless, and the moonlight cools my cheek and washes the scene beyond the glass with a quiet radiance, touching it with the pristine grace that is a visible reminder of what, from the first, I wanted Snow City to be, and what (I fervently hope) it yet can be in spite of all that has happened in the last two days.

And as though that light and its concomitant grace falls not only upon the outer world but upon my inner turmoil as well, I am reminded of the rough kindness and unexpected gentleness of G-shot. And of the respect tendered to me by the Boss. And more: *A service organization*, the Boss termed himself and his colleagues (I, for the moment at least, determinedly leaving aside the matter of hurting people when they deserve it); and his offer of supplemental employment smacked not at all of the loutish or the intimidating: it was a request, no more. Even now, I have no doubt that, should I decline his offer, I will hear nothing more of it...though I am equally sure that from now on, come performance nights, my last set will find him at a back table in the Blue Rose, listening to the chaconne, his eyes misting for whatever reason he has chosen not to tell me.

Gangsters here can weep. They can ask rather than demand. They can respect rather than order.

Good thoughts, all — or at least a rationalization sufficiently plausible to allow me to sleep — and I return to my bed. And dreams of my current world (unfortunately unremembered) and nightmares of my former world (mercifully forgotten) finally take me and grant me repose until just before noon the next day.

Shopping to do. Errands to run. Save in passing, there is no time for sightseeing, which I regret extremely. Perhaps Snow City's underworld (if such it be) is indeed made of more humane stuff than I might expect...but, then again, perhaps I only want to think of it that way. A few hours of leisure at the mall or in the park would do much to reassure me, but I have a life here in Snow City, and therefore I must attend to the mundane business of day-to-day existence. After that, it will be time to prepare for the evening's performance.

And he *will* be there. I know it.

I purchase groceries, deposit checks at the bank, receive a trim from my hairdresser (who remains steadfastly obdurate in her prejudice against waist-length braids on women in their 30s), and at last stop in at the music store near the mall to replenish my store of guitar strings.

"Savarez yellow-card?" asks the shopkeeper, who knows full well what the answer will be.

I nod. "If you please, Mr. Anthony."

Zachary Anthony, as dry and gray as Mr. O'Dally is flush and corpulent, shakes his head. "Extra-hard tension's going to take a toll on those hands of yours someday, Echo. Are you sure you don't want to back off to red-card?"

"Very sure, and without the least reservation." I smile. The shop, wood floored, old and brown as an owl, with a brick facade and tall, streaked windows providing a double helping of sunlight, is full of guitars, accordions, violins...all manner of instruments, their gear and tackle and trim, and Mr. Anthony peers at me through half-moon glasses, shaking his head amusedly as I rattle on in my horribly convoluted speech. "I am obliged to confess that, doubtless owing to my astonishing lack of technique, I cannot coax a reasonable sound out of my instrument with anything less than high tension."

He turns to the shelves. "That's a Ramirez you play, isn't it?"

I laugh. "I indeed wish it were so. But alas, I must be content with a Kohno. Perhaps not so august a pedigree, but a sweet sound, and the instrument is most tolerant of my inadequacies."

"A Kohno's a fine instrument. Masaru-sensei's work is second to none, and his son's carrying on the tradition in fine style." He pokes among the shelves, pulls a box toward himself. "Three sets, as usual?"

"Three, indeed. My monthly budget will hardly stand for more, I fear."

Three sets in hand, he turns to the register, an old fashioned brass contrivance with oversized keys and scrollwork that would not be out of place amid the works of a Victorian clock tower. "Well, three sets is plenty: one for playing, one for spares, and one just in case. If you took to buying them by the gross, they'd just get stale on the shelf, and I wouldn't see my favorite customer for months at a time."

I would blush at his words, but a glimpse of a familiar black limousine cruising along the street in front of the shop has seized my attention as forcefully as if someone had taken hold of my nose and turned my head.

"Echo?"

"Ah...yes...yes..." I have completely lost the train of the conversation. "You are doubtless right, Mr. Anthony."

He rings up the sale. "I'm always right, Echo. You know that. So listen to me: that Kohno of yours is a wonderful instrument, but a player of your caliber really deserves to have a Ramirez *1a* in her hands."

I manage as wry a grin as I will allow this strange and idealized version of myself. "Which the kind gentleman would, of course, be happy to sell me."

"Oh, I'd have to special order it, and depending on backorders and whether you wanted Brazilian or Indian rosewood and such, it might take a while to get here." He makes change, hands me money and strings. "But, mind you..." A wink. "...my motives are always entirely altruistic."

The afternoon's clouds have been steadily building, and by the time I step back out onto the sidewalk, a light rain is falling...one that will, I know, soon turn heavy. I open the umbrella that until then has been hanging uselessly on my arm and start toward the bus stop, parcels in hand and the precious strings tucked into my purse. A Ramirez, I reflect, would indeed be nice. But in order to beat my Kohno at its own game, it would definitely have to be *Clase 1a* — fine woods, crisp timbre, the potential for a multitude of tonal nuances — nothing less. And *that* I cannot afford. Indeed, though Mr. O'Dally pays me well enough, I will never be able to afford such a thing on the income I receive from the Blue Rose.

The thought comes idly and unbidden: what if I played at the Boss's nightclub? *More than adequate compensation*, he said.

I give my head such a violent shake that several passersby turn their heads in my direction as though concerned that they are witnessing the onset of some kind of fit. I manage to dispel my passing fancy before anyone calls for an ambulance, however, and continue on, chagrined at what I can only perceive as weakness. Taking money under such circumstances! And...such disloyalty to my Kohno! My Kohno, which has been such an unswerving companion and confidante, allowing me to earn a living, comforting me during the first confusing days and weeks of living in a dream made real, and even (my thoughts running on in spite of my best efforts) bringing me into contact with...

...such interesting people.

With such interesting offers.

Defeated once again in my efforts to control my wayward musings, I pause on my way to the bus and plunk myself down on a bench at the pedestrian mall, heedless of the wet that soaks my skirt.

A gangster.

And yet he wept.

And he seemed so nice.

It is some minutes before I finally lift my eyes. Straight into *hers.*

She is staring in my direction, but she does not see me. Lost in her inner world, she does not appear to notice much of anything. But she is sitting in her accustomed place, on her bench, in the pouring rain.

Completely dry.

The clock tower strikes the half hour. She rises and runs. I, sitting alone on my own bench, my bags and umbrella falling unnoticed into the puddles, bow my head, my hands pressed to my face.

⊱❦⊰

In as much of a mental blank as I can muster, I prepare myself and my guitar for the evening's performance. All is as it always is, as it always has been throughout my time in Snow City. Inspect. Tune. Warm up. Practice. I note fret wear on the wound strings, but though there are new strings to be had, now is not the time to change them, for new strings will take a day or two to stretch out and hold their pitch, and I cannot be constantly retuning in the middle of a piece.

String replacement will be a task for a day off, then, and yes, Mr. Anthony is probably right: perhaps extra-hard tension will bring arthritis on a year or two early. But the yellow card Savarez allows the Kohno to sing brilliantly, and at any rate I intend to let old age take care of itself. At present, I am thirty-five, and I have other things on my mind. Music. Making a living. Existing in my idealized perfection.

Realizing that my idealized perfection contains blemishes of which I was not previously aware.

Practice. And more practice. My fingers flow into the intricacies of Dowland and Bach, and when, just before my Spartan dinner, I take a minute to check my e-mail, my fingers tap keys in half-conscious chordal patterns and bass lines as I respond to a missive from an uncle — Seymour — who is a minister at a small church in an equally small town in Montana. An uncle I have never met and to whom I cannot possibly be related because I simply did not exist in Snow City earlier than three months ago.

Or did I? Was there, perhaps, another Echo Japonica, one who lived happily and productively in this world — preexistent, not dreamed — before my consciousness somehow usurped her identity? Such thoughts and attendant qualms come to me upon occasion, reinforced, to be sure, by external evidence: income tax records dating back the requisite number of years, a driver's license renewed fourteen months ago, pay stubs dating back to my (or someone else's) first days at the Blue Rose along with a framed (first tip!) dollar bill I have no memory of receiving...letters, bills, documents of every sort that testify mutely to a life lived in Snow City for much longer than I can recollect.

Whose life have I stolen?

As I tap away, politely declining yet another invitation to spend a week or two in the guesthouse at Uncle Seymour's ranch — relax, take it easy, surely city life must wear on one after a while, so come smell the wildflowers and perhaps do a little horseback riding — I look up from the computer and catch a glimpse of myself in the mirror on the far wall. Big blue eyes. Blonde braid. I did not look even remotely like this...before. But...but who did? And where is she now?

My performance that night is adequate. I am a professional: I will have it no other way. But though Luigi and Mr. O'Dally obviously notice that I am withdrawn and cool, my thoughts shadowed, they do not press me for reasons. Nor do I lift my eyes from my strings as I play: even during the easiest and most trivial of my pieces, my head is bent over the neck of my instrument far more than necessary...for fear that I will espy that gray-clad figure sitting at a back table.

Only once in the course of the evening do I edge toward personal interaction, for after my second set, my curiosity and worry about my hypothetical predecessor at last get the better of me, and while allowing myself a cup of tea at the counter during my break, I turn to Luigi, who is wiping up the remains of a latte left by a clumsy customer.

"Luigi...I find I have a curious question that I am impelled to ask you."

He brightens: a break in the clouds over this gloomy musician's head? "I'm at your service, Auntie Echo."

"Did I..." I do not know where to start. "Was I...that is to say... was there anything..." I falter, unable to find the words. How does one ask something so seemingly idiotic?

Luigi considers me. He is young and intelligent and frequently flippant. But there is a place for flippancy, even in Snow City. "Just spit it out, Auntie."

With difficulty, I swallow the last of my tea. "I have been playing guitar at this coffee shop for years now, have I not?"

"Yes." The Mediterranean lilt. "Of course you have."

I press on despite my fears. "Did I by any chance start to act somewhat strange about...about three months ago? Somewhat different than before? Somewhat...one might say...weird?"

Luigi finishes mopping the latte, rinses the cloth abstractedly, and puts it aside. For a good minute, he looks serious, even thoughtful. Then: "It's a little hard to say, Auntie Echo. You've *always* acted a little weird."

I sigh. Of just such stuff are quandaries made. But I nonetheless thank him...and spend the last part of my break hiding in the back office.

And when I take the stage for the last set, the Boss is there, at his usual table, with G-shot.

Waiting for the chaconne.

I keep my mind on my music, but though I lose myself in Dowland, I nonetheless hope, in the back of my mind, that the old lutanist can once again work the softer, gentler magic of pre-Baroque polyphony, and can thereby soothe whatever demons conspire to bring such sorrowful tears to the man who hides so considerately in the shadows.

And perhaps the antique cadences do just that, for tonight my subsequent excursions into Bach bring intent listening from the gray figure, and as, finally, the last, trembling, double octave D of the chaconne fades away, the tears of the previous nights are supplanted by a deep sigh, as though — at least for a short while — a heavy burden has been set aside.

As I pack up in the back office, I half worry that I will be offered another ride home. But by the time I leave the building, the Boss and G-shot have discretely retired, and I take the bus back to my apartment in the company of genial but relatively uncommunicative strangers who merely nod when I board and then return their attentions to their books and their e-readers and their smartphones, favoring me with nothing more demanding than cordial smiles as I descend to the sidewalk at my stop.

For me, then, another sleepless night as the rain, returning with renewed vigor, patters down on the apartment building, splashing on my small balcony and streaking my bedroom window with mazy rivulets. Now heavy, now no more than a mist, its variations allow me to mark the progression of my white, insomniac hours, and toward dawn I begin to doze off.

And then I am awake, bolt upright in the darkness, listening. Hearing those footsteps. Approaching...receding.

Scrambling to the window, I catch a last glimpse of amber hair flicking around a distant corner, flashing palely in the glare of a streetlight surrounded by a halo of rain and mist.

My world has been invaded by my past. The mirror of my fantasies has cracked, turning distorted with unknown tears and darkling requests for music. But though over gangsters and their bosses I have no sway, the passage of the strange, amber-haired, green-eyed girl from the pedestrian mall gives me one small, perhaps trivial, opportunity to gather in the shreds and tatters that have begun to fray the edges of Snow City, to knit up what, admittedly, might in the end prove to be no more than a single sleeve before it ravels beyond all repair.

No headlong plunge down the stairs, therefore. No frantic rush along the street. No losing myself in the nocturnal turnings of the city and thereafter succumbing to irresponsible and senseless hysteria. Tonight I am deliberate, careful. I dress for the weather, methodically donning clothes, coat, and galoshes and equipping myself with an umbrella, and I descend the outside stairs step by step, all but certain I know where the girl is going; and though, yes, I am intruding — perhaps irresponsibly, perhaps unwarrantedly — into her life, I cannot but feel that I *must* intrude, if only to throw my weight into the pan of the scales opposite that which contains such things as limousines and gangbangers and G-shot's laconic *"It fit me, mama"*.

The night city is quiet. I step through the pooled radiance of streetlamps, pass by winking stoplights, and skirt the windows of shuttered shops until I reach the mall. She is not there. No, and she will not be there until the next afternoon, for such appears to be the pattern into which she has fallen. But I remember the look of hopeless longing on her face as she stood in the alleyway across from the high school, and I therefore continue, leaving the mall behind and making my way along streets and around turnings.

A last corner, and the school, veiled by rain, comes into view. I — the stranger, the intruder, the ghost — pace along the pavement, placing my steps with care: just enough noise to advertise my presence, not so much as to sound unduly alarming. And when I reach the mouth of the alley, I stop, eyes downcast.

"Good evening," I say. I do not have to see her. I know she is there. "My name is Echo Japonica."

"H-hello..." comes the uncertain reply. "Have you been following me?"

"I have not. But I knew where you would be."

"H-how?"

"I saw you here on a previous occasion." I do my best to keep my voice noncommittal. "You were standing in the rain in the daylight, and now you are standing in the rain in the night. It is not right that you be out alone in the dark and the wet. So I wonder..."

I risk a glance at her. Yes: in the rain and at night. But not a drop of water on her.

"...I wonder whether I might once again be so bold as to offer you the sharing of an umbrella."

Her voice drifts out of the dim alley like a distant hand groping through miles of mist. "Why?"

"Because you are a child."

The hot denial comes quickly. "I'm not a child!"

I nod, sighing. I should have expected it. "And I, for my part, find it difficult upon occasion to believe that I am an adult. But, leaving aside the question of our respective ages: share an umbrella with me, I pray, and I will see you home directly."

"I...I don't..."

I sense — no, I *know* — what she is about to say, and it frightens me. Has Snow City fallen so far? Frayed so terribly? Raveled so completely?

"...I...don't have a home."

Homeless, then? Horror follows horror. This should not — *cannot* — be happening here.

"I mean," the girl goes on, her words spilling forth in fits and starts, "I've got a home, and I've got a family. But they don't...they don't want me. They turned me out. They told me...they told me to go away and never come back."

I stare at her. Well-spoken, polite...vulnerable, perhaps, but with an edge of determination, she seems so unlikely a candidate

for abandonment that for the better part of a minute I can find no words with which to reply.
"What about friends?" I manage at last.
"They run away...now."
Which explains the scene I witnessed the other day: the students' uneasy expressions, the agonized guilt of the older sister.
I cannot let this happen. Unbidden, I step into the alley and, uninvited, shield the girl with my umbrella...which appears to be entirely superfluous: there is not a speck of water on her save for the tears trickling down her cheeks.
Has nobody spoken to her like this before, asked these questions, offered the slightest shred of help, of comfort?
What is happening?
"Child," I say, "regardless of your family, regardless of your friends" — We are face to face, almost touching. I have never allowed anyone else in Snow City such intimate proximity. I never dreamed that I would ever permit such a thing. — "you surely cannot be living on the street."
Anger flares...accompanied by a kind of vague shame. "Stop calling me a *child*. My name is Charity. I'm sixteen years old and I'm not a child!" And then: "And in any case, I'm..."
She looks away quickly.
"...I'm not living anywhere now. At least...not...not really *living*."
I stare at her.
"There was an accident," she says, the water falling all around and she dry in spite of it. "In January. A car. I was killed." She lifts those green eyes to me, and I see in them what I, concerned until now only with surface appearances and bare facts, did not see before: a window into unknown depths, into abysses of knowledge that lie beyond all dreams, all nightmares, all imaginings.
"I..." I stare, stupid and bewildered.
"Don't you see?" she demands. "I'm *dead*. I'm a *ghost*."
The tears take her then, and she begins to sob uncontrollably.

CHAPTER FOUR

A ghost living with a ghost.
That is what we have become, Charity and myself. Though I have, previously, clung to a detached, wraithlike existence on the borders of social intercourse, this is nonetheless my city and my world, and in them I am an adult, and Charity (despite her heated denials) is a child, and I cannot and will not allow her to wander the streets — without friends, without shelter, without family — while she, in effect, presses her hands futilely against the transparent but adamantine glass of mortality that separates her from all her loves and hopes.

I brought her to my apartment. There was no question about it, not a moment's hesitation. To the shelter of my umbrella I added an arm about her shoulders, and then from her I took her wandering and her flight, guiding her along the dark streets, steering her through the lights and past the silent shops, helping her unbelieving steps up the stairs, and swinging my door wide, allowing what warmth and comfort my spare accommodations might offer to reach out and embrace her.

"You're sure you want this?" she said at the threshold. "Even though —?"

"I have no doubt whatsoever," I replied. "Enter and be welcome. This is your home."

Green eyes turned my way, wide with disbelief. "I'm...I'm home?"

I nodded, a mist of rain drifting across the landing. "You are home indeed, Charity. Welcome home."

And at last she entered, the words *I'm home* a near-inaudible whisper on her lips.

What does one do with a child? Not hard. Shelter her. Feed her. So now Charity is at my small dinette table — I had to fetch a chair from the bedroom in order to provide seating for two — staring at the bowl of oatmeal and dried fruit I have put before her.

And at that moment I realize my potentially disastrous *faux pas*. Charity is a ghost.

I fumble with my words, trying to sidestep the overly formal phrasing that rises instinctively to my tongue. "Can you...are you able to...?"

She saves me the embarrassment with a cheerful nod. "I can eat. I don't have to, but I can. I've stolen a hot dog or two, so I know everything in that department works. It's just that I've..." She contemplates her bowl. "I've never had oatmeal made with soy milk before. Or with wheat germ and raisins and stuff."

I am still embarrassed. Before, I was concerned about projecting my inner demons upon the girl. Now I find I am doing the same with my dietary preferences. "I can make something else if you so desire," I say. "Soy milk provides a creamier texture, so I have found. And as for the wheat germ and the raisins..." I feel myself color. "My personal idea of comfort food, I fear. My apologies for inflicting it upon you."

To my relief, she shakes her head vehemently. "It looks delicious. And...I..."

The ache in my stomach twists like a knife. "You have not eaten in days have you?"

The rain cannot dampen her, but her tears can. "Months. Hotdogs, yeah, but not a real meal. Not since...then."

"Eat now, then," I say. "And then I put you to bed, and you sleep at home."

She picks up her spoon, but: "Why are you doing this?"

I can never tell her the real reason for my actions. Fortunately, however, there is another reason, one at once less frightening and easier to understand. "Because this is simply what people *do*," I tell her. "We take care of one another. Particularly —" But no: I will not again risk alienating her by stumbling into the "child" trap. "It is simply what is *done*."

"I wish..." For a moment, her eyes clench. "...I wish my parents knew that. I wish my friends at school knew that."

No more than an insignificant span of table separates us, but I will not leave her alone again. I drag my chair up beside her, and I guide her hand, dipping her spoon into her oatmeal and bringing it to her lips. "They are simply afraid," I say. "And in any case, now is not the time to worry about that. Come, now. Eat. There is always tomorrow."

At the first taste her eyes widen. "Maple syrup?"

I finally realize that the unfamiliar expression on my face is a smile. "Maple syrup," I confirm. "It is, in my opinion, far superior to the insipidity of common sugar."

She nods, and of her own accord scoops more of the cereal. "You're right," she mumbles through her second mouthful.

Finding herself at last in the company of one who will listen, she tells her story. She tells it slowly, between mouthfuls of the oatmeal she eagerly spoons into her mouth as though the simple fact of eating food at a table with another person is in itself a shelter from the irregularity of her continued existence.

There are long silences between her sentences. Sometimes between her words. I just listen.

"Things were pretty normal until it happened," she says. "No big family blow ups. No real problems. There was mom and dad. I was the younger daughter, Faith was my older sister. Still is, I guess. Though she probably doesn't want to think of it that way anymore."

I remember the girl at the school...and the turning away.

"It happened in January," she continues. "Faith was going to be taking the SAT right after the holidays. That, and she had a report she had to write for school." She lifts those green eyes, all full of knowledge the nature of which she herself may not suspect. "I mean, nobody in their right mind does homework over Christmas vacation, right? But...anyway...she and I'd both slacked off pretty good. But we shared chores at home, and it was her turn to go shopping. She was swamped with getting ready for the test and writing her report, so she asked me to trade. She'd cook dinner and I'd do the shopping.

"It was January, and it was cold. But we'd had a few warm days, and the snow had melted and then frozen up again. We all knew it was bad for traffic, but...well, I was crossing the street and I didn't even see the car that hit me. I just heard a sliding sound."

She hangs her head as though confessing a shameful secret.

"And then everything went black. Maybe if I'd been more careful, checked the signal twice and then made sure the traffic was really stopped...I don't know. Sometimes I feel so stupid about it."

Her shoulders tremble. I put a cautious hand on the one closest to me. "I cannot see that you are in any way to blame for what happened."

She does not seem to hear me. "Anyway, there I was in this big dark place, and I'm like, 'OMFG, I'm dead.' I think there was a light. I'm pretty sure of it. And, yeah, I've seen the TV shows:

47

you're supposed to go toward the light and all. And it's supposed to be all wonderful and warm and everything. But..." She stares at her bowl. "But...but I didn't want to go there." She lifts her gaze to me, and her eyes are frank, open...and immeasurably deep. "I didn't want to be dead. I wanted...well, it wasn't that I was afraid, or that being dead was a bad thing or anything like that. It was just that..." Her hand clenches her spoon. "I wanted to be with my family. I wanted to be with my friends. I wanted to go to school. I wanted to be normal, and just...just *be*. There I was in that big dark place, floating around, and I was feeling really, really cheated, because...because it just wasn't *right*. What's so great about being dead if everything you want is what you can't have? I didn't want warm, bright places. I wanted home. I wanted mom and dad. I wanted my sister. I wanted my friends."

She puts her spoon down, puts her face in her hands. "So I got mad. And I started yelling about...all that. That it wasn't fair. That everybody who had anything to do with whatever crazy system it is that makes up life and death was just plain freakin' *wrong*. And that they shouldn't beat up on people who just want a life." She lifts her head, blinks at me. "I used a lot of bad language."

"I confess I cannot blame you."

She picks up her spoon again and shoves oatmeal and fruit into her mouth. "Anyway," she mumbles, "I kept yelling that there was *no way* that I was going to the light, and that I wanted a ticket straight back to where I *belonged*, and that they could take their little nicey-nicey afterlife and shove it right up..."

She gives me a wry look. "You were my age once. You know how girls can be."

I nod, even though I have no idea.

"So, anyway...someone must have gotten tired of hearing me yelling. So..."

She sags, drops the spoon.

"So...?" I ask.

"So, I got what I wanted. Next thing I knew I was on the street corner, there was snow all over, and there wasn't a sign of the accident. I checked a newspaper and it was...like...a week later. I guess time goes different over there. Or else I was yelling for a really long time. I don't know which. But about then is when I realized that my heart wasn't beating, and that I felt kinda...thin and floaty. So I got scared, and I ran home, and that's...that's...that's..."

She slumps against me, crying.

"That's when it...when it got really bad. I went inside, and Faith took one look at me and ran like hell and locked herself in her room. I mean, I knew I was dead, so I checked the mirror, but I didn't look like a zombie or anything. There wasn't anything rotting. I looked pretty normal, in fact. Just like I did before the car hit me. Same clothes, and not a mark on me. Maybe a little pale, but nothing much. And then Faith must have called mom and dad on her cell, because they both came piling in so fast they nearly crashed their cars in the driveway. And when they saw me they were...like...way beyond freaked."

I must speak. I cannot help it. "They did not take you back?"

She straightens, mops her tears with her napkin. "Mom and dad are really conservative and real religious. They started yelling at me to get out of the house because they were sure I was some kind of devil." She shakes her head. "They weren't making a lot of sense, but it sounded like they'd decided that since heaven had obviously kicked me out, I had to be evil or something. It was like... getting hit with a baseball bat. I took off running." She finishes mopping and hangs her head. "So first I'm alive, and then I'm dead, and then I'm alive again...but not really. And I'm on the street."

"Your friends?"

"I went to their homes to see if I could...crash on the sofa or something. Same thing. *Night of the Living Dead.* In Technicolor and 3D." She tries to laugh, but she chokes. "So I just started wandering. Day after day. Week after week. I didn't pay much attention to time after a while. Mom and dad and Faith were a lost cause — I think Faith feels real guilty because I'd taken her place for shopping that day — but I tried to be at the school every day when it let out, hoping that someone would...well...give in and give me a place to stay. No dice. But I kept trying."

She goes back to her oatmeal. "The cold didn't bother me, the snow didn't stick, and I couldn't get wet, so staying outside wasn't really a problem. It just made me feel bad, like I'd lost everything. And It didn't take me too long to figure out that I didn't really have to eat, and that sleep was sort of optional, but I tried to sleep anyway, because sleeping made me feel like there was at least *something* normal in my life." She wrinkles her nose. "Or death. But it's hard to sleep when you feel...you just feel so empty."

"I understand."

"Do you? Really?"

I nod. "Yes. I understand very well. And, I pray you...let us leave it at that."

She manages a smile. "There's always tomorrow, right?"

"Always."

Her eyes: uncanny again. Fathomless. "So how come you're not running away from me?"

I give her a pat on the head (she winces in disgust) as I rise, and I begin to clear the dishes. "Because whether you are alive or dead, you still need someone to take care of you."

She frowns. "Are we back to that child stuff again?"

The matter-of-fact tone in my voice surprises even me. "No. But you are young, and you are still of school age, and you have friends to make once again and a family to reclaim. So you need help." I shrug. It is obvious, is it not?

Well...perhaps not.

"You won't turn me out?" There is a note of real fear in her voice. "Even though I'm dead?"

Hands full of dishes, I pause behind her chair. I have myself known too much rejection, have seen too many starving children, heard too many imploring voices for my words to be anything but the absolute truth: "Never, my dear Charity. Never. I would not think of it."

"*Why?*"

I could not even begin to explain it to her, and it occurs to me that, strange though her existence might be, it is no more strange than my own.

A ghost...living with a ghost.

And, later on, after I have tucked her into my bed and made up a futon for myself in the living room, as I lie dozing and wondering about what changes this strange living arrangement will bring to my existence, I hear the bedroom door open. In the faint light, I see Charity, and I hear her tread softly across the hardwood floor, and then she has slid under the comforter with me, cuddling against my side.

Her body is cool, its temperature no different from that of the room through which she passed. Life left her months ago, and this corporeal form she wears is, after all, no more than an illusion. She warms, though, taking her heat from me just as she took shelter and food, and then, after single sigh, she is off among her dreams, eyes closed, amber hair spilling along the pillow and whispering across my fingers.

For a few minutes, I wonder what dreams might come to the dead. Dreams of life, perhaps? And do the living, therefore, dream of death, wandering among the shades of past and present, mingling with those among whose company they will eventually be numbered? But finally, reminding myself of my own words — that there is always tomorrow — I, too, drift off, my arm wrapped protectively about her shoulders, my sleep mercifully dreamless.

Tomorrow does indeed come, and with it...

I open my eyes. The room is bright with sunlight. Charity is no longer at my side. But... "I am of the considered opinion," I say aloud, "that I smell...heaven."

"It's actually breakfast," Charity replies from the far side of the serving counter. Her hair is tied up, she has donned one of my threadbare aprons, and as something hisses and sizzles on the kitchen stove, she wields a spatula like a mace of office. "My family always said I was a pretty good cook. And you looked so peaceful there on the futon that I let you sleep."

The clock says noon — my usual rising time because of my musician's late schedule — but we sit down to a meal of bacon and eggs...neither of which I usually keep in the refrigerator.

"I hope you don't mind," Charity explains. "There really wasn't anything in the house. What have you been eating, anyway? Oatmeal and more oatmeal? I mean, it was good and everything, but you can't just live on oatmeal."

I tilt my head inquiringly as she adds a piece of toast to my plate. "You hope I do not mind...what?"

"I...uh..." Charity blushes. An unusual state of affairs for a ghost. I am, in fact, not sure how she manages it. "...raided your purse and went out early to shop. The change and receipt are on the counter. It really didn't come to all that much." Her eyes drop guiltily...but she *is* a good cook. The eggs are perfect, the bacon pure ambrosia, the toast a complement to both. And there is coffee: my new associate seems to have precisely intuited my preferences regarding what I like in my cup.

"As it happens, my plans for this day did include some shopping," I lie shamelessly, "which is why the cupboard was rather bare. And I trust that, henceforth, the two of us will find it well within our abilities to keep the larder adequately stocked."

The crisis has been successfully averted, but another, I realize, looms. My work at the Blue Rose has provided sparingly for my rent and board, with just enough left over for guitar strings and an occasional garment. But now, with two abiding under my roof, how will I manage to stretch the budget?

Again: time for that tomorrow. Today...

Well, today seems to call for even more expenditures. There will indeed be the question of grocery shopping, but:

"We need to purchase some appropriate clothing for you, Charity," I say as we wash dishes together. "You cannot go about in winter coat and snow boots indefinitely."

"They're all I have," she admits. "They're what I was wearing when I —"

"Shh. We shall not talk about that. You are here, and it is early summer, and you must have something reasonable. I confess, however, that I will more than likely prove an utter dunce when it comes to young fashion, and therefore I expect that you will be the one to choose. I beg you, however: as I am of a rather conservative bent, please do your best to refrain from anything too...too...uh..."

"Tarty?" It is the first honest, unabashed smile I have seen from her.

"That...would be the word, yes."

"Don't worry. I'm much more goth than tart." She catches herself. "OMG...that *sooo* fits now."

"I pray you, my dear: do not dwell on it."

But how often have I ever taken my own advice, what with my incessant brooding over my status in Snow City? I...a ghost. A stranger. Watching the life of this world go on outside my window. Sitting in the mall — watching again — not participating, hiding behind my guitar...

Charity dries the last plate. "Do you always talk so funny?"

My turn to blush. "I am afraid that it is my way."

She shakes her head, smiling. "It's kind of cute, really. Though I think a lot of people wind up not understanding you." Her words falter then, and she doffs her apron slowly. "Uh...how do you want me to call you?"

"In what way do you mean?"

"I mean...like *Ms. Japonica*, maybe, 'cause you said you're conservative. Or maybe something else?"

"I assure you, I am not so much the fuddy-duddy as to insist upon honorifics. Echo will do quite nicely, thank you."

She brightens. "Echo, then. And I'm Charity, of course. Charity Monthage. Call me Charity. And...and...and...well, like I said, I've got a big sister, but...she...she..."

She falters completely and presses the wadded-up apron to her eyes as her shoulders tremble. I kneel and put my arms about her, once again struck by the chill of her body. "We will reunite you with your elder sister eventually, my dear. I will in fact do my best to return your whole family to you. But for now, I pray you, think of me as your *other* big sister. We are together now, and together we will face the world."

Her face is still buried in the apron. "Big sister Echo?"

I smile. "Little sister Charity?"

"I'm still a ghost."

"I know. I am, too. In a way."

She shifts her face from the apron to my shoulder. "Thank you."

And so begins our strange life together. With oatmeal, and that first night spooned together in slumber, and breakfast, and later that morning...with Charity into my makeup before I am out of the shower. "Don't you have anything darker than brown in eyeliner, Echo?"

"No," I call to her from the bathroom. "For better or for worse, I am decidedly blonde. Black eyeliner would have the unfortunate consequence of making me look d—" I catch myself just in time. "Would make me look quite ghastly, I assure you. And have you come to filching my cosmetics?"

"All mine were at home. Or in my backpack, which I don't have. But I gotta wear *something*, or I'm gonna look...well..." I avoided the word, but she says it herself. "...dead."

I stick my head around the doorframe. "Your words earlier left me with the decided impression of an inclination towards goth."

Charity has my liner and mascara in hand, and she is frowning at the mirror in the bedroom. "Well, brown, then, I guess. Goth, yeah, but since I really am dead, I probably better not lean into it, huh?"

Though her own words cannot but hurt, she makes light of her condition, quite obviously determined to stare it down as best she can. What, then, to say in the face of such pain mixed so inextricably with such courage? I have no idea. I had not expected any of this. Will I prove, in the end, any better a parent than those who turned Charity away over the mere technicality that she has no heartbeat and that she breathes only out of habit?

I pray I will.

"Fix your face as best you can," I tell her simply. "We will find something more appropriate at the department store."

To my relief, Charity's tastes in clothing prove to be simple. Skirts, occasionally. Jeans and T-shirts, mostly. Running shoes and one good pair of heels. Unfortunately, all must possess at least a modicum of style and are therefore a bit more on the expensive side than I might wish, but between my checking account and running my credit cards up a little beyond what I find entirely comfortable, I foresee that I can manage.

Charity, though, intuits my mental calculations. "I'll go with just this and this and this," she says, selecting from her considerable pile a skirt, a blouse, and a single pair of jeans...and leaving everything else on the dressing room rack. "Will that be OK?"

I ponder her sudden resolution. "You seemed to be quite particular toward those black shorts." I am careful to leave out the adjective *expensive*.

"I think that...maybe...well...maybe I'm a little too pale for them," she says. Untruthfully. "But do you think you can swing some lip gloss, Echo?"

"I think lip gloss will be quite manageable. Something for your eyes, though?"

"Oh, I don't know..."

I lean down to her ear. "We must get you your own cosmetics," I whisper. "It does not do at all to share such things."

She grimaces wryly. "Right. I could get some terrible disease and die."

"Now, now...I will not have you abusing yourself. We can certainly afford some eye makeup. And then..." I check my watch. "And then I fear I must hie myself to my guitar and prepare for work tonight."

"You're a musician?" She all but bounces. "I saw the music and the guitar case and everything, but that's your *job*? Oh, that is so *cool*!"

"I perform at the Blue Rose come evenings," I explain, "but... um...I confess what I play might be considered rather sedate by your standards, though I do have a small repertoire of pop and jazz."

She grips me by the arms and stares up at me with those fathomless eyes. "I am absolutely, positively, freakin' sure that underneath that conservative exterior of yours is a real headbanger," she declares. Loudly.

The clerks, the customers: they are all staring.

I am crimson.

Charity looks around, sees the eyes fixed on us. "Don't worry," she assures everyone. "It's all right. I'm dead."

The staring stops. Instantly.

She tugs on my arm. "If you're sure you can swing this stuff, let's get out of here," she says. "And then you get ready for work, and I've got...a little errand I need to run."

Eyes. Fathomless, yes. Canny, very.
"What...may I ask —?"
"No you may not."
"Because I would not let you?"
Eyes hot, hands on hips. "You just try and stop me!"
"Oh, dear God."
"You're out of your depth, Echo. Just accept it."

She pulls me toward the cash register, then. "And in case I forget to tell you," she says, "you're the greatest. And I love you."

I fumble with my purse and wallet while the girl at the register stares at Charity. Does she...see? Does she...know? Does she...believe what Charity just announced to the entire store?

At least she is not screaming and running away.

"Charity," I say, instinctively trying to shield her from what might prove, in the end, to be future disappointment, "I appreciate your sentiments, but you must remember that, though I give you my most heartfelt promise that I will do my best by you, you nonetheless hardly know me."

"But, Echo..." The depth in Charity's eyes seems to go on forever. "...isn't that what love is all about?"

I am still pondering her words as I watch her lose herself among the other patrons in the shopping mall, already wearing her new pair of jeans and the blouse that — though it *is* a trifle tarty — I had not the heart to deny her. Off on the errand of which she will not speak.

I go back into the clothing store and buy the pair of black shorts.

Then, home. No message from Charity on the answering machine (and I realize that future budgets will, doubtless, have to provide for a cell phone). I put her new skirt and shorts in her bedroom (*Her* bedroom? How quickly I have been seduced!) and, with a sense of relief, turn to the comparative normalcy of my guitar, even though its touch and the pieces I practice put me inescapably in mind of the Boss and his discomfiting request.

And, yes, the Boss is at the Blue Rose that evening, sitting at his usual table — alone this time — arriving early, staying through all three of my sets, listening intently to my progression from trivialities to upbeat jazz and pop to the profundities of Dowland and Bach.

He leans forward so far during the chaconne that his chest is all but pressed against the tabletop.

It seems that, despite my initial resolve, I have by now become inextricably enmeshed in the affairs of Snow City. My days as a hermit, as a wandering ghost flitting at the fringes of the world I dreamed into existence, are over. Seduced, trapped, pent in a prison of relationships of my own free will, I am indeed, as Charity so aptly put it, out of my depth.

The apartment lights are on when I return, and a number of freshly washed dishes in the drainer and the faint odor of cooked hamburger tell me that my girl returned some hours before. The bedroom door — closed — indicates that she has retired, and so I settle my instrument and gig bag in their usual places and prepare to sit down with a cup of tea, intending to watch a few minutes of a movie until I can contemplate repose. I am, however, diverted from my course by the discovery of several plastic bags of clothing, shoes, and cosmetics set beside the sofa. Curious, I poke carefully among folded pants, skirts, blouses, T-shirts, and assorted shoes, underwear, and makeup... all of which appear to belong to a much younger woman than I.

The conundrum resolves itself when I find a note on the counter beside a backpack containing high-school textbooks. Judging from its numerous revisions and crossed out words, it is the rough draft of a fair copy left somewhere else. And the location of that somewhere else becomes quite clear to me as, munching thoughtfully on the sandwich left in the refrigerator for me by ghostly but affectionate hands, I read the words:

Faith,

Thanks for keeping my stuff safe. I'm sorry it's not working out between us. I understand. I love you anyway, and I don't blame you at all for what happened.

I've got a place to stay now, so don't worry about me wandering around at night, but I need some clothes and stuff, because the lady I'm with isn't made of money, if you know what I mean.

I'll be around if you ever want to talk. Take care, and if you can manage it without giving them a heart attack, please tell mom and dad that I still love them, too.

Hugz,
CHARITY

And, down at the bottom of the page, printed in big, block capitals:
YES, ECHO, I BROKE INTO THE HOUSE AND GOT MY STUFF.

I am still laughing quietly at her outrageous spunk when the bedroom door opens. Charity is standing there in pajamas.

"Was it OK?" she asks. "To do that, I mean."

"I suppose so. It is, after all, your home."

She shakes her head. "It's not my home. Not anymore. Not since they turned me out. This is my home here. As long as that's all right with you."

I meet her eyes. "Perfectly all right. And I am quite glad of it. And..." I nod toward the fragment of bread and meat still in my hand. "...thank you for the sandwich."

"No prob. Thanks for the clothes and...and..." She blushes again. "...and especially the shorts. They're totally awesome. But I..." She looks away. "I get lonely and scared when I'm by myself. I guess I spent too long...out there."

Her gaze turns back to me.

"So can I sleep with you again tonight?"

I set down my empty cup. "Surely."

CHAPTER FIVE

"I'm sorry, Ms. Japonica, but I can't violate municipal and state regulations. Charity Monthage is deceased, and is therefore ineligible to attend classes. And in any case, since you have no family or legal connection to her, you have no authority to enroll her in school."

Bureaucracy, it seems, is alive and well even in my cherished fantasy world, and the high-school principal, entrenched behind his scarred but sturdy oaken desk and surrounded by aging file cabinets, shelves of text books, and racks of dusty, three-ring binders, has just now put the last nails in Charity's coffin...sealed and buried though that particular container has been these last several months.

I glance at Charity, who is sitting beside me, dressed modestly of her own (mostly) volition, looking pale, yes, but very much present, very much *here*. She sighs and drops her gaze to the scuffed linoleum floor.

I expected this, her attitude clearly states.

I half expected it as well and prepared for it as best I could, but I have few resources with which to prosecute my aims.

"Charity Monthage is sitting across the desk from you, Mr. Phelps," I say. "Can you indeed find it within yourself to deny her readmission?"

His face is even paler than Charity's. "You put me in a difficult position, Ms. Japonica. I have Charity's file right here in this folder. I reviewed it this morning. It clearly states that she was killed in a car wreck in January. A copy of her death certificate is included."

Charity's eyes widen, and I recognize her wry, quite literally graveyard twist of humor bubbling to the surface. "You've got a copy of my death certificate? Can I see it?"

Mr. Phelps looks at me. I look at him. "I find myself," I say, "somewhat of the opinion that it is only just."

His hand shaking, he extends the document toward me. "You... you can't take it out of the office," he stammers.

"No prob," says Charity, snatching it. Her eyes, green and deep, scan the document. "It's all in medical-ese," she mock-complains, "but...hey! It says I died of severe, multiple traumatic injuries and consequent rapid exsanguination! OMG, that is sooo rad! How often do you get to die from traumatic injuries and rapid exsanguination?"

Mr. Phelps looks to be on the verge of fainting.

"Charity, my dear girl," I say to her (softly), "you are frightening the poor man to death."

"To death?" Her eyes narrow. "Good. Then that'll make two of us, and maybe he'll freakin' understand."

I turn back to the principal. "I'm terribly sorry, Mr. Phelps. Charity's nature partakes greatly of the irrepressible."

He nods vacantly. "As...as always, as I recall...yes."

Charity hands back the document. "Thank you, sir," she says politely. A glance at me, then back to Mr. Phelps. "I am sure you will appreciate the fact that very few individuals are afforded the opportunity to peruse the declarations of their own demise."

I frown. "I will not have the idiosyncrasies of my speech ridiculed by a sixteen-year-old girl."

Charity grins at me. "What are little sisters for?"

My turn to sigh. Irrepressible, yes.

Back to the principal. "Mr. Phelps," I say as diplomatically as I can, "I am greatly appreciative of your kindness in seeing us this morning and quite sensible of the near-insoluble conundrum with which we have presented you. But if Charity is in fact dead, then, in effect, she possesses *no* interested family, and I am free — nay, necessity and common humanity impel me — to take the place of the responsible adult in her life. I have already provided her with food, clothing, and shelter, and it is therefore only logical that I also represent her interests in resuming her studies."

For a moment, my words appear to sway him, but then he glances once again at the death certificate. "I'm afraid that returning Charity to her classes is impossible, Ms. Japonica. "Months have passed since her...uh..."

He looks to Charity. She musters a hopeful smile for him.

"...demise. She is hopelessly behind in her studies."

"I got my textbooks," Charity puts in. "I've been reviewing like crazy. And reading ahead. I'm not dumb. I can catch up."

"And...and...and..." Having now found a foothold, Mr. Phelps refuses to relinquish it. "...as for the matter of guardianship, Ms. Japonica: do you have any official notice of your legal status regarding Charity?"

"None whatsoever," I admit, surrendering my last hope.

Mr. Phelps puts the document back in its folder and closes the manila cover. "I'm afraid my hands are tied."

"But..." Charity is on her feet. "Mr. Phelps, you *know* me. And you're the freakin' *principal*!"

For a moment, he appears to see her as she is: not as a ghost, not as a spirit, not as the damned thing her parents have chosen to call her, but as a simple girl, sixteen, determined to return to school, to friends, to the day-to-day life of an adolescent teetering on the verge of womanhood. But, then, once again, that terrible turning away: "Ms. Japonica," he says almost reluctantly, "my hands are tied. There are rules."

I feel my heart clench. For all this — school, normalcy, friends — Charity battled the very forces of life and death. And won.

All for naught, as it turns out.

Perhaps home schooling? And slow, steady efforts to effect a reconciliation with her friends and family? Am I — the hermit, the recluse — up to such a challenge? The very fact that I quail at the thought tells me that I am not. And yet...I *must*.

Charity stands, tugs at my arm. "C'mon, Echo," she says. "Let's go. You gave it your best shot."

As far as best shots go, Mr. Phelps obviously feels that he has not risen to the occasion. His tone is crestfallen as he rises to see us out. "If there is anything I can do," he says, "please let me know."

Charity is on the verge (I sense it plainly) of letting him know exactly what, in her opinion, he can do, but at a glance from me, she bites back her words, and together we make our way down the hallway toward the outside exit. From behind the closed classroom doors — the doors which will, to Charity, remain closed — the drone of instructors' voices and students' questions and answers accompany our hollow footsteps.

"You picked this time so that classes would be in session and I wouldn't have to face anybody, didn't you?" she says.

"I did. I confess it. There is no use complicating matters even further than they are already."

She hangs her head. "I'm just a burden for you."

My arm goes about her shoulders as we step out into the sunlight. "One never so willingly undertaken, I assure you."

Our visit to the bureau of vital statistics turns out to be equally futile. Even in an era of computers, it seems, one cannot simply click a box, press "enter", and change someone's status from "dead" to "living". Until closing time puts an end to the tedious affair, the two of us are shuffled from office to office, from clerk to supervisor and back again.

We come away with nothing to show for our day's labors. Charity is dead. Gone. It does not matter that she eats, sleeps, speaks...and weeps. The world is finished with her. There is no returning. Though she may sit, as physically present as myself, before desk after desk, her existence cannot and will not be officially corroborated.

Is this then, how ghosts have always been made? Attempted returns met first with fear, then with denial? How many spirits have come back, pleading to be accepted, only to meet with the same impenetrable barrier as now confronts Charity?

How many have given up? How many still wander?

Charity, I am determined, will not wander. Nor will she be denied. The method of returning her to recognition, however, eludes me, and I go in to work that night with my shoulders knotted and my mouth clenched with frustration and not a little anger at the trivialities that separate my girl from her wishes and taunt me with my impotence.

Just what kind of a shabby little bastardized and ill-conceived world have I begotten?

My emotions run deep enough that my sets go badly, my fingers fighting me fret by fret and measure by measure. And then, in the midst of my second set, the thought that not once — not once! — during the course of our interviews with the principle of the school and the supervisors and underlings at the bureau did anyone save myself speak directly to Charity drives for an instant all thoughts of music from my head and leaves me frozen motionless upon the stage, the angry blood pounding in my temples.

When I come to myself, I find the coffee shop dead silent. The customers are staring at me. Mr. O'Dally is staring at me. Luigi is staring at me. The Boss, at his usual table...is staring at me.

And closer, just beyond the lip of the stage with a latte before her, Charity herself. Staring at me. With those green, impossibly deep eyes.

I cannot continue the piece. I cannot, in fact, recall what piece I was playing.

"I find my instrument has come out of adjustment," I lie to the house. "I will be back shortly to continue the set. Thank you all for your patience."

Mr. O'Dally and Luigi are all care and concern. Is there anything they can do? Water? Aspirin? A cold cloth? But Charity takes charge. "I think Echo just needs a short break," she says, taking my hand and relieving my nerveless fingers of my guitar. "She's had a rough day. Where does she usually go between sets?"

She gets me settled in the back office, and a glass of water clears my head. "Do you need something stronger, Echo?" she asks. "Coffee or something?"

"I will be fine in a minute or two, Charity. The water is proving to be of great benefit. But what has brought you here? And at such a late hour?"

She shrugs. "I got tired of studying — not that it's looking like it's going to do me much good — and I didn't have anything else to do. Sleep's optional for me, like I told you, so I came down to listen. You sound great. Particularly those rockers you were doing. Knew it. First-class headbanger material."

"Thank you." I put my face in my hand. "You are indeed overgenerous, my dear. Particularly considering that I fell apart so disastrously a minute ago."

Her eyes turn owlish. "It was everything that happened today, wasn't it? Got to you, huh?"

I nod...and then look up as the door opens. It is Luigi. Looking very frightened. The Boss, right behind him, shoulders his way into the office and dismisses the younger man with a nod.

"It is perfectly all right, Luigi," I call weakly. "The B— I mean, Mr. Maxwell is a...a..."

"A concerned friend," explains the Boss.

Luigi blinks, torn between disbelief and terror. "Uh..."

The Boss turns to Luigi. "You've got customers at the counter, my man."

Luigi leaves. Quickly. The Boss closes the door.

Charity's large eyes have grown enormous. "Echo! You know Boss Maxwell? That is so...so...so uber-cool!"

I am awash. "You...know the Boss?"

"Are you kidding? *Everybody* knows Boss Maxwell. I mean, everybody knows *of* Boss Maxwell."

I am still awash. Everybody except me, it appears.

The Boss bends down to her. "I don't believe I've had the pleasure, Miss...?"

Forthright as usual, Charity offers her hand. "Charity Monthage," she says. "How do you do, Mr. Maxwell?"

"My...ah...ward," I manage.

"Little sister," Charity corrects me. "Sort of. And chief source of hassles and really bad days."

I explain...partially. "Charity's family turned her out."

The Boss takes her hand gravely. "I am quite well, Charity, thank you. And you can just call me Boss. Now then: your family has turned you out? Have you been in some kind of trouble? Misbehaving? Disrespecting your momma and papa?"

"Nothing like that." She sighs: of late, she has made the confession so often that for all the trepidation with which she faces another utterance of it, she might was well be mopping the kitchen floor. "It's actually pretty stupid. I got killed. Traffic accident. I'm dead. I wandered around for months before Echo took me in.

We've had a bad day because nobody'll let me back into school or even treat me like I'm a real person." She shrugs. "Because I'm dead."

The Boss holds her hand a moment more, appears to note its temperature, then releases it. After taking a moment to feel her forehead, he drags up a chair and sits down, holding us in his dark gaze. "Maybe you both better tell me about this."

⋈

The Boss listens in silence as Charity speaks. I put in a word or two when the narrative concerns me directly, but no more: this is, after all, Charity's story and Charity's grief. And she has, this day, had quite a sufficient number of adults ignoring her, talking over her, leaving her out of any meaningful discussion.

The Boss's dark face darkens even more as Charity describes our futile efforts earlier in the day.

"So the principal just stonewalled you at the school," he says at last, "and then you got the old bureaucratic runaround at the department of records."

Charity nods glumly. "That's about the size of it. People would hardly even *look* at me."

"Well, now..." He puts his large, callused hands on his knees. "... that won't do at all." A glance at me. "That why you've been muffing tunes right and left this evening, Ms. Japonica?"

Blushes and humiliation come easily to me these days, it seems. "Yes. I fear that anger and frustration have periodically gained the upper hand."

"Put the day behind you," he says. "Go out there and play. And I want that chaconne. For the rest: leave it to me. I'm going to talk to some people. Tonight's Friday. Give me until Monday afternoon. You off then, Ms. Japonica?"

"I have Mondays off, yes."

"Good, then you've got your afternoon free. You and Miss Charity go back to the school and see the principal at two o'clock on Monday. Two o'clock, mind you."

"But I daresay he will not —"

"Oh, he'll see you, don't you worry about that."

"And when we see him...?"

The Boss's smile is bland...with occasional hints of razor blades. "Ask him again about getting Charity back into school. I'll take it from there." He regards my girl for a moment. "You're a very fortunate ghost, Miss Charity. You've got friends."

Charity lifts her eyes to his face, and if the Boss is shaken by what he sees in them, he does not show it. "Friends?"

"Ms. Japonica is your friend, isn't she? And I'm your friend, aren't I?"

"You're my friend too?"

He nods gravely. "I make a point of being friends with all the right people, Miss Charity."

"Boss Maxwell's my *friend*? That's...that's..." Caught between enthusiasm and deep humility, Charity finally takes the middle course and bobs her head at him. "Thank you."

On her shoulder then, he lays a large hand. Despite myself, I am looking at that hand, thinking about how it must have come to have those scars and those calluses, and wondering how it is that he can rest it so gently upon one so fragile, so vulnerable, one who nonetheless demonstrates such fortitude and will in the face of the utter negation of existence that has come upon her.

"My pleasure," he says. His gaze flicks back to me. "Monday at two, then. And mind you: two sharp."

For some reason, despite the aura of threat and violence that continues to hang about the presence of the Boss — and the flat contradiction that aura holds for everything I want to believe about Snow City — his words settle me enough that I find myself able to return to my second set and acquit myself with relative professionalism, particularly when I see that the Boss is now sharing his table with Charity, and that the girl's eyes, though still disturbingly deep, are shining with joy.

Boss Maxwell. And everybody knows of him? Except me?

What on earth was I dreaming when I made Snow City?

Between a back rub from Charity and a cup of tea from Luigi, I find I am fortified well enough for the third set that I disgrace neither Dowland nor Bach. And when the last notes of the chaconne reverberate through the quiet coffee shop, the Boss is nodding approvingly, and Charity (still beside him) is clapping along with the other patrons.

Sleep does indeed appear to be optional for Charity, for that night, when I visit the bathroom between bouts of nightmare-riddled sleep — dreams of that other place, dreams of what happened there, dreams of what I myself had to *do* there — I hear papers rustling in her bedroom, pages turning. She is obviously studying, reviewing her lessons, plunging ahead into the material covered by her classes during her months of wandering. And it strikes me that Charity fully believes that she *must* study, that she *must* review and learn as much new material as possible, because she believes that she *will* return to school.

The Boss has said so, and so it will be.

And beyond all my rational doubts — the Boss no more controls the school board than he commands the winds and tides — I find myself believing as well. Somehow, it will happen. Charity has two friends...and the hope of regaining many more. And with friends (even if they do not command school boards, winds, or tides), anything is possible.

But it is with a resurgence of doubt and a stubborn ache in my stomach that, come Monday, Charity and I present ourselves at the school at two o'clock. Sharp.

If the Boss has spoken to some people, that privileged group obviously does not include the principal, for when we enter the office, Mr. Phelps looks up from his files and papers with an expression of outright annoyance. "Ms. Japonica," he says, "I believe I made myself perfectly clear to you the other day —"

Anger gets the better of me once again. "Mr. Phelps, I believe I might be so bold as to point out that there are three of us in this office. You, me, and Charity. And I would consider it a mark of what is obviously your innate good breeding if you would please include Charity in your remarks. In other words, if you are going to deny her readmission to school, pray be so kind as to deny it to her face, and please refrain from pretending she does not exist. I assure you that, without a doubt, she is as real as you or I."

Mr. Phelps is speechless for a moment, but he is nonetheless shaking his head. "I told you before that I don't make the rules," he says when he finds his voice. "I still don't. I can't do anything for you."

I notice with some annoyance that his choice of words is so neutral as to leave the question of addressee completely open.

"Good day," he says, returning to his paperwork.

Charity looks at me, her eyes bleak. But I feel a presence behind me, a very large presence, one that all but fills the open door of the office. And when I glance back, I find G-shot standing there like a basalt monolith. Behind him is the terrified face of Mr. Phelps' secretary, and then G-shot enters the office, steps aside, and the Boss strolls in.

Everyone knows Boss Maxwell. At least, everyone knows *of* him. And Mr. Phelps appears to be no exception.

The Boss is, as usual, unfailingly polite. "Are you having some difficulty with my nieces' request, sir?"

I blink. His...his *nieces?*

I see from the expression on Mr. Phelps' face that he is momentarily taken up with cogitating upon whatever hypothetical (and quite tortured) set of familial relations might result in an uncle-niece connection between the Boss and the two women in the office. His disorientation wears off quickly enough, however, and after opening and closing his mouth several times, his eyes take on a look of apprehension: this *is* Boss Maxwell, after all. "Your... nieces?"

"My nieces," says the Boss. "I believe their request is pretty reasonable. Miss Charity is of school age. And I understand that education through high school is compulsory in this state.

"But...Charity..."

"Technicalities."

"You want me to —?"

"Let her back in school." The Boss's tone makes it more than adequately clear that he is being more than adequately patient with a more than astonishingly obtuse individual.

"But..."

"Yes," says the Boss with a sigh. "Your position." He reaches into his coat and comes out with...not the Glock I am half-expecting, but with a folded piece of legal-sized paper. "I trust this will put an end to your difficulties."

Mr. Phelps takes it, unfolds it as though it can be nothing less than his own death warrant, and reads. "How...?"

The Boss shrugs. "I talked so some people."

I myself have no intention of asking what was said during those talks or how it was said. Ever.

Mr. Phelps reads the document once more. "Ah...I think..." He glances at G-shot. G-shot nods amiably at Mr. Phelps as though considering just where to begin the process of dismemberment. "I think there will...will...be no problem at all."

Mr. Phelps looks at me, then. "I expect Charity to be in school tomorrow, then, Ms. Japonica."

The Boss's gaze shifts not a whit, but his lips purse disapprovingly.

I stand firm. "If you would be so kind, sir," I say to Mr. Phelps, "you will please address your answer to the appropriate individual."

G-shot, the Boss, and an angry blonde. Not to mention a ghost. Mr. Phelps appears for a moment to be uncertain of whom he should be most afraid. But at last he turns to Charity.

"Miss Monthage," he says. "School tomorrow?"

⇥⊣+⊢⇤

But winning over Mr. Phelps is one thing. Winning over classmates and sister is another matter entirely. And though Charity continues her studies throughout the night, I myself find sleep not at all optional...but nonetheless entirely elusive. As a result, though my musician's schedule customarily has me leaving my bed at noon, I am this morning sharing breakfast with my girl at half past seven, and preparing to escort her to school.

"You really don't have to do this, Echo," she tells me as she shoves books into her backpack. She is wearing her new and much-loved black shorts and her bordering-on-the-tarty top: clothing-wise, at least, she will fit right in. "Actually, it's pretty embarrassing to have an adult holding my hand like this. I'm not in kindergarten after all."

"Under normal circumstances, I would be wholeheartedly in agreement with you, Charity, but I cannot help being somewhat of the opinion that, under the circumstances, you may be in need of additional moral support. These are, after all, the young persons who have been fleeing from you these last months."

Charity nods unwillingly as she checks the time. "It'll be nice to have somebody watching my back, for sure. Well, OK. But we'll have to run to catch the bus."

Catching the bus, however, proves unnecessary, for when we reach the street, we find, waiting at the curb, a gleaming black limousine. From behind the wheel, G-shot nods a stolid greeting, and the Boss himself stands at the open rear door, bowing us in.

Charity unconsciously catches my arm. "Looks...looks like we're going in style."

We are indeed. We arrive at the school a quarter of an hour before classes are to begin, at a time (carefully calculated, I am quite sure) when the greatest number of students are to be found loitering on the grass, the steps, and the pavement in front of the school doors. And as the long limousine rumbles into position directly in line with the front walkway (I cannot dissuade myself from the suspicion that the convenient gap in the line of parked cars has been somehow prearranged), the effect upon the assembled students is, I confess, infinitely satisfying.

Even more so is the that of the Boss stepping out and swinging the door wide for his passengers. I can see the name *Boss Maxwell* framed on any number of lips, but when he reaches in and hands Charity out as though it were prom night and he her favored beau, every face in the crowd goes utterly blank.

The combination of the limo, the Boss, and Charity has apparently succeeded in creating a cognitive short-circuit in the entire group.

As I, feeling somewhat like a tedious afterthought, clamber out of the vehicle on my own, the Boss, with Charity at his side, squares his shoulders and straightens his tie. His dark, dark glasses glint in the morning sun. "All right, listen up," he says to the crowd. "We got a homie here been away for awhile, been on her own for awhile, been *on the street* for awhile...and wants to get jumped back into the gang. What do you say?"

Stunned silence. Everybody knows the Boss. At least, everybody knows *of* the Boss. But his reputation is quite obviously so overwhelming that it has stunned his audience into speechlessness.

"I'm listening, people."

The Boss, as far as I have been able to ascertain, is unfazed by Charity's condition. Ghosts, it appears, hold no intimidating qualities for the man, and it occurs to me that this is possibly because he has, in his career, personally produced not a few of them. But though he appears to be completely without apprehension of any sort when it comes to the undead, he has obviously never attempted to coax a group of high school students toward the same point of view. Hence, he stands, a dark figure in the bright sunlight, his expression one of consternation.

I venture to speak. "Perhaps a gentler hand, sir?"

"Hmmm? You want to give it a shot, Ms. Japonica?"

Charity is tugging at his sleeve. "Boss, I'm not sure that's a good idea. Nobody's going to understand a word she says."

"Give the lady a chance, Miss Charity." The Boss smiles. "I'm sure someone in the habit of reading Jane Austen novels will be happy to translate for the rest." He raises his gaze to the students. "This here is Ms. Echo Japonica. She's been looking after Charity. She's also her legal guardian."

I blink. "*That* was the paper you gave Mr. Phelps?"

The Boss nods. "Yes. I'll get you a certified copy in a day or two." He eyes me from behind his dark glasses...and I sense the presence of an amused twinkle. "You got yourself an official family now, Ms. Japonica."

Taking encouragement from the Boss's words, Charity pipes up: "She's a working musician, guys. She's really cool. Listen to her, for God's sake!"

Blushing crimson appears to have become a normal state of affairs for me, but underlying my embarrassment is a deep sense of anguish, for returning Charity to her friends has become, in my eyes, an outward symbol of my own inner redemption: having so obviously created Snow City lame, halt, and crippled, I must do everything within my means to correct its deficiencies. And I greatly fear that this, my first labor, may prove far more arduous than a little housekeeping in the Augean stables.

With my arm about Charity's shoulders, then, I attempt to find language that will not completely bewilder my listeners.

"Yes, everyone, Charity has come back. And as I have seen you turn away from her after school, I will assume that you are all doubtful and perhaps even afraid of her."

I see comprehension on the faces of the students and am hopeful that my linguistic convolutions may yet be held off long enough for me to make myself clear.

"Maybe," I continue, "some of you are under the impression that Charity returned because those on the other side of life rejected her. Nothing, however, could be further from the truth. Maybe some of you think that, as a result of her misfortune, there is something amiss with her. But that is not true either. The fact is, Charity has come all the way back from...from that other place...to be with you. To be your friend once again. She was offered light and bliss, but she turned away from them because, in her opinion, her light and her bliss lay here. At home. At school. With her family and her circle of friends." My tears are running freely now, and I hope I am not deluded in thinking that I see their counterparts on the faces of some of my young listeners. I certainly see them on the cheeks of the dark-haired girl who so resembles Charity, and I therefore renew my efforts. "Perhaps her family does not yet understand, but all of you have your own minds to make up, and this morning I beg you to favor her with your goodwill and your acceptance. She has come so far and has endured so much to be numbered among you once again. Please give her a chance."

No, I am thinking, *give* me *a chance. A chance to prove to myself that Snow City and its world still possess that redeeming grace of which I dreamed, that perfection I longed for, that completeness for which I searched. Please...*

"Please take her back into your community." My throat is tight. The scene has blurred with my tears. "Please recognize that friendship is not something that ends with death, nor even with a return from death. Please understand that friendship remains forever, regardless of situation, state, or circumstance."

How I wish it had been so in my old world! But it was not. It never was. And now I am begging these children not just to renew their bonds with Charity, but to renew my faith in my own creation. Gangsters, ghosts, familial rejection: by the choice of a handful of adolescents, all might be transformed.

"The...the...friendship is still there," I choke. "Charity — your friend — is offering it to you. Please take it."

A bell rings, announcing the beginning of classes, but no one takes notice. After a minute, Mr. Phelps, the principal, strides out to see what is happening that is causing such a callous disregard for school protocol, but one look at the Boss causes him to retreat into the shelter of the entryway. Several teachers, following, see Charity, turn pale, and join Mr. Phelps.

At last, movement in the crowd. It is Faith, Charity's dark-haired sister. But as we watch, she slowly turns away and hurries into the building, head bowed, arm dashing the tears from her face.

My arm is about Charity's shoulders, and I feel her sag, as stricken in death as anything living could possibly be.

Not her sister...please. If her own sister cannot accept her, then what chance have we?

But though my unskilled but impassioned monologue has proven ineffective, Faith's rejection has broken the spell, and the gathered students are exchanging glances, casting wary looks at the school doors, turning back to regard Charity (so I deeply hope) with new eyes. A tall black girl strides to the fore, then, cornrowed hair bright with beads, dark eyes flashing clear and defiant, coltishly long legs carrying her straight up to Charity.

"Hey, Rebekah," says Charity.

"Hey, Charity." The black girl regards her for a long moment, and from the demeanor of the other students, it appears that she is a sort of ringleader among Charity's classmates. "So you're really dead? Nobody made a mistake? Girl, we been wondering about that ever since you started hanging around, but most of us been too scared to ask."

A long sigh as Charity nods. "I'm really dead, Rebekah. I'm a ghost."

Rebekah pokes Charity's shoulder lightly. "I thought ghosts were supposed to be, like, see-through or something."

"I guess I tried harder than most."

"Did it hurt?"

"You mean the accident? I didn't feel a thing. It happened too fast."

"And now? Whatcha feeling now?"

"Kinda floaty. Like a soap bubble."

"Well, you sure feel more solid than a soap bubble." Rebekah ponders her. "An' you wanna come back?"

"I miss everybody," Charity says simply.

The dark, defiant eyes turn to the Boss. "You OK with this, Boss?"

"I wouldn't be here if I wasn't," says the Boss. "Charity's all right in my book."

Rebekah turns to the other students. "Charity's dead and all, and she's a ghost, but Boss Maxwell says she's OK. That's good enough for me. Anybody not down with that?"

There is a general murmur, but I cannot decipher it. One of the smaller girls, however, seems to have turned a light shade of green, and clapping a hand to her mouth, she runs for the doors.

"Betsy Morris," Rebekah calls after her, "if it's the can you're heading for, remember that you're all alone and we got that Hanako ghost in the third stall!"

Which stops the panicking Betsy in her tracks and sends her backpedaling away from the door, caught between two unknown horrors. But the winter was cold, and the sidewalk has heaved, and Betsy, lacking a reverse view, catches her heel on an uplifted slab near the top of the stairs and pitches over backward, fully airborne.

"OMFG!" It is Charity. Freeing herself from my arm, she lunges forward, pushes past Rebekah, and winds up sprawling headlong directly under the hapless Betsy, who is thereby saved, if not from a broken neck, then at least from numerous scrapes, contusions, and perhaps a concussion or two.

It takes a minute and several pairs of hands to untangle the girls and get them on their feet. Betsy has given up her foray into the chartreuse but is by now almost as pale as Charity.

"Char?" she says, looking into those unnervingly deep eyes.

"It's me," says Charity. "Honest."

"You saved me."

"Well, what are friends for?"

"You're...you're still my friend?"

Charity spreads her hands. "That's kinda-sorta up to you, Bets. This isn't Zombie Apocalypse."

Rebakah is frowning. "Boss Maxwell isn't good enough, Bets? You gotta have Char turn herself into a doormat for you?"

Charity is half exasperated, half hopeful. "Hey, guys, everyone, look: if that's what it takes, I'll be a doormat, OK?"

Impulsively, and with the expression of one hurling herself into a vat of ice water, Betsy hugs Charity. "You're c-c-cold," she says, shivering.

Charity clings to her friend as though to a life preserver, eyes closed, tears starting. "It kind of comes with the territory. But nothing's rotting, believe me. I check every morning. Honest."

Betsy shudders at Charity's sense of humor, but hangs on nonetheless.

Rebekah turns, then, and addresses the crowd, loudly enough to include the teachers and the solitary student hiding inside the doors. "Anybody got a problem with this?"

A general murmur, another exchange of glances, the shaking of many heads. I cannot see what the teachers are doing, and Faith is well hidden in the shadows beyond the doorway.

But no, in general there seems to be no obvious problem, and with Rebekah on one side and Betsy on the other, Charity is led toward the school. "Let's get you to class, girl," Rebekah is saying, having now consigned both myself and even the Boss to the inconsequential category of *adult*. "We saved your seat. Teacher wanted to shift things around, but we wouldn't let her. I guess maybe we sorta knew you'd be comin' back."

At the doors, Charity pauses and, for a moment, returns her gaze to us, her pale face radiant. Her friends. She has them again.

And maybe...just maybe...someday, her family.

In another half minute, the area before the school is empty save for the Boss and myself. My tears are still streaming, and heedless of my stockings, I sink to my knees, my hands to my face. "Dear God...it is happening. Please...please let it keep happening."

The Boss kneels beside me, his arm lapping gently about my shoulders. "You're not from around here, are you, girl?"

CHAPTER SIX

I leave the Boss's question unanswered, and he does not press for a response. Instead, beyond directing G-shot to drive back to my apartment, he is silent, musing at the passing streets as though making of them an obscure oracle, one that tells him of matters in which I might or might not play a part: Charity, the chaconne, his offer of a position at his club, the inner workings of Snow City and his seeming ability to bend them to his will.

Finally, "Get some sleep, woman," he says as he hands me out of the limousine into what seems to me at the moment to be the obscenely bright sunlight. "I doubt you closed your eyes all night."

Technically, he is wrong: I closed them often enough. The action, however, led to nothing that resembled sleep. But I simply nod my thanks, drag myself up the stairs to my rooms, and collapse, fully clothed, on the futon in my living room.

My sleep is visited by dreams of Charity. In the classroom. Sitting between Rebekah and Betsy. Raising her hand eagerly and answering questions posed by a somewhat white-faced teacher whose pedagogical studies have (quite inexplicably) never touched upon any methods for imparting knowledge to the deceased. But necessity at last prompts the instructor to ignore both what she cannot change and the novelty of her position, and Charity is back among her scholastic community, doubtless finding herself offering more than a few explanations during lunchtime, but otherwise quite happy to remain firmly midstream in her interior river of contentment.

Hearing Charity's key in the apartment door lock, I open my eyes...remembering Faith.

What about Faith?

Charity peers in. "Did I wake you?"

"Not as far as I am aware. Is it so late? School is over?"

"Yeah. I got a lift from one of the kids with a car."

"We will need to equip you with a bus pass, I imagine." More expense, but I push the thought aside as I stagger up from the futon. "I think I have need of coffee."

Charity drops her backpack by the door. "I'll make it. And then..."

She does not finish her sentence, but trips happily into the kitchen. So comfortable is she with the mundane actions of life that at times I find it hard to believe she is a ghost. And yet at other times I catch a faint hint, as of transparency, about her, a clue that she is perhaps not quite so real as she seems.

Floaty, she said of herself and, living as I have at the fringes of this world, I myself have felt, upon occasion, much the same: detached, insubstantial. A part of this place, and yet not, straddling two mutually exclusive states of being and yet somehow holding to both.

For a moment, I sound my sensibilities. Floaty? Still? Yes or no? And with an upwelling of emotion made of equal parts fear and relief, I discover that the answer is *no*. Not anymore. Not since I claimed Charity. Certainly not since she claimed me. Now part and parcel of Snow City — and most assuredly out of my depth — I can no longer afford the luxury (or perhaps the self-indulgence) of floaty.

Once again, Charity creates unerringly my preferred brew, and I change into a robe and slippers and sit on the sofa by the window, sipping the bitterness as I look out at the greening mountains. Dark vales and ravines. Rushing streams. Peaks that, despite the advance of warm weather, still retain a touch of snow.

Faith.

That turning away. That retreat into the school. That look on Charity's face.

I put the thought aside. "And then what?" I say, looking up from my cup. "You did not finish your thought."

"You want something to eat?" Charity calls from the kitchen.

"I am quite sensible of the generosity of the offer, but the coffee is fine for now. Your thought, pray?"

Charity reenters the living room and sits on the floor in front of me with a glass of milk and a plate of cookies. "I can't have you sacking out on the futon anymore," she says between sips and bites. "You're on a different schedule, and you need to sleep. You can't keep getting up when I do. You get off work at...what? One or two in the morning? And then you have to come home and stop shaking before you can sleep. That makes it about four. Now me, I have to get up at seven for school, pull myself together, and bomb out of here about eight. With you sleeping in the living room, that's going to get old for you real fast."

She looks toward the windows, but I can tell she is not seeing the mountains, and her expression is heartbreakingly similar to that which she wore as she watched her sister's retreat.

"I don't want you to start resenting me," she says.

"I most certainly do not resent you."

The memory of Faith hangs in the air like a shroud, but she casts aside her pensiveness and breezes on. "So I want you to take your bedroom back, big sister. Sleep's not that critical for me, and I can sack out on the futon when I feel like going offline. Which means that, in the morning, I've got the kitchen and bathroom clear and I don't bother you."

"I will be more than happy to get up if you need me to."

Her deep gaze flicks back to me. "That's just it. I don't need you to. I can make breakfast, wash up after, and even leave lunch for you. Actually, I'd like to. Leave lunch, I mean. You've done all this great stuff for me and it's only fair that I do something for you in return." Her eyes turn sympathetic. "You sleep, Echo. You work hard at night, and I go to school during the day. It's complicated, but we can make it work."

I cannot quite shake off my perception of Charity as an abandoned waif, and I am therefore reluctant to consign her to a futon in a corner of the living room. But her words do indeed make sense, and her fear of resentment and subsequent rejection is — though objectively baseless — quite real, and so we spend an hour or two rearranging the household. "Believe me," she says as she hangs tomorrow's school outfit on the coat hook by the door, "I won't make any noise in the mornings. I'll be as quiet as..."

She giggles. Nervously.

"...quiet as a ghost."

The giggle turns abruptly into a choke, and I am across the room in an instant, hugging her close as she buries her face in my robe and sobs for all the fear and the loss, cries for today's hope and happiness, and weeps for her sister, Faith, who still wanders alone...in a deeper, darker, and even more unsympathetic wasteland than Charity herself ever encountered during her months of abandonment.

⇌

Our routine quickly settles down. Charity to school in the morning. I to work in the evening. Quite often, Charity's friends stop by for afternoon and weekend study sessions so as to help her catch up with her missed class work, and day by day, owing to both her friends' efforts and her own nocturnal exertions (most every night I return from the coffee shop to find her at the dinette, doggedly poring over her textbooks) we see her grades rise steadily from above-average to near the top of the class, and this is particularly fortuitous considering that the end of the school term and final exams are drawing near.

But her sister still wanders apart. Admittedly, Faith is second year while Charity is first year: they share no classes. But in the course of the day, they do pass one another in the hall, and Charity has yet to meet with any reaction besides that terrible, uncompromising...turning away.

Fear? Guilt? Some stubborn and unyielding combination of the two? I do not know, but on a day of rain, one of my days off, I ride the bus to a stop near Charity's old neighborhood, my destination the address I gleaned from one of her textbooks by holding the flyleaf obliquely to the light so as to reveal the faint palimpsest of numbers and letters she had made such a diligent effort to erase.

My umbrella-sheltered steps take me into an affluent area of lush lawns, winding driveways, and gated entryways. With the approach of summer, the weather has turned warm, and flowers are blooming, trees are well-leafed, and where old ivy creeps over old brickwork, it glistens a deep green. My braid is heavy with moisture and my shoes, despite my care, are soaked both by drift from splashing raindrops and by surprise attacks from unforeseen puddles.

Charity's old neighborhood: money, luxury. And what have I offered my dear girl in its place? Comparative squalor. Near penury. Penny pinching. A futon in a corner of a living room. Irregular hours. Bus passes and scrimping on clothes.

She deserves better.

And yet here, in this upper-class ghetto, she found not acceptance, but rejection. She was turned out, ordered away, denied shelter.

She deserved better.

The address brings me at last to an out-of-the-way street where old houses are, for the most part, set back among old trees. Here I confront a rambling abode in the Spanish style, with red tile roofs, white walls, an enormous front yard bordered by a split rail fence adorned with rosebushes blooming a dark and venomous red, and a driveway that stretches alongside the house and back through a wrought iron gate that not only hints at more house and yard and garden beyond it but gives a glimpse of (of all things...particularly in this region of mountains and snow), a swimming pool.

Charity's house.

"At least she is cherished now," I murmur as I walk up the drive and turn onto a brickwork path that, after a right-angled bend, leads directly up to a covered front porch with a wooden door so massive and thick with moldings and hardware it would not be out of place on a mausoleum.

A ring of the bell, and as I wait, my eye drifts back toward the small garden effectively enclosed by the path, the house, and the driveway. Azaleas, camellias...and in the middle, a curious post, about three feet high. It looks to have been roughly sawn off, and after a moment I perceive, beside it, a small shrine — Saint Francis, I believe — lying tumbled among the shrubs like a flower untimely severed and left to rot.

Affixed to its base is the other part of the post.

Lopped, and left. And as I puzzle at the meaning of it, the door opens to reveal a woman with severely coiffed, salt-and-pepper hair. Her face is hard, set, and her eyes are already regarding me with suspicion as her mouth clenches in preparation for (I suspect) a quick rebuff to any overture.

She does not resemble Charity in the slightest. For which I am profoundly grateful.

"Have I the honor of addressing Ms. Monthage?" I ask.

"I'm Mrs. Monthage, yes," she replies. Perfectly proper, with just the right hint of a rising inflection on the last word. And yet there is something cloyingly menacing about her tone.

Dismissal hangs in the offing, and I try not to hesitate. "I pray you will forgive me for intruding upon you in this unconscionable fashion. My name is Echo Japonica, and I harbor the great and most undeserved hope that you will speak to me with regards to your daughter."

"Are you from the school? Is she in trouble? Is she sick?"

I assure Mrs. Monthage that the answers to all three questions are most definitely in the negative, and I am thereupon invited into a small, dark entryway decorated in a pseudo-Spanish style, then beckoned down a passage that, bordered on one side only by a waist-high partition topped with artificial greenery, reveals thereby a large, almost garish living room only a little smaller than my entire apartment. Wing chairs upholstered with floral cloth, a coffee table that, were it properly felted and cushioned, could double as a billiard table, a long sofa. One wall is mostly taken up by a fireplace capable (should the need arise) of serving as a two car garage, another is broken by a set of archways that give onto a formal dining room with heavy chairs, a heavy table, sideboards to match, and a wheel-shaped, imitation-candle-lit chandelier seemingly large enough to invite stopovers from Jupiter-bound spacecraft.

"I'll get coffee," says Mrs. Monthage. "You *do* take coffee, don't you?"

She whisks through a door at the far end of the corridor, and I am left alone in the still room. The general color scheme is brick red, rose, and dark wood, but though the overall effect should be one of sunlight and warmth, particularly considering that a tall bay window looks out onto the rose-bordered front yard, the feeling is one of inertia and cold, and I find myself shrugging my sweater closer to my shoulders.

In a minute or two, Mrs. Monthage bustles back in with a tray. Coffeepot, cups, sugar, cream. She has already decided that I take my brew with two lumps and plenty of cream, for that is what is contained by the tiny, porcelain cup she puts into my hands, a fixed, brittle smile on her red-rimmed lips. "There now..." she is saying. "What can I do for you, Miss Juniper?"

"Japonica, if you please, ma'am."

"I'm always glad to talk about Faith, Miss Juniper. Such a devoted child. Pliant, as I'm sure you understand. Just as a child should be. Putty in her parents' hands. Does well in school...a perfectly normal girl, perfectly normal...yes..."

She rattles on as though the death of a daughter six months before has left no more of an emotional imprint than a brick dropped into a pool of quicksand. Half-consciously, I scan the room. Photographs and paintings of Mrs. Monthage, of Faith, of someone I assume to be Charity's father...but nothing to indicate another daughter. No Charity. No picture. No memorial. No keepsake. She might well have not existed, all memory of her having been terminated as brutally and inarguably as that severed stump that once held the shrine to Saint Francis.

"I am," I admit, "somewhat familiar with Faith, and of her most praiseworthy accomplishments."

Mrs. Monthage agrees wholeheartedly with me. "A wonderful girl. Of course, it's not my place to take any pride in what she's done. Showing pride that isn't mine to show might make her prideful herself, and that's the road to perdition, don't you agree, Miss Juniper?"

I give up on the matter of my surname. "I have indeed always been of the opinion that a modest demeanor is best."

"You seem like such a sensible woman, Miss Juniper," she says and, seeing that I have managed to choke down the unbearably sweet slurry with which she initially presented me, hastens to replenish it. "Or would you prefer three lumps?"

"Ah..." Discretion is indeed the better part of valor. "Two will be fine, ma'am."

"Such a well behaved guest," she murmurs to herself, "and with such a nice opinion of my only daughter." (I notice the stress she puts on the word *only*.) "Now, Miss Juniper," she says, putting the cup with its vile contents into my hands, "what can I do for you regarding Faith?"

Sensing dangerous if not outright lethal ground, I make a point of setting the cup down on the tray before I reply. "Actually, Mrs. Monthage, it is with regards to your younger daughter, Charity, that I have come to speak."

"Charity? I have no daughter named Charity."

For a moment, I flounder. Could the address have been wrong? Perhaps Charity foresaw my intrusive snooping and deliberately pied the textbook inscription so as to prevent me from finding her house. But my gaze flicks once more to the photographs, and there indeed is Faith, and the family resemblance removes all doubt.

Screw your courage to the sticking place, is the phrase that runs through my mind, but I am vaguely aware that those particular words led, in the end, to disaster.

"Your other daughter, ma'am," I try again. "She was killed in an automobile accident in January."

I see Mrs. Monthage's lips go flat against her teeth, her narrow eyes narrow more. I suspect I have by now most certainly taken myself well outside the category of *well behaved guest*.

Which turns out to be exactly the case. "I *had* a daughter named Charity," Mrs. Monthage admits after a lengthy silence during which I can imagine the coffee in the pot and the cups skinning over with ice. "She was, yes, killed in January. I'm going to have to ask you to leave, Miss Juniper."

I keep my seat on the sofa. "Ma'am, Charity still loves you and the rest of your family, and it is her great and sustained wish that she can effect some kind of reconciliation."

Mrs. Monthage turns away dismissively. "How can you know what the dead want?"

"Ma'am," I say, risking all, "Charity lives with me. I took her in. She has returned to school, resumed her studies, and has been reunited with her friends. She would dearly like —"

"*Demon!*" She whirls on me, and for an instant, I an unable to take my eyes off her mouth, the overly red lipstick encircling the whiteness of teeth clenched seemingly to the point of shattering. "What came back is a demon!" The words hiss out at me. "You're damned, woman. You're consorting with devils. Whatever you're seeing is possessed, a corpse that has no place among the living."

"Madam, I most humbly beg to differ —"

"My minister knows all about such things, and he has instructed me, my husband, and my daughter well. Avoid sin and all near occasions of sin! Get out of my house, you vile thing! Charity is dead and gone. What's assumed her form is damned forevermore, and there's no doubt it's determined to drag the rest of us with it!"

In the face of such an assault, I take my leave as best I can. "Please forgive me for having intruded upon you," I tell her as she herds me toward the front door.

"Get out!"

I try one last time in the entryway. "Your daughter deeply desires to come home, Mrs. Monthage. Will you deny her the embrace of her family?"

She flings the door wide. "*That is not my daughter!*"

Outside, the rain is pouring down, puddling on the lawn and in the garden, splashing on the stump of the Saint Francis shrine. "Is there no hope at all?" I ask.

And for some reason, my question brings her up short...but only for a moment. "Hope? *Hope?*" she screams at me. "There is no hope. There never was a hope. There will never be a hope! Now get out before I call the police!"

I stumble onto the porch and down the steps to the walkway. The rain falls, soaking me. In the confusion attending my departure, I have forgotten my umbrella, and I will not brave an attempt to reclaim it. By the time I have walked the several blocks to the bus stop, then, I am wet to the skin, and it is only through the kindness of a stranger who offers to share his umbrella that I am spared a twenty-minute wait in what is rapidly assuming the proportions of a deluge.

I leave behind a standing puddle on the floor of the bus when I disembark, and then I must endure another round of despondent slogging through falling water in order to reach my door. Which, though the sound of the television tells me that Charity is home, I find to be locked.

The landing is exposed, and though I attempt to remind myself that a little more rain cannot possibly make me any wetter, I am nettled enough to knock on the door a little harder than would otherwise be my wont. "Charity! Open the door, please!"

I rummage in my purse, but my emotions weigh upon me, and my key proves elusive. "I'm getting dressed!" Charity calls through the closed (and locked) door. "I've been trying on the stuff I stole to see if it still fits! Hang on for a sec!"

"I might remind you," I call back, "that the rain is heavy, the landing, roofless. And due to unfortunate circumstances, I have no umbrella. I have discovered, moreover, that much to my surprise, I do not appear to be waterproof."

A long silence. At last the door opens. Charity is standing there in the entry, clad in clothing so mismatched that she might well have upended a bag of cast-offs over herself. I notice a hint of tears in her eyes, but I am too wet and miserable to comment on it as I step gratefully into shelter.

Charity turns away, wiping her eyes. "You're making fun of me."

"My dear girl —"

"You're twigging me because I can't get wet. I can't even take a shower or a bath. It's like I'm wearing a raincoat all the time. Nothing gets wet. The only clothes I've got that get wet is the old stuff I stole from the house! For God's sake, I'm surprised my freakin' *eyeliner* sticks!" She plonks herself down on a dinette chair and buries her face in her hands.

Volatile teenage hormones? The grief of a ghost who has had her status thrown in her face once too often? Judging from my interview with Mrs. Monthage, I can well imagine how Charity's post-demise homecoming played out, and I am again impressed with the girl's strength of will.

To have gone through...*that*...and yet be so upbeat and strong.

But she is not upbeat now, and her strength is showing some cracks. "When it started to rain, one of the kids made a joke — I know he didn't mean it to hurt, but it did — that they could use me as an umbrella. And it just...it just...*hurt*. It's like...like I'm back in school, and I'm back with my friends and all, but I can't ever forget that I'm really a ghost."

I am still standing — dripping — in the entry. The apartment seems so small. The pile of cushions where Charity sleeps — in the living room! — seems so horrible. My wet-to-the-skin state seems so indicative of my own damp-spirited existence in Snow City, an existence I have with such infinite lack of consideration inflicted upon Charity, who (I have no doubt at all) had, at her parents' house, her own bedroom, her own television and DVD player, her own cell phone and computer. I can offer her none of these.

And now, unwittingly and unintentionally, I have hurt her.

There is nothing wrong with being a ghost, I want to say, but I cannot. I was a ghost in Snow City for too long, and I am just now realizing that I cannot recommend that particular state to anyone. But I do not speak, and Charity finally looks up. "What...what happened to you?"

"I...I appear to have forgotten my umbrella," I say, hoping to leave it at that.

"Where did you go?"

"Out. Just...just out."

Unconsciously, I put a hand to my face, and then I find I am on my knees in the entry, my shoulders shaking, the disastrous meeting and its resultant distress at last catching up with me.

I feel arms about me, then. Charity is beside me, kneeling. "You went to my house, didn't you?"

"I did. I had an...unfortunate interview with your mother."

"Mom's...pretty whacked out, isn't she?"

Demon, her mother called her. *Possessed. Devil.*

How much of that did she say to Charity? To her face? Doubtless, all of it.

I nod absently in response to Charity's question, but now, recalling the encounter, something about Mrs. Monthage's words — something she said — niggles at the back of my mind.

Something does not match up.

It will not come to me, however, and so: "Were you raised Catholic, Charity?" I finally ask.

My eyes are closed, but I feel her nod. "Raised," she says. "Pretty much lapsed. I didn't really care about it all that much. Now..." She lifts her head, and I open my eyes to find them staring into hers.

Impossibly deep. Abysses of knowledge.

"...now I'm not sure what I'm supposed to be. I don't think anything in the Bible really covers my situation. Well, maybe it does, but I'm a little afraid to look."

"Was...ah...is there a Saint Francis shrine in your front yard?"

"Oh, *yeah*," she says, immediately brightening. "There sure is! Man, I love that thing. I really like the idea of someone taking care of the birds and animals. I even thought about becoming a veterinarian. That is...before January. But...did you see it, Echo? Isn't it cool? I mean, it's just like a little house with open sides, and Saint Francis standing in the middle of it with trays all around him for birdseed and stuff. And it has this cute little copper roof my dad always kept shined."

I nod. "I saw it. Yes."

Indeed, I saw it. Lopped off. Gone. Left to rot and corrode among the leaves and flowers that will, come autumn, fall and decay, and then be buried in the winter snows.

"It is quite lovely," I tell her. "Perhaps we can arrange for something like it here."

But even as I speak, I know that my tiny apartment is no more fit for a shrine than it is for sheltering a teenage girl, ghost though she may be, helpful though she may be, needy though she may be.

Needy beyond my darkest imaginings.

I look down. Charity is wearing her mismatched assortment of clothing and, as she predicted, they possess no particular resistance to water. "I am soaking you," I murmur.

"Don't worry," she says, her hurt having evaporated, "I'm waterproof, remember?"

"True, and I affirm to you without hesitation that I will never use you as an umbrella, no matter how pressing the need."

She giggles. "For you, Echo, anything. I was willing to be a doormat. I guess I can manage an umbrella."

"Let us think no more of that. We shall towel off, put on something dry, and have an early dinner. Would leftovers be acceptable?"

Her green eyes flash. "I'm not touching that egg foo yong even if I *am* dead," she declares.

"Then let me unearth another umbrella, and we shall go out. I know of an Italian eatery, and as it is not far from here, we shall not find ourselves overly inconvenienced even should the storm become a veritable Niagara."

But the rain has greatly diminished by the time we leave the apartment, and the walk to the restaurant proves less than arduous.

But all the while I watch Charity wolfing down spaghetti and meatballs, I am, mentally, tallying up household expenses, comparing it with my income, and coming time and again to the same conclusion: over the long run, I cannot suitably provide for this girl on what I earn from my performances at the Blue Rose.

Upon our return, then, after I have disposed of the offending egg foo yong and gotten Charity settled among her cushions and comforter, I sit alone in my bedroom, considering the task I have set before myself.

Finally, I open my purse and extract a business card. The number printed on it returns my gaze for some minutes before I am able to find the courage to pick up the bedside telephone.

I dial, there is a ring, and then a familiar voice: "Maxwell."

"Ah...Boss?"

"Ms. Japonica! A pleasure to hear from you. How may I be of assistance?"

I open my mouth to speak, and just then the oddity in Mrs. Monthage's words comes back to me. Did she say *hope*, or was it actually *Hope*? A virtue...or a name? Faith we have, and Charity too. But...

But what of Hope? Another sister? And does that absent being have anything to do with the viciousness with which the Monthage family is determined, on the one hand, to demonize Charity and, on the other, to deny her very existence?

"Ah...Boss..." I say, dragging my wits back together, "I was wondering..." Can I really bring myself to say this? To gather together all my dreams of a quiet, sheltered life in Snow City and kick them bodily into the dustbin?

It seems I must.

"...wondering whether...whether I might impose upon you for an opportunity to meet and...and possibly discuss your most generous proposition."

CHAPTER SEVEN

My request is, the Boss assures me, no imposition at all, and it is in fact granted the very next night, after I have finished my sets at the Blue Rose...ending, as usual, with the chaconne and with, as usual, the Boss's shadowy presence at his back table.

As I am packing up my kit, G-shot sidles into the office. (Indeed, I somewhat doubt the door is wide enough to admit him any other way.) "Boss wants to know if you're still OK with talkin' tonight."

I took the precaution of very deliberately pacing myself during my sets, husbanding my strength for the main event, which on this particular night, will occur *after* my performance. "I perceive no obvious impediment."

G-shot frowns, mystified. "Well, if what you mean is what I *think* you mean, it's just that he don't want t' be takin' advantage if you're tired."

I am decidedly *not* tired. As usual, navigating the technical and emotional hurdles of an evening's music has banished fatigue and thoughts of sleep alike, and I follow G-shot out to the street with a clear head...clear enough to notice that, near the counter, the Boss is speaking with Mr. O'Dally. And that Mr. O'Dally is nodding...if not enthusiastically, then at least vehemently.

The Boss joins us in the limousine a few minutes later. "I don't want you jumping into something that's going to make you uncomfortable," he says, settling in and nodding for G-shot to pull out. "I don't work that way. I'm here to make people happy and maybe make a few bucks doing it, and though I've found that there are all kinds of ways for people to be happy, getting their arms twisted when they don't need twisting or don't deserve twisting isn't one of them."

"I do not appear to be understanding you."

"I want you to scope out the club before you commit yourself. It's a pretty different scene."

I nod, but I cannot escape the plain facts: for Charity's sake, I need more money, and therefore, different scene or no, I must steel myself to a serious consideration — and probable acceptance — of the Boss's offer.

G-shot takes us into a section of the city with which I am, to my surprise, dimly familiar: dark streets filled not with jubilant crowds or lighthearted college students or expectant theatergoers...but rather with shadows: furtive shapes that, at the sight of the approaching limousine, step into the blackness of alleyways or melt into the ill-lit lobbies of cheap hotels or turn away in order to conceal faces, identities, intentions.

I recall it now: I wandered here some weeks ago, the first time I attempted to follow Charity into the rainy night. I became lost, and G-shot found me.

And now I have returned. Not following this time, but being led.

"This is a part of town where you don't want to be walking alone, Ms. Japonica," the Boss remarks casually, as though commenting on the weather. "Oh, nobody'd really hurt you. That's not the way things go here, and in any case if they did they'd wind up having to talk to *me*, and they surely don't want that."

I catch myself looking at his rough hands, illuminated intermittently by the passing of widely separated streetlamps.

"But they'd sure scare the hell out of you," he continues. "So just be careful. In any case, on your nights here, G-shot will be picking you up and taking you home. *If* you decide you want the position, that is. I'm not assuming anything at this point, though your current employer is willing to free you up on Thursdays: slow night for him, and most of his student clientele are cramming for tests on Friday." He catches my uncertain look. "Oh, he's more than happy to have you on Thursdays. Don't you worry about that. What I'm saying is that he can *spare* you on Thursdays. So if you decide that my place isn't your cup of tea, your position at the Blue Rose won't change a bit."

He is being more than generous, not forcing me, not urging me, always leaving me a way out. But under the circumstances, I feel ever more constrained.

That sense of constraint falls heavily upon me when we pull up in front of a pair of broad, glass doors framed in polished brass. A doorman, uniformed, stands in front of the entrance, but his stance and his musculature convince me he is in reality more of a bouncer. Flanking the doors are framed announcements of bands booked into the club — French Dip, Termynal Balystyks, Champagne — and above is a twenty-foot wide sign, scintillating with a million tiny LEDs:

CLUB PIZZAZZ

It is *nothing* like the Blue Rose.

The Boss grins at me. "My club. I like to think of myself as someone who brings a little pizzazz into people's lives. What do you think?"

"It is indeed quite impressive," I say, only half conscious of my words because I am staring at the pictures of the musicians.

Everything from hair bands to punk rock to rap groups with a superabundance of turntables and samplers to jazz ensembles with gleaming horns and upright basses. "But are you not worried that the appearance of a mousy guitarist with no more than an acoustic instrument and nylon strings will bring consternation to your patrons and perhaps even foment rebellion?"

"You just let me do the worrying about that, Ms. Japonica," says the Boss as the doorman hastens to swing the door wide for him, circle the car, and hand me out. "I have a feeling they'll appreciate something a little different."

While I will admit the possibility, I am not reassured when we enter the club.

Flashing lights, pounding music, the oppressive din of a hundred shouted conversations. Men on the prowl for women. Women on the prowl for men. Older men secure in their knowledge that status and wealth will easily provide them with a panache equal to or even exceeding that of their younger counterparts. Girls — of much too tender an age, I think, but hopefully surpassing that of consent — stripped well beyond the borders of decency, dancing on raised platforms or draping themselves on poles, jiggling with abandon or writhing suggestively, doing their best to increase the surging energy of the throng.

Here there are no thinkers, philosophers, or contemplative students such as patronize the Blue Rose. Instead: boisterous, party-minded residents of fraternity houses and members of sports teams determined to break, bury, and trample their training regimens. Hoods and punks. Molls and trollops. Whoops and whistles greet each of the live band's new forays into the realm of heavy metal and power pop, and the musicians themselves are obviously thoroughly enjoying themselves as they push (and not infrequently exceed) the limits of good taste with their gyrations and deliberate double entendres.

But though my own stage presentation is far removed from what I see here, still I am not so different from those who now fling themselves about the spotlit platform and attack their instruments with such vehemence that they might well be assaulting strings, keys, skins, and brass disks alike with lethal force. For I too am a performer, and all who make up our kind live to communicate feeling and emotion, exist to say something with the tools with which Providence has graced us; and I myself have been known upon occasion, even in the middle of the deep intensity of a Dowland fantasia, to free my right hand momentarily from the strings and clench a fist as a sustained chord, ringing, shouts the profundity of the lutanist's vision across the coffee shop.

But...play here? Me? With my humble Kohno? With my Giuliani, my Scarlatti, and my Dowland and Bach? And the chaconne? What about the chaconne? A quarter of an hour of angled and intricate counterpoint thrown into the maelstrom that is Club Pizzazz?

I fear the Boss has misjudged not only the tolerance of his clientele, but the abilities of his prospective musician as well.

Flanked by the Boss and G-shot, I am escorted without incident through the maze of tables and booths, but as we skirt the dance floor where a hundred forms of subtle and overt courtship rituals are being vigorously prosecuted, I am painfully aware that I too am being examined, considered, even mentally undressed by various individuals of the male persuasion, the curves of my body and the set of my breasts entered into several dozen mental spreadsheets, the bottom line of which contracts into a single calculus:

Beddable...or not?

"I dunno, Joe," I overhear during a dead silent upbeat from the stage, "she *is* a little like a mouse, ain't she?"

In *my* Snow City?

The downbeat comes, and with it a crashing wall of sound as my escort and I round the end of the bar. The Boss gives the man in charge a nod, receives a polite half-bow in return, and then we are at an employees-only rear door flanked not by uniforms but by the hoodies and dark glasses I saw the first night the Boss visited the coffee shop. The men wearing them are solid, stolid, and bedrock strong, and they acknowledge the Boss's presence with identical grunts, all the while (obvious even through their dark glasses) keeping an eye on the crowd.

"Everybody having fun?" the Boss asks.

"Righteous time, Boss."

"Staying this side of trouble?"

"Yup."

"Keep 'em there and we'll all be happy." And, leaving G-shot with the hoodies and the dark glasses, the Boss takes my arm and leads me through the door and up a flight of deep-carpeted stairs to a second-floor office furnished in dark woods, mahogany furniture, and velvet draperies. A window looks out over Snow City, presenting a pleasantly serene nightscape of lights and the occasional bit of traffic.

With the closing of the heavy office door, the din of the stage band fades to the rhythmic, almost comforting thud of the kick drum. The Boss offers me a seat (gratefully accepted) and a scotch (politely declined in favor of water), then eases himself into the leather chair behind his desk, puts his feet up, and leans back with a sigh. "You hate the place, don't you?"

I nearly drop my glass. "I...ah...would not go so far as to express so extreme a reaction, but I must admit a certain disbelief that my musical talents would find a cordial reception here."

"Don't be so sure." Loosening his tie, he rises and goes to the window, contemplates the quiet view. "I'll tell you a story. Back when I was in college — didn't finish: they weren't teaching me anything I didn't already know — well, back then I didn't give a damn about classical music. Heard it on the radio, heard it on recordings. Whole thing left me cold. The moderns *still* leave me cold, I should say. But the old stuff, when they knew about tunes and how to turn a nice phrase, before folks started frettin' and fumin' over criticism and that sort of foolishness...now, *that*, I found out I liked. But I didn't find out from the radio or from recordings. It was from a guy who played piano at my college. Music major. There was a piano in the lounge at one of the dorms, and one day he sat down and just started playing. Oh, I don't quite know *what* he was playing. I asked afterward, but the names he rattled off just went by me. Still, though, hearing him and watching him play *live*...now that was something else, if you know what I mean. A gent who was a real musician making all those sounds just flow out from under his fingers...well, I'll tell you, that put an entire new face on classical for me. It wasn't something that came out of a box. It was something that people put their bodies into: heart, soul, blood...everything. And from that day on, I heard classical different. Went to concerts. Listened to guys and gals play at the mall. Spun some CDs occasionally. Because what I was hearing had stopped being something manufactured by a music company and had started to be something made by *people*."

He swings around and fixes me with his shaded eyes. "People like you, Ms. Japonica. So here's your chance to make some converts. You go out there and play your pop and your jazz, sure, but you play that other stuff too, and you show my folks what music is really made of. That it goes beyond a good stage show, and that there's not only cake with frosting, but a good solid bowl of meat and potatoes to the meal."

I feed Charity. I feed her shelter and esteem...and (dare I say it?) even love. I spoon all of it into her hungry soul like, yes, meat and potatoes. And now the Boss is offering me a chance to feed many more, to nurture those who, unforeseen and unlooked for, have somehow found their way into what is proving to be a much broader and widely compassed conception of Snow City than I ever imagined.

Staying this side of trouble? the Boss asked. And, yes: all those people down there in the club...finding happiness — sometimes violent and uncomfortable happiness — but staying this side of trouble.

Still, "I do not wish to disappoint you," I tell him in all honesty, "but I fear that this endeavor might in the end prove to be beyond my powers."

"Willing to give it a try, though?" the Boss asks. As though reading my thoughts.

I am silent for a moment, but the silence stems not from hesitation or unwillingness, but from my astonishment at my own temerity. "Yes," I say at last.

"One set tonight, after the band finishes? Test drive?"

I nod. "One set. A sampler. A-and..."

He waits expectantly, already knowing what I will say.

"And I will play the chaconne."

※

A few minutes later, I find myself in a downstairs dressing room, being fussed over by two of the girls from the dancing platforms. One — tall, black, and amply provided with the sort of curves that make me feel like a wilted stalk of celery — takes me firmly in hand.

"We got a rep to uphold here," she tells me, her hands already undoing the fastenings of my dress, "and we sure can't have you going out on that stage looking like somebody's maiden aunt. I'm Dolores, by the way, and that's Grace over there. She's picking out an outfit for you." I am already half undressed. "Candy," she calls out to a girl just coming in, one of those who were so contorting themselves on the vertical poles out front, "can you get this braid out of Blondie's hair and get hot and heavy with the curling iron? She's going on stage in a few minutes."

I am still playing catch-up, and have not even consciously registered the intentions regarding my hair. "A-an outfit?"

"These duds aren't going to get you anywhere but into a convent, girl. You might be playing unplugged, but you need a little jazz and some razzmatazz if you're gonna be hanging with Club Pizzazz."

I am decidedly of the opinion that I do not want jazz *or* razzmatazz, but Dolores, Grace, and Candy overwhelm my meek objections, and in a surprisingly short time I am curled, ringletted, pushed up, made up, low cut, lace stockinged, miniskirted...and tottering on five-inch heels.

I am afraid to look in a mirror, but I do anyway. I recognize the woman I see reflected in the glass no more than I did the one I regarded when I first awakened in Snow City.

"*Now* you be smokin', girl," Dolores is saying as her cohorts nod enthusiastically. "Oh, Sweet Judy Blue-Eyes. And all that hair! Get yourself out there and knock 'em dead."

In truth, I feel half knocked dead myself, and my thoughts are spinning as, leaning heavily on G-shot's arm to avoid pitching headlong from my unaccustomed and wobbly height, I take the stage. The band has finished, and much of their equipment has been cleared away, leaving — center front — an open area with a solitary chair, footrest, and microphone at the ready.

It is very late by now: the crowd has thinned considerably since the departure of the band, and we are near to closing time in any case. The thought strikes me that perhaps Charity might be worried that I am not yet home. But I made a point of telling her that I would be having a meeting after my Blue Rose performance, so doubtless she is still at her books, hard at work and oblivious of both the time and my absence.

I manage the last steps to the chair alone and unaided, and the Boss himself strides across the stage and puts my guitar into my hands. I am hoping that he will make some explanation of my presence and my repertoire, but he takes the microphone only to say, "Ladies and gentlemen: Ms. Echo Japonica," after which he replaces the mike, moves it into position, lowers his dark glasses enough to give me a wink, and departs, leaving me standing front center stage, being ogled by the male patrons, critically evaluated by the female patrons, and openly stared at by the wait staff...all with expressions indicating unmistakably that they are wondering what on earth this strange lady with an even stranger-looking guitar intends to do.

I share in their bewilderment.

But when the spotlight envelops me, I bow politely to acknowledge the tentative applause and take my seat...to be immediately confronted with a problem: in five-inch heels, putting my left shoe on the foot rest will be an exercise in absurdity. Not to mention exhibitionism.

Candy, the owner of the shoes, is at a table with a male companion who seems transfixed by her well-displayed endowments. She seems worlds away from the brightly lit stage, but not so far that she cannot immediately understand my predicament. "Slip off your right shoe," she mouths at me.

Kindhearted people. Helpful people. Perhaps my dream of Snow City still breathes. Gratefully, I doff the shoe, shove the footrest aside, and remind myself that, in a skirt this short, I will have to keep my knees firmly together in order to avoid presenting another sort of entertainment altogether.

I try my strings. My guitar is in tune (though I wish I could say the same for myself), and as I take one last look at the expectant house, a flash of movement from a perch up on the side wall of the room draws my eyes: the dreadlocked sound engineer is giving me a thumbs-up. The microphone is live.

One set. A little bit of everything, and it *will* include the chaconne. Since my mind has gone distressingly blank regarding the matter of where to begin, I allow my hands to find their way into Carcassi and Giuliani: trivial music, true, but something to settle me and perhaps warn my listeners that for the next forty minutes they would do well not to expect ear-shattering volume or digital effects. And, yes, as I feared, I see looks of consternation: the Boss has brought...*this*...to Club Pizzazz? Whatever could he have been thinking?

I see women grabbing their coats, men escorting them to the doors.

But I am not so shy and retiring, nor so much of a creature of habit, that I let my dalliance with custom dictate the entire course of my set, and after "Lesson XXIII", that delicate but profound meditation by Fernando Sor, I launch into my pop and jazz arrangements. Gratifyingly, this results in renewed interest on the part of my remaining audience and, working now in partnership with the amplification lent to me by the club's sound system, I let my fingers tighten on the strings more than is usual for my Blue Rose performances, ripping out chords percussively and flashing through arpeggios and scales with an occasional jerk of my head and a resultant swirl of wildly curled hair.

Yes, people, it *is* a strange guitar. And it is nylon strung and acoustic. *But let not its simplicity deceive you.*

I am heartened when I look up to see couples on the dance floor. The college students and theater goers at the Blue Rose were content to listen, but here my audience desires to *move*, and though I slip an occasional minuet and gavotte — leaning heavily on the accented beats — into the sequence of pieces, I see the dancers adapt to the changing rhythms almost instinctively, the girls cuddling close to the boys, feet lifting and falling not with a pounding rhythm, but with a light touch: this night, angels might well be pirouetting on the parquet floor of Club Pizzazz.

And then Dowland: the slow, chromatic scale that begins "Farewell", a harbinger of his lengthy exploration of the limits of Elizabethan polyphony and chromaticism. The atmosphere changes, the dance deepens, and I dig further into the strings, tearing Dowland's melancholy from my instrument as, on the floor, couples are moving into an intimacy over which the old lutanist extends a hand of benediction.

"Farewell" ends, and a glance at my watch tells me that it is time to begin the chaconne.

I can take for myself no credit: it is not my spell under which the dancers have fallen. It is that of the masters in whose shadow I labor, in whose eyes I am quite content to perceive the merest glance of approval. Tonight, however, with the sound engineer having been forward enough to add a slight reverb and a very discreet chorus to my guitar and the Boss standing to one side of the big room, arms folded, watching both me and my audience, approval seems to be lavished upon me unstintingly. Despite my nerves, despite my unsettling appearance, despite the novelty of my clothing, I, too, have been overtaken by the flood of music, and my fingers feel no fatigue as they launch into the opening statement of the great piece, the immense, block chords ringing clearly.

For a moment, I am afraid I have lost my audience. This music is simply too complex. But in response to my apprehensive glance, the Boss gives an encouraging nod, and the sound engineer backs off on the chorus enough to let the full-throated sound of my beloved Kohno reverberate through the room, sweet and clear.

And the dancers...respond, changing their footwork, shifting from the lutanist's solace to the Kapellmeister's profundity, finding within the angular and skewed abstractions of Bach's absolute music something human, something humane. An intimacy beyond the physical, a blending of spirits and of pure hearts unburdened of calculation or quest for brute gratification. Minor leads to major and the delicate interplay of starkly discrete melodic voices, an interplay that tips into near-violence as a storm of chordal work first bursts forth in fury, then settles into limpid serenity, and now I see teardrops glistening on the faces of the dancing couples, kisses exchanged, embraces that call forth the unreserved and unconditional giving of self to self, the honoring of the other, the vision of the beloved — even if that vision is only for an hour, a minute, even a few seconds — in the deepest, most profound bestowal of trust, affection, cherishment...everything that I ever dreamed of for Snow City, everything I wanted to find, everything I had, for so long, sought and longed for; and I discover, as the chaconne shifts back into a tangle of near-dissonant melodic minor, that I myself am now lost in the mazed polyphony, that my own eyes are misting, adding their brimming gleam to the myriad, sparkling, compassionate tears that have arisen throughout the room.

Dancing, slow dancing, to the prolonged, three-beat intricacies of the chaconne. And together, we all, all of us, musician and listeners, dancing fingers and dancing feet, take shelter — as so many have before us and so many will after — in the arms of the master.

A swirl of notes, a light-speed, scalar rise and precipitous drop, and then we are caught in the strong reassurance of the final measures, chord stacking atop chord in a resolute restatement of the opening harmonic structure that brings us all safely back to the ordinary world. But not unchanged or untouched are we: those who dare make their foray into the limitless realms of Bach's creation cannot but return with widened hearts and souls, and my audience, having listened not just with their ears but (through the agency of the dance) with the entirety of their physical beings, have perhaps journeyed farther than most.

It is the better part of a minute before the applause begins, hesitant at first, as though afraid to break the spell, but growing in intensity, and at last surging wave upon wave.

Mentally offering my thanks to the master, I sway, too dizzy with the hour and with my exertions to even think about rising from my chair. But G-shot, ever massive, comes to my rescue, himself bending to refasten my shoe (about which I have completely forgotten, leaving myself open to a potentially lethal plunge off the stage), afterwards taking me by the hand, helping me to my feet...

and keeping me from pitching forward as I bow with propriety and gratitude to the audience that has so kindly followed me into what for them cannot have been anything other than uncharted territory.

Across the room: the Boss. And an inquiring lift of his eyebrow. I nod.

Proposal accepted.

A short time later, G-shot is driving me home in the limousine, taking the streets moderately and the turns slowly until, back in my familiar neighborhood, we at last pull to a stop in front of my apartment building.

"Oh, yeah..." He reaches into his coat pocket and extracts a piece of paper. "Boss said to give you this. Thursday's your night now — three sets, jus' like at the Blue Rose — and here's your week's pay in advance."

Mechanically, still somewhat stunned by the evening, I take the paper. A check. I glance at the amount written on it and am staggered.

More than adequate compensation? Much, much more than adequate! But...why so much?

And all for the chaconne?

"Need some help up the stairs, Ms. Japonica?"

It is only then that I come to myself enough to realize that I am still in the clothing I wore onstage: by the time I finished packing up, The girls had left, and I myself was too awash to remember to change. "I...I think I may be able to manage."

Climbing three flights of stairs in five-inch heels? Perhaps not the most insane thing I have done this night, but very close. And yet, even carrying my guitar and my gig bag, I negotiate the steps without mishap.

The sky is lightening in the east as I enter my apartment, but inside it is quite dark. I am well past my hour, I know, and Charity,

I am sure, must be asleep, so I strive to be quiet when I set down my instrument and bag and shut the door behind me.

But then there is a blaze of light, and I see Charity sitting bolt upright on her futon, one hand on the switch of the end table lamp, the other clutching the comforter to herself as though to ward off some nameless evil. Her large eyes widen at the sight of me, and for a moment her mouth opens and closes futilely, speechless.

"Who are you and what have you done with Echo?" she demands at last.

I manage to reach the sofa before my tolerance for the heels gives out, and I do not so much sit down as topple.

"In all honesty, my dear girl," I say, "I confess I have not the slightest idea."

CHAPTER EIGHT

Charity brings herb tea, but it is some time before I can rouse myself from my stupor. At which time I peel off my alien garments and fling myself into the shower in a desperate attempt to regain my normal self...while Charity, perched on the closed lid of the toilet, enthusiastically affirms and reaffirms her approval of my novel change in style.

"I mean," she rattles on over the sound of the shower, "I never knew you could look so...so...I mean, Echo, you are such a total *fox*" —

"And at my age, too," I murmur under my breath, wondering whether I am finishing her unspoken thought.

— "with those big eyes...and all that hair! You look like the lead in one of those guns-'n'-girls anime series or something!"

"I am of the considered opinion," I respond from within the torrent of gratifyingly hot water, "that my 'big eyes and all that hair', as you put it, were applied with some kind of epoxy. I have been at them for ten minutes now and they have not budged."

"Probably used gel on your hair, and fried it in with an iron."

I think back to the dressing room. That is, in fact, exactly what the girls did. "Is it a life sentence I have been given, then?"

"Nah. It'll come out. Just drown it and use lots of shampoo. And I've got some super-strength eye makeup remover in my bag. Lemme go get it."

I stick my face out from behind the shower curtain long enough for Charity to apply what I infer to be some species of industrial-strength solvent. Gratifyingly, the mascara, shadow, and liner at last dissolve, and the hairspray and gel give up soon after that.

"I'll always see you now as that total hottie," Charity assures me (unreassuringly) as I wrap myself in a robe and proceed to towel my hair. "I just *knew* you had it in you! A-and whoever thought of that push-up bra, for sure...like...ought to get a medal or something. Knees clasped to her chest, Charity glances down for a moment. "I guess...I guess I don't have a lot that's pushup-able," she says.

"Oh, my dear girl, they come. They always do. Pray, give it time."

In response to my words, my ward makes something of an odd face, but then appears to shake off whatever thought momentarily possessed her. "Anyway, you can't keep borrowing your stage clothes, so we'll have to do some shopping together."

The truth of her words is undeniable, but I quail at the thought of the type of stores I will have to visit in order to acquire the necessary paraphernalia...as well as at the potential expense.

And then I remember: the Boss's check. An immense amount for one night a week. Money will not be a problem. Neither for clothing nor for housing. In fact...

Was not housing the whole point of the night's endeavor?

"Ah...I believe that very soon we will be changing residences, Charity. To something larger. You will have your own bedroom."

She blinks in surprise, lifting her eyes — those deep eyes — toward me as I explain that I cannot in all conscience continue to relegate her to a corner of the living room. She is sixteen years old, and she deserves — nay...*needs* — a certain degree of privacy.

But her living room futon, earlier, gave me a glimpse of something that — now that I can confront the mirror with some equanimity — returns to mind: Charity, frightened.

"Did something happen while I was gone, my dear? I recall your discomfiture upon my return being rather more than might be occasioned by the appearance of an overage trollop."

She blinks again — translating — and at last appears to remember what she obviously meant to forget. "Oh...that. Well, yeah. I was studying and all, but when I took a break, I looked out the window, and there was this weird guy down on the sidewalk."

"Weird?"

"All in black. With a black hat. Not a...not like one of those private detective hats you see in the movies. It was kind of like with a real broad brim. But what really creeped me out was his eyes. I couldn't see his face, but I could tell that he had really weird eyes. Like, crazy eyes."

"You could not see them, though?"

"I just...sort of saw them. Without seeing them."

She half turns away as though any further explanation would be an admission she has no desire to make.

"He was kinda tall," she continues. "Thin. Really thin. And he was looking up at the building. But...I mean...I could tell he was looking at our window. Actually, like, I could tell that he was looking at *me*."

Snow City or not, my dealings with the Boss and his associates force me to ask: "Some kind of criminal?"

"No..." But her voice trails off, decidedly unsure. "Anyway, when you came up the steps, you sounded so different...with the heels and all...I was afraid it was him."

"So you were hiding."

She gives an embarrassed laugh. "Yeah, well...kinda stupid, huh? In the living room, of all places. And behind a comforter. And...I mean...what's he going to do with me, after all? I'm dead, right?"

There are so many terrible things having nothing to do with physical death that can be done to a young girl...but not in Snow City, not in this world, and I breath a silent prayer of gratitude that merciful and instinctive foresight prompted me to excise those particular horrors from my creation. But despite Charity's brave words, she looks to be on the verge of tears, and I kneel and wrap my arms about her as though she is the frightened, needy child she actually is. "Sometimes, my dear," I tell her, "I sincerely believe that you are more alive than I will ever be. But as for the man, I suspect he is one of the Boss's...ah...employees. I am certain that Boss Maxwell is keeping an eye on us. For some reason which I confess I cannot fathom, he is intent upon hearing me play Bach's 'Chaconne in D Minor' on a regular basis."

"That's how you met? Playing at the Blue Rose? Playing the... what? Chaconne?"

"The chaconne. Yes."

Surreptitiously, she blots her eyes on the front of my robe. "What's a chaconne, anyway?"

"It is rather like a passacaglia."

"Oh, now that's a *biiig* help."

I laugh. "A passacaglia is a set of variations over a repeating bass line."

"Like jam bands do?"

"I will assume for the sake of simplicity that such is the case. Now, a chaconne, in contrast, is a set of variations based on a repeating *harmonic structure.* Vitali and other composers wrote chaconnes for various instrumental ensembles. But Bach wrote one for solo violin, which has, happily, been transcribed for classical guitar and other instruments."

I have lost her. "Harmonic structure?"
"Ah...chord changes."
"Gotcha. *Really* like a jam band, then. But it sounds like it might be kinda hard."
"Bach's music is...yes...rather challenging."
Her smiles come through at last. "Well, what's *not* challenging is breakfast. And then I go to school and you get some sleep. And after that we go shopping." A sly grin. "OMG, you are such a fox, Echo. For sure we are sooooo getting you back into a push-up bra."

⇌

Charity makes good on her threats that afternoon, dragging me off to the mall as soon as she comes home from school, and then dragging me further...into a number of stores I would never, ever, under any sane or normal circumstances, have entertained even the slightest thought of patronizing.

"Are these fashions not a little...ah...young for me?"

"You're a stone gorgeous thirty-five, Echo." Charity is pawing through racks of clothing with the intensity of a fox excavating a rabbit warren. "Flaunt it. Actually, if you're playing at Club Pizzazz, you've *got* to flaunt it. It's the style. You gotta be fly. You gotta Mac out." She glances sidelong at me. "I know, I know: that movie's dated."

I have utterly no idea what she is talking about, but a short while later, she is fussing over me in a dressing room as I once again regard a perfect stranger in the mirror.

And she did indeed get me into a push-up bra.

"This leaves absolutely nothing to the imagination," I murmur, turning this way and that, hoping to find some redeeming shred of virtue in my appearance.

"It's not supposed to."

"Charity...this is just shy of pornography!"

"What's pornography?"

Charity, I know, is nothing if not savvy. Not the slightest bit naive. Apparently, my dream of Snow City omitted yet another scourge of my former world...and I am reminded of the time my girl's history text (in the course of one of my feeble attempts to help her with homework) blandly informed me that the years between 1914 and 1950 marked a period of very profitable cooperation between the United States, the Soviet Union (which, after a brief experiment with communism, settled into a benevolent socialism), Germany (headed, in the 1930s and 1940s, by an urbane, popular, and very pacifistic gentleman by the name of Adolf Hitler), and Japan (then simultaneously engaged in a mutually advantageous free trade agreement with China, Korea, and Vietnam).

And no mention at all of anything particularly unusual happening on September 11, 2001.

"Thank you," I murmur softly...though to whom I am not quite sure.

"Makeup!" Charity is exclaiming. "We need makeup! *Lots* of makeup! Honestly, Echo, you ought to be wearing this kind of stuff *all the time!*"

But I am decidedly *not* wearing "this kind of stuff" when, the following afternoon, I approach the door of the rectory at Saint Ignatius church, the center of the parish to which (so I have learned after some clumsily oblique inquiries) Charity's parents and sister belong.

After a rather basilisk-like appraisal by the housekeeper, I am ushered into a quiet sitting room; and I spend only a few minutes examining the crucifix on the wall and the bookshelves of religious texts before a man in a black suit with a Roman collar enters and introduces himself. "I'm Father Henry, the senior priest here at Saint Ignatius. Call me Hal if you want. Don't worry about the 'Father' business: this is the 21st century after all, and I'm supposed to be on your side, right?"

My stage manner makes itself known, and I bow politely. "Echo Japonica. Ah...Echo, if you so desire."

"Echo, then. Please..." He gestures toward the chairs.

The uncushioned seat I take is not what I would enthusiastically deem "comfortable", but it serves its purpose, and, with the priest listening intently, I explain my situation, Charity's situation, and my reception at her parents' house.

When I finish, Father Hal sits back and ponders the ceiling while I attempt to keep myself from twitching. After all, Charity's mother did explicitly inform me that her "minister" had told her to avoid the girl and all near occasions of the girl.

But the priest surprises me. "Died," he murmurs, "and came back. Now, I think I'd be inclined first off to assume *angel* rather than *devil*." He leans toward me then, elbows on knees. His dark hair, parted to one side, is flecked with gray, lending a serious, competent look to one who otherwise might appear almost too young for his collar. "I remember Charity's death," he says. "Her mother and father were very distraught. Her sister, too. But, actually, the parents were even more distraught than is usual, and believe me, I've celebrated my share of funeral masses for children. The ushers literally had to hold them up at the graveside service."

"Faith blames herself for the death. Charity went on errands in her place that day."

"Understandable guilt on her part, then. I'm not surprised she's having difficulty facing her sister."

"Yes. Quite understandable. But when I attempted a reconciliation, or at least the first steps toward a reconciliation, Charity's mother was insistent that her minister had branded the girl a demon, and for that reason my efforts proved futile."

His eyebrows lift. "Her...minister, you say?"

"Yes."

"She didn't say *priest?*"

"She distinctly used the word *minister.*"

He passes a hand over his clean-shaven cheek. "Well, that explains a number of things, I suppose. Charity's family hasn't been to mass or received the sacraments since the funeral services. No one here at Saint Ignatius has seen them anywhere near the church. In fact, I ran into the father and mother at the grocery store some weeks ago and they...what's the term?...cut me dead." He shrugs despondently. "They appear to have left the Church and found someone else to attend to their spiritual needs."

"Whoever they have found certainly seems a rather intolerant sort."

"Just so." Father Hal purses his lips contemplatively for a moment, then: "But how is Charity? How is she getting along? Is she well? Is she happy?"

"She is back in school, I am delighted to say. She has reconciled with her friends. She is indeed dead: there are some...symptoms... but nothing overly outré. She is generally content, even blithe, but she occasionally demonstrates a sense of humor so black that I can only describe it as infringing upon the ultraviolet. Her status pains her, of course, but her family's rejection pains her more."

"Died...and returned," he ponders. "And all out of love. I'd definitely have to say *angel*, and I'd very much like to meet with her."

"You are not..." I frown, trying to make some sense out of what I want to say. "That is...you do not appear to be demonstrating any particular distress at Charity's clearly unorthodox situation."

"It gives me something of a turn," he admits, "but you have to remember, Echo, that the Church was founded on miracles. And I suppose I'm something of an optimist. There are enough devils to go around: let's keep our eyes peeled for the angels who walk among us."

I nod. "Charity is nothing if not angelic. Rambunctious, perhaps, and with that black sense of humor that, I think, disturbs even herself upon occasion, and...somewhat precocious; but if anyone should detect even a shred of perdition in her, I would be hard pressed not to doubt their sanity." Father Hal smiles, and I give him my card. "You can reach me at this number. I fully intend that Charity and I will be moving to larger quarters soon, but I shall keep you appraised of our whereabouts. And I have no doubt that she would be happy to see you, considering that you are most certainly not the individual who is filling her family's heads with such utter claptrap about devils and demons."

He glances at the card. "Classical guitar? You're a musician, then. Where do you play?"

"At the Blue Rose coffee shop," I say, wishing I could leave it at that, but honesty and his collar force me to add, "a-and at Club Pizzazz."

He lifts his eyes from the card, stares at me in surprise. "Was that *you* the other night? I'd never have recognized you without your, uh, costume...but, as Saint Paul wrote, 'now I see clearly'." In answer to my bewildered look: "The monsignor and I were there having a drink together," he confesses with the air of a boy caught in the act of filching cookies. "It was a very difficult, very late-running day, and we also try to make a habit, pun intended, of showing our collars in unexpected places, if only to remind people that God, too, shows up when you're not expecting Him." A grin. "Though I don't suppose you'll take that as much of an excuse. But you...that guitar...and there at the end..." He sighs, shaking his head. "Bach's violin chaconne, wasn't it? You were amazing!"

Priests...at Club Pizzazz? It *is* the 21st century, I suppose, but I blush...for several reasons. By the time I take my leave, however, I have regained my composure, and Father Hal cordially promises that he will be in touch: dead though she may be, Charity is nonetheless one of his parishioners, and as such she remains under his pastoral care.

My composure, however, is short-lived, for when I reach the sidewalk and turn toward the bus stop, I catch a glimpse of a figure — tall and thin, clad all in black, and wearing a broad-brimmed hat — slipping out of sight and into the shadows between the church and the rectory. One of the other priests? No: I am sure it is not. And therefore I pause warily, peering into the gap between the buildings. There is a walkway, carefully trimmed foliage, flowers, intimations of a back garden: a pastoral haven in an urban landscape. But no dark figure. No trace of any recent passage.

Although it is perhaps but a case of nerves and no more, I cannot shake the feeling of being watched during the bus ride home, even though I discern no black-clad figures among my fellow commuters, and the sensation only intensifies as I climb the stairs of my apartment building. Yet, though I turn and turn again to scan the street below, I see no one.

The apartment is uninhabited when I return, but there are messages on the answering machine: one from Charity (having been supplied with an appropriate allowance, she has gone with friends to get hamburgers after school)...and one from the Boss.

"I understand you're in the market for a rental house, Ms. Japonica," comes his voice — matter-of-fact as usual, smooth and mellow with only the slightest hint of potential violence lurking just under the surface...as usual — "and I think I may have found something that will suit you very well. Give me a call when you get in and we can hop over and take a look at it. The owner tells me he's very flexible with his hours: any time that's convenient for you, he's your man."

The message ends, and I reset the machine. Am I, then, so transparent that the Boss has already guessed that my living arrangements must change? But impulse — or perhaps instinct — takes me of a sudden to the window, and I snatch the curtain back...to see a dark figure stepping into the cover of the apartment building across the street.

I dial the Boss's cell number with a growing sense of disquiet and, when he answers, inform him that, yes, I would be very happy to look at the house. We agree upon a time and, "Oh," I remark, "I do greatly appreciate the fact that you have a gentleman keeping an eye on Charity and myself, but I assure you that such concern is unnecessary. To the best of my knowledge, we need no greater-than-average supervision."

The Boss's voice suddenly drops a semitone or two. "You're being watched, you say?"

"Yes. I believe I was followed when I called upon a parish priest this afternoon, and now I suspect there may be someone outside the apartment building. Charity saw someone as well the night I played at the club."

"Well now..." Another semitone, but the Boss is obviously making a firm attempt to be casual about the matter. "...I can't say I've arranged for anything like that, but a few of the boys might have taken it into their heads to protect my Thursday-night investment... as I'm sure they're thinking this whole thing is. I'll have a talk with them and let them know they can step it down from red alert."

"I'd appreciate that. It is..." I glance toward the curtains. "...a trifle unnerving at times."

"Don't you worry a bit, Ms. Japonica. I'll set everything right as rain."

But when I hang up, I am certain that what Charity and I have seen has nothing at all to do with the Boss or his associates. And when, again on impulse, I step to the window and twitch aside the curtain, I again see the watching and waiting shadow melt into cover, and I know that its eyes — *weird eyes*, Charity said of them, *crazy eyes* — are fixed upon me.

I mention nothing of the watcher or my visit to the rectory when Charity comes home. I do tell her that the Boss has very likely found a house for us, assuring her that any proposed domicile must of course meet with her approval before I will agree to any rental arrangement. Beyond that, we continue with our usual routine, and after dinner and dishes, I pack up my guitar and my gig bag, don my performance attire (as opposed to my "stage clothes") and, bidding Charity good night, leave her to her books and her cramming: finals are almost upon her, though I have no doubt that her grades will be at or near the top of her class.

With a sense of relief, I detect no watcher as I descend the stairs and wait at the bus stop. The rainy season having been left behind, the evening is warm and cloudless: stars are appearing in the deep indigo sky while Venus glitters brightly in the west, and when I reach my customary stop and walk the last few blocks to the coffee shop, my steps are light. No push-up bra, no more than a trace of makeup, comfortable clothes, and sensible pumps: Snow City tonight is the embodiment of perfection.

Except, perhaps, with regards to the matter of illumination in the Blue Rose.

"Has my eyesight unaccountably taken a turn for the worse?" I ask Luigi when I step through the double door into what seems a dark cavern...though it at least *smells* like the Blue Rose. "Or is the light in here somewhat less than usual?"

"Ah! *Il padre* put in some new dimmers, Auntie Echo," comes Luigi's lilt. "Are they not..." I assume that he is pausing to wave his hand in his customary Italianate gesture, but as he is no more than a blur in the darkness, I would be hard-pressed to say for sure. "...just the thing?"

"Loath though I am of being thought predisposed to ill-founded or fanciful conclusions," I return, "I am rather of the opinion that I will not be able to find the stage, much less my frets and my strings."

"Intimacy, my dear Auntie Echo! Intimacy! Your own wonderful music put father in mind of it. It is all so...ah...so..."
"Intimate."
"Exactly."
Despite my best efforts, I feel an eyebrow arch. "Is your father, by any chance, in the store at present?"
"He's off running some errands."
I grope my way to the back of the room using the candles on the scattered tables in much the same manner as an airliner uses runway lights, and save myself from smacking into the rear wall more by feel than by sight. As it is, however, the forward end of my guitar case thuds into the plasterboard hard enough that I expect Luigi — or, rather, Jake — will, come tomorrow, have an appointment with some spackling paste and paint.

As usual, I tune and prepare in the back office. I keep the lights low in order to save my night vision, all the while attempting to convince myself that everything will be better by the time I reach the stage. The dimmers will surely have been raised...or perhaps by some providential Divine intervention, I will have been graced with the perceptive acuity of a bat.

The clock ticks toward my start time, and I open the office door to find that, if anything, it is even darker in the coffee shop than before: the dimmer settings have not changed a bit, but the last traces of the sunset's afterglow are even now fading from the sky, taking with them the spill of light from the front windows.

And Mr. O'Dally is still absent.

I find myself oddly wishing for the push-up bra and the five-inch heels: such accouterments might summon forth the welcome presence of a spotlight, and there would be no worries about having to play by means of some novel application of the Braille system. I must, however, make do with what I have, and as I fumble my way to the stage, I am mentally revising my setlists, giving priority to works I can play by feel, cobbling together a series of pieces that will allow me to negotiate tonight's performance without serious mishap. Thankfully, I find my chair in its usual place and settle myself, but a stray glance toward the back of the room reveals a darker obscurity, visible only by virtue of the flickering candlelight on the table before it: the Boss.

The chaconne.

Play the chaconne...by *feel?* Me? Impossible. And yet, so it seems, I must. Perhaps I might ask the Boss to have a word with Mr. O'Dally about the lighting? But no: I have imposed upon him enough, and I will not burden him with the task of solving such niggling problems as, upon occasion, plague all musicians.

Luigi finally comes to my rescue — this time in all sincerity — with a lit candle and a stand. "I think the dimmers might be just a little *too* low, Auntie Echo" he murmurs to me as he carefully positions the light. "I'll talk to Dad about it when he comes in."

I whisper my thanks, but even with the candle, the illumination remains somewhat less than optimal. Dressed in performer's black as I am, I doubt that anyone in the coffee shop will be able to make out much more than my light-colored Kohno guitar, my hands, and my pale face and hair.

Fortunately, I *can* make out my strings and my frets now, and with an inward sigh of relief, I return to my usual setlists. Simple pieces to start with, lighter and more driving pop and rock for the second set. And when I take the stage for the third time, I see (vaguely) not only that the Boss is leaning forward expectantly — he seems to have discovered an appreciation for Dowland as well as for the chaconne — but that (clearly) Luigi has considerately refreshed the candle...and added a second.

Which is immensely fortuitous, considering the exactitude with which I must now play. Dowland starts off easy enough — though nothing to which the great lutanist has put his hand can be deemed completely effortless — with light dances, and then Bach begins to flow. Not the chaconne. Not yet. For now, selections from his suites for lute and (where the whim came from, I cannot say) his "Prelude, Fugue, and Allegro".

It is in the twisting course of the fugue that I sense a certain disquiet in the air. Given time, any performer develops a sense of the listeners' mood, how they are responding to the music, whether it is time to abandon a given program and try alternative selections; but this feeling is something I have not previously encountered. It is like the edge of a nightmare half-remembered upon waking, one that prompts the sleeper to curl into a ball beneath the covers and weep, though the tears' origin remains unknown. Or like the gloomy melancholy of a fellow traveler on the bus, a dour gaze cast fixedly upon the floor mats speaking eloquently of profound mental distress.

Even in Snow City, I consider as I reach the final measures of the fugue and glance down to make sure that a particularly difficult string crossing goes smoothly...

...only to be transfixed by the sight of the ruby-red dot shining on the back of my hand. A vibrant, shimmering point of laser light that slowly rises along the upper part of my guitar and from there toward my chest.

The screaming, insane incongruity of such a thing and what it means at first freezes me, freezes my fingers, turns my feet and face to ice, and leaves me motionless...rooted to my chair.

This cannot be happening...not here...

The dot continues its upward drift, forced by the ambient darkness to feel its way slowly toward my center of mass: my chest, my heart and lungs, my main arteries and critical organs.

"What the *hell?*"

The Boss. In the silence left by the sudden cessation of music, his voice rings like a hammer striking a steel anvil, freeing me from my immobility and allowing me to throw myself to the left just as an eyewink of light and ported gases flares momentarily from the darkness of the coffee shop and the muffled crack of a suppressed firearm cleaves the intimacy, the quiet, the music...all asunder.

I am spun to my right as the bullet, missing me, plows into my instrument, slamming the Kohno's body into my ribs and turning the bottom half of the guitar into a splintered mass of cracked soundboard, broken bracing, and pulverized lacquer. Overbalanced, I fall heavily to the floor as panic seizes my audience and brings them — screaming, crying, — to their feet. Footsteps in the darkness now: pounding, fleeing for the front door, surging toward the rear exit; but my eyes are gripped and held by the sight of my beloved Kohno lying shattered and broken in the fading light of the now guttering candles, and as I watch, helpless (as, so it appears, I have always been helpless, whether in my old world or in Snow City) the tension of the strings drags the instrument — curving, buckling, collapsing — inward, the guitar finally imploding with a dull crunch of fractured wood and fragmenting finish, destroying itself beyond all possibility of restoration or repair just as my dreams of Snow City have, with that single shot, vanished, utterly disintegrated in a burst of focused hate and rcified violence.

CHAPTER NINE

"Echo! Oh, my freakin' God...Echo!"

Charity is folded in my arms — or, rather, I am folded in hers — as I sit on the rear step of the ambulance, a blanket clutched about my shoulders in an attempt to hold at bay the cold that, despite the warmth of the night, persists in digging ever deeper into my bones. My right arm, salved and bandaged, is throbbing after the extraction of numerous splinters, my left arm stings from a double injection of antibiotics, my ribs ache with bruises, and I have had neither the heart nor the strength to move since the EMTs finished with me.

Charity sobs. "I heard all the sirens. The neighbors across the landing had the news on and said you'd been shot. I...I ran all the way here."

About us, the street is full of black-and-whites, flashing lights, crime scene investigators. The area in front of the Blue Rose is cordoned off with yellow police tape, and the whole block has only recently been released from lockdown.

"The Kohno took the bullet, Charity," I tell her. "Should I scar from the splinters, I will bear the marks proudly, in honor of a noble instrument." I blear at her, a storm of emotions beating upon me. "But...you ran? My dear girl, our apartment is nowhere near!"

Charity nods defiantly. "I ran. I couldn't catch a bus, so I ran."

"For miles?" Not a drop of sweat on her. Not a hair out of place. Not gasping for breath. Perfect. Just as, I realize, she always is. Angelic, indeed: untouched by the smears of mortality. "B-but surely you must be exhausted!"

As usual, when acknowledging the irregularity of her circumstances, she shrugs uncomfortably. "It doesn't work that way for me."

A police detective was beginning to question me when he was interrupted by my girl, who, hair flying and green eyes wide, defying all warnings and shouted orders, threw herself over the police tape and through the blockading scrim of officers in order to reach me. Now he shakes his head resignedly, steps forward, and attempts to resume his work. "Ms. Japonica...did you see the shooter?"

"I must confess I did not," I say. "Owing to the shop owner's recalcitrance regarding adequate illumination, I was unable to see anything save for the incontrovertible evidence of the laser sighting mechanism."

The detective looks baffled.

"Echo always talks like that," Charity explains. "It's her way of keeping people at arm's length."

I stare. In a handful of words she has explained not only my language but my entire life in Snow City.

"She's saying that it was too dark to see him. Or her."

Tiredly, grieving over the loss of the last shred of my world's innocence, I nod.

The detective makes another effort. "And did you happen to see where he — or she — went after the shot was fired?"

I shake my head. "All was confusion and darkness. Perhaps the Boss —" But I catch myself. Doubtless the Boss wishes to be left out of any...inconvenient inquiries.

And then I realize that I have not seen or heard any sign of him since his exclamation in the coffee shop. G-shot and the limousine are missing as well.

Fortunately, the detective misunderstands. "We've checked with Mr. O'Dally," he informs me. "He wasn't there during the shooting."

I take refuge in my fatigue. "Just so. Just so."

"Can you think of any reason anyone would want to harm you, Ms. Japonica?"

Harm...me? In my own world?

"Do you have any enemies?" he persists.

A fleeting memory of Charity's mother, red-rimmed mouth tight, ordering me out of her house, blazoning the name of demon upon her daughter.

Enemies?

"I...I cannot imagine anything of the sort."

Or have I already imagined it?

"I'm afraid we'll have to hold what's left of your guitar as evidence, ma'am. Ballistics will be getting involved, and we'll...."

To my ears, his words fade off into nonsense, nonsense buried in a chaos of thoughts. Police. Weapons. Ballistics. Evidence. Did I really build into my fantasy all these mechanisms of horror? My first months here, I saw nothing like this, read nothing about this, could imagine nothing of this. But it was here nonetheless.

Or was it? Am I, in actuality, continuing to build my dream? Having first created my ideals, am I now, day by day, constructing, extending to its logical conclusion, the dark and frightful underbelly of what I once called civilization? The barest thought of the idea is repugnant to me, yet here it is, seemingly reinventing itself despite my wishes, mortaring itself together brick by brick, event by event...atrocity by atrocity.

Everything I tried to escape.

Charity steps between me and the detective, firmly ending the interrogation. "We're losing her, sir. She's had too much for one night. Can I take her home?"

The detective: notebook open, pencil poised. "And you are?"

Not a trace of hesitation or apology. "Charity Monthage. Echo is my legal guardian. I live with her."

As it has become quite obvious that there is nothing more to be gained from badgering a bedraggled and near-hysterical musician, he takes our telephone number and address, puts his card into my strengthless fingers, and lets us go. Nonetheless, we arrive home in the back of a squad car, and two police officers check the grounds and the apartment thoroughly before they allow us to ascend the stairs.

"Thank you, gentlemen," I manage through chattering teeth. Chattering...though not with cold.

"Our pleasure, ma'am," says one of the officers, holding the door open for us.

Our pleasure. I cling to the words. Surely here is some trace of humanity and grace still clinging to Snow City.

"Please," I whisper. "Please."

"C'mon, Echo..." Charity sits me down at the dinette and begins rummaging through the kitchen cabinets. "I'm going to make you some soup. It's canned, but you know we buy the good stuff."

When the telephone rings, I start so badly that I nearly upend the table. By then, Charity has the soup hot, and she gently pushes me back down into my chair and sets a bowl and a spoon in front of me before she goes to pick up. I stare at steaming chicken noodle, wondering whether I can actually eat it. Wondering whether I can eat anything anymore.

"Japonica-Monthage," Charity answers the phone, and then, after a moment: "Yeah, I know...sounds like a law firm. Hang on, Boss. She's right here."

She brings the cordless phone over and I press it to my ear, almost relieved to have been reprieved from the soup.

The Boss, as it turns out, did not desert me at the coffee shop: rather, having seen that the shot missed and that my physical injuries were relatively inconsequential, he went in pursuit of the shooter. G-shot, however, waiting outside by the limousine and quite familiar with the sound of a suppressed firearm, had already collared the man as he burst out of the front door...and had persuaded him that his greatest desire was to examine the car's interior.

At this very moment, in fact, some of the Boss's associates are also persuading him. In a back room. Somewhere.

"They're getting some info," says the Boss. "More than he'd give the police. I'm all in favor of Miranda, you know, but sometimes you have to be a little more...sincere...with people."

I do not know what he means by "sincere", and I assume that, as is the case with many things concerning the Boss, I do not *want* to know.

"You ever heard of someone called Brother John?" he asks.

"Brother John?" I repeat out loud. "I confess I have not." I turn to Charity, avoiding the still steaming but faintly accusing sight of the soup. "Charity, have you heard of a Brother John?"

"What? Like in 'Frére Jacques?'"

"Ah...I think not." I return to the phone. "Is that the individual you have detained?"

"Nah, we've got some slimy little weasel who knows how to use a Sig nine-millimeter and a laser sight. But what we've pried out of him so far is that Brother John ordered the hit. Something to do with you being at odds with the natural order, whatever that means. It's not much, I'll admit, but everything else he's spouting is shout-'n'-holler Jesus and God forever and demons everywhere." His tone turns somber, resigned. "Some people use crack, I guess, some use religion."

I begin to suspect then that the mysterious Brother John was the individual outside the apartment. And outside the rectory. *Weird eyes...crazy eyes.*

But...crack?

Here?

"Anyway, we're working on showing our sincerity a little more" —

I shudder.

— "but I'm beginning to think he doesn't know much beyond what he's already told us."

My mouth has unconsciously fallen open, and Charity, determined, dips up a spoonful of soup and feeds it to me. "Chew, swallow, repeat," she orders, dipping a second spoonful. "*You're* not dead, so you need this."

"Don't you worry, Ms. Japonica," the Boss continues, "this piece of trash might think he's buds with God, and he's powerful afraid of this Brother John, but you can be sure we'll put the fear of the *Lord* into him."

I half expect to hear screams and the rhythmic thud of bastinado in the background of the connection but, unaccountably, I hear only the sound of crickets and cicadas. "Where are you, Boss? If I may be so indiscreet."

"Outside your apartment building. It's me and G-shot right now, but I'll have some of the boys out here 24/7 to make sure you're all right."

I am awash. "But...but the police executed what I assume was a diligent search before they let us out of the car."

A chuckle. "Oh, Ms. Japonica, I'm disappointed. You really ought to know by now that we're much better at not being found than the police will *ever* be at finding us. Now, you get some sleep and call me on my cell when you get up. I'll have someone come by and run Charity to school. All this 'natural order' stuff is a powerful bother to me, and I'm not taking any chances."

Sleep? Can I really sleep? But body chemistry will not be denied, and between emotional shock and the ebbing of adrenalin, I am nearly unconscious as Charity, taking pains not to poke my bruised ribs, gets me into pajamas and under the covers.

"My Kohno," I murmur, fading into merciful blackness. "Everything..."

"Shh...." says Charity. "Shh.... Time enough to think about it tomorrow. You taught me that, big sister."

<hr>

The knowledge that I can no longer count on the sanctity or the safety of my world comes seeping back to me as, come the next afternoon, I struggle up from sleep, first into a drowsy layer of continuing hope, and then, when I rise...and feel the throb of pain from my wounds...into the pitiless glare of reality.

My window shows me no watcher outside. Nothing, in fact, out of the ordinary. Snow City continues its apparently ideal life, but where before I was slowly becoming aware only that its surface perfection masked secrets of a darker, more disturbing nature, now I am faced with the existence of what might well be a lethally virulent contagion.

I do not see the men the Boss promised. But I know they are there.

A message is waiting for me on the answering machine: "Don't forget to call me, Ms. Japonica," comes the Boss's voice, the ominous rumble in its tone seeming now to have become a permanent fixture. "We need to go have a look at that house. And a few other things have come up."

I decide to let him wait while I shower and examine my wounds. The splinters, I decide, were more than adequately excised by the EMTs, and my bruised ribs will mend in a matter of days. No infection, thanks to the antibiotics, but the supplementary tetanus shot aches such that the combination of stiffness and pain may well prevent me from performing for several days.

My Kohno.

Weeping, I allow myself to slip to the floor of the shower, allowing the water to drench me with warmth. I can heal — at least my body can — but my Kohno cannot. The guitar that sustained me throughout my life in Snow City is gone. Reduced to a useless pile of leavings and broken bits.

Much like its owner.

But despite apparent — and apparently increasing — failings, Snow City was not created lightly, nor was it founded and constructed without a substantial amount of grit and determination. Snow City was, and is, my dream. And into its building went weeks, months, years of longing and yearning; white, insomniac nights of heartache and idealism; dogged and belligerent rejections of all the disease-ridden hate so freely vomited forth by my old world. Defective? Perhaps so. Failing? Perhaps yes. But as the water sheets over me, I once more gather together the determination, the longing, the grit, and — yes — even a little anger.

And I rise.

I will not lose Snow City.

Staying this side of trouble? the Boss asked.

Yes, I decide. I will stay this side of trouble. And I will do everything within my power to keep Snow City this side of trouble. Governments and politicians brought my old world to its knees with their squabbles and their equivocations and their petty disputes over territory and their foolish displays of puissance. But Snow City is mine, and I have no patience with those who would, bit by bit, chip away at its foundations and then claim ignorance and good intentions when the whole edifice comes crashing down.

I finish my shower, dry off, dress, and call the Boss.

"I've been putting out some feelers," he tells me. "This Brother John turns out to be some kind of renegade minister. Off the wall. Crazy. Makes the Tennessee snake handlers look like a Quaker sewing circle. Started out as Methodist or something, but got himself tossed out over what some of my contacts called 'doctrinal disputes'. Which I translate as 'knock-down, drag-out fights over who's going to hell, when, and why'. Brother John seems to think almost all of us are. Now. For whatever reason happens to come to what's left of his mind at the moment. Anyway, he's gotten himself a number of followers. Some people seem to like that sort of thing. That sense of belonging and being right. Maybe we all do, I don't know. Sometimes I wonder what's buried inside all of us, why it's necessary for folks like me to keep other folks in bounds. Why so many of us just want to have somebody else tell us what to do so that we don't have to deal with all the hassle of making our own decisions. Anyway, Brother John seems to have put together a nice little congregation that'll do anything he tells them to."

He mutters something about "bat-shit crazy, all of 'em," but I am thinking of Charity's mother talking about her "minister". And about demons and devils. The connection is blatantly obvious to me, but I cannot, of course, prove it.

I blink, startled by my own thoughts: I do not *have* to prove it.

And with that inner permission, the pieces start to fall into place. My interview with Charity's mother. Her irrational flare of anger and denial of her daughter. Her minister. The family forsaking its customary place of worship. That strange reference — oblique, admittedly, to the point of absurdity — to hope. Or, rather, to *Hope*.

And that shot.

"I am quite beholden to you, my dear sir," I tell the Boss. "And, as I should by necessity mention, deeply in your debt."

"Nonsense." The panther thrum is by now almost reassuring. "You've given me the chaconne, and you're performing at my club. I'm in *your* debt, woman."

"About the chaconne...and performing..." I falter, unsure of what to say.

"Ah, yes. Your guitar. We can talk about that when I see you."

"See me?"

"We're going to look at a house, remember?"

We pick Charity up from school, the eyes of the other students once again growing wide at the appearance of the Boss's limousine, and I note, with a glow of happiness I thought I had lost forever, the hugs and affectionate pokes given my ward as she trots down the walkway to the open door of the vehicle. Our course, however, does not take us directly to the house, for at my request, we first attend to some long overdue business.

"Cell phones?" says the Boss. "You can get set up just about anywhere, but I have a friend at a store run by one of the big carriers. He can get you fixed up right proper."

Charity's eyes are bright. "Can I do a smartphone, Echo? I mean...I know that's...like...asking a lot...but...well..."

I assure her that she can have whatever she likes. My Kohno might be gone, but I can at least manage a smartphone for my girl.

The purchase turns out to be surprisingly complex: there are many models and variations, all with roughly similar but nonetheless distinctly different features and appearances. For myself, I fear I disappoint the clerk greatly when I explain that I simply want something capable of making and receiving calls with a minimum of fuss, and that I do not require access to games, the internet, e-mail, or any form of interplanetary communication. But his expression brightens considerably when he turns to Charity, for my girl knows the jargon, knows the equipment...and knows exactly what she wants.

"This one just came out, and it's got that whopping memory for songs and other stuff," she explains as her fingers flash across the demo model's touchscreen. "It's not equipped for flight, but that's about the only thing it can't do."

After a glance at the Boss, who is standing off to the side with the attitude of a benevolent uncle, the clerk turns to me. "I can give you a great deal on the package."

"That would be...most gracious of you," I assure him.

"My folks must have tossed my old phone," Charity goes on. "It wasn't with my stuff. Maybe they buried it with me." She ponders the demo model in her hand. "I wonder: if I dial my old number, would I be connected directly to the afterlife?"

Which prompts the clerk to cycle through several changes of indeterminate expression. Finally: "This is...ah...some sort of... gift, then?"

"Charity is my ward," I explain.

"Yeah," says Charity without looking up. "Mom and dad sort of disowned me when I died."

Instant silence.

"It is a figure of speech," I assure the clerk.

I am filling out forms and reading through paperwork when Charity tears her eyes away from her newly acquired treasure. "This is the one with the tracking app on it, isn't it?"

Tracking app? I wonder.

"Yes it is," says the clerk. "But you can turn it off."

I am out of my depth. "May I be so bold as to ask for an explanation?"

My initiation into cellular thaumaturgy continues: while most portable phones provide a GPS link — mostly for the benefit of 911 calls — the model with which Charity is so enamored sports a more active variant: it actually tracks the phone's movements and makes them available for download to the owner's home computer, thus providing a detailed map of one's wanderings.

Charity's expression is, decidedly, saying *no*. My instincts are, with equal conviction, saying *yes*. I recall the hatred of the mother, the strangeness of the renegade minister, and most of all, the image of that ruby dot, drifting upward and centering on my chest a split second before the Boss's words freed me from my immobility and saved my life.

Charity and I huddle for a discussion in a quiet section of the store. It is not an argument by any means. Our relationship plumbs depths that make the usual quarrels between adults and teenagers the stuff of trivial absurdity. "Given all that has happened," I explain, "I would be more comfortable, and greatly reassured, were I, in an emergency, able to find you."

"You don't trust me to call?"

How can I explain what it is that I fear when I myself do not know? I have my memories of my old world, and I have my experiences of my new, and together, they join voices into one, irrefutable, cautionary refrain.

I go down on one knee before Charity. "I trust you implicitly, my dear girl. I trust you more than I trust any other soul in this entire world, including myself. But strange things have been happening of late, and I think it important that we leave the tracker option available."

Charity's deep eyes are probing me, evaluating the rationale of my request, considering my motives...which I am certain she sees much too clearly, though their details and genesis might yet remain obscure to her. "Well...OK," she says at last. "But on two conditions."

"You have but to name them."

"One, that you don't snoop."

"You have my word. Emergencies only."

"Two..." An impish grin. "You get a phone just like this, and you leave the tracker on, too. If you snoop, I snoop."

"Done," I say, and we seal our covenant with a handshake. "But you must play the role of Virgil to my Dante and be my guide through the dark wood: I have not the faintest idea how to operate this sort of device. I would wager I would have a better chance of piloting an airliner."

She smiles...and adds a hug to the handshake. "Stick with me, big sister. I've got your back."

In contrast to the cell phone purchase, the house rental proves effortless. I could not ask for more: three bedrooms, hardwood floors (I confess a preference for slippers and socks in the house), a big living room with a large window looking out on a tidy front lawn, a secluded backyard, a delight of a kitchen with cabinet space galore and a convenient pass-through to the dining room...and all of it a five-minute walk from Charity's school.

Light, light, light: not a shadow to be seen. Walls are freshly painted, floors polished, appliances spotless, and the bedrooms are begging for an opportunity to provide safe, restful repose. Pricey, yes. But given my position at Club Pizzazz, quite affordable.

Which brings me once again to the uncomfortable question: what, exactly, *is* my position at Club Pizzazz? And, for that matter, at the Blue Rose?

"I can't speak for Mr. O'Dally," the Boss admits after Charity, trailing the landlord and G-shot, has raced away to explore the rest of the house, leaving the two of us to confer privately in the sunny living room, "but your spot at the club is not going away, and I'd wager Mr. O'Dally's going to keep you on at the Rose no matter what. But for now I'm of a mind that you need a break from Snow City, Ms. Japonica. You've been playing music five nights a week for...well...years now, as I hear it. You've had a traumatic experience, to say the least. And we've..." He ruminates for a moment. "...got a bit of trouble on the home front, if you take my meaning. Though I don't particularly like the idea of not hearing you play the chaconne for a while, it might be time for you and Charity to have a little vacation."

"Am I understanding you correctly, sir? You want the two of us to go somewhere?"

"At the risk of sounding like a bad movie, Ms. Japonica, that's exactly what I'm saying: I want you both out of town. In my experience, if a body feels strongly enough to take a shot at someone, that body isn't going to stop with one try."

I glance nervously down the hall. No sign of Charity or the men. Nevertheless, in a whisper: "Do you think they might try to harm Charity?"

The Boss keeps his voice equally low. "Can't say for sure. But I'd feel better if the two of you were someplace out of the way — safe — for a couple weeks. You got anywhere like that you can go, Ms. Japonica?"

I have come to a stunned but defiant acceptance of what happened the previous night, but the thought of anything of the sort being directed at Charity is, to my mind, obscene. Get her out of town? If necessary, I will get her entirely out of the country. "I believe I can arrange something. But in addition to the police doubtless wanting another interview or two, Charity has final exams beginning tomorrow, and I am unwilling to pull her away from them: her schoolwork means a great deal to her. And...a two week absence at most: she has taken it upon herself to enroll in summer school in an effort to bolster her intensive scholastic review."

"Spunky girl." The Boss nods. "Very good, then. I'll have a friend in the department fast-track the police work, Charity can take her tests, and we'll keep a close eye on you both until you're safely away. I'll have a chat with Mr. O'Dally, too: your gigs will be waiting for you when you come back in time for summer school. Will the house do?"

"I like it very much" —

And Charity, bursting back into the room just then with G-shot and the landlord close behind, is waving her arms enthusiastically. "It's perfect, Echo! I *love* it! Which bedroom is mine? I'll flip you for the one with the pink trim!"

— "but I am somewhat concerned about the size. How will I ever keep it clean?"

Charity has foreseen that concern. "We'll *both* keep it clean," she declares. "We'll make a schedule. Dusting, vacuuming, mowing lawns, raking...all that good stuff. Oh, Echo...we gotta do this!"

On my face, I feel a shade of a smile I thought I had lost forever. "I think you have your answer, Boss." I turn and bow to the landlord. "We wholeheartedly accept your terms, sir."

"Don't you worry about the size," he assures me as I deal with paperwork and write a check for the deposit and first month's rent. "Rooms always look smaller once you get the movables in."

I think of my few meager sticks of furniture and suppress a wry smile.

"And..." The owner of the house is old, his hair white and thin, the skin on his arms brown and sere from summer gardening, the lines on his face burnt deep by the sun. "...you know, I'm getting on, and I've been thinking it's time to let some of my properties go. We can talk about a rent-to-own agreement if you decide you like the neighborhood."

Snow City again. The Snow City I always wanted. I feel my eyes ache and half turn away to hide the tears.

"Thank you, sir," I tell him. "I am infinitely obliged."

"Backyard!" shouts Charity, and she is off once again...with a not-overly-reluctant G-shot at her side. The landlord, with a glance at the Boss, assures me that my references are of the first water and hands over the keys.

"All yours," he says, and takes his leave.

The Boss and I are once again alone in the living room. From the backyard come Charity's cries of delight and G-shot's pleased laughter. I am terribly conscious of my own voice: muted, apprehensive. "What else do I not know?" I ask.

"That's about it. Didn't have a chance to get much more out of the shooter."

"I assume you turned him over to the police?"

"Ah...no. He's dead."

I feel as cold as I did when watching the laser trace its way toward my heart. "You did not —"

"No, we didn't. You know my views on hurting people when it's not called for."

Despite myself, I cannot but notice a few additional bruises and deep gashes in his disfigured knuckles. Just before he senses my gaze and shoves his hands into his pockets.

"He killed himself. The boys went out for coffee, and he got his belt off and...well..." He inhales deeply, exhales. "That was that."

"He did it himself?"

"Yes. Nobody else could get into that room. It was his own doing." Again that slow breath: inhale, exhale. "Kind of makes you wonder just what Brother John is really like, doesn't it?"

Despite my unwillingness to make the connections, all the pieces are falling together with the force of converging avalanches. And Charity comes rushing in at that moment, unflushed, unbreathing, not a drop of sweat on her, but eyes shining. "Oh, Echo...can we have a dog?"

I must get this child away from this place as soon as I can.

"We shall have to discuss that at length, my dear," is all the reply I can find. "First, of course, we must move in and get settled."

"Don't you two worry about the moving," comes the Boss's deep thrum. "You take your trip, and me and the boys will get your things over from the apartment." Our eyes meet, and I know that it is not simply convenience he is offering.

Charity blinks. "We're going somewhere?"

"After your exams," I assure her. "So much has been happening, I thought a vacation might perchance be in order."

"Oh, that is so cool! After last night, you *definitely* need a break, Echo."

And then she is off again, re-inspecting what she has already inspected and settling her claim firmly upon the bedroom with the pink trim. But G-shot comes back from the limousine a few minutes later with a black, padded pouch made of woven nylon. He hands it to the Boss. The Boss hands it to me. "Know how to use one of these?"

The weight and feel of the pouch have already told me what to expect when I pull back the zipper. "Unfortunately," I say, my voice all but choking, "I do."

"Sakes alive: all *sorts* of surprises from you, Ms. Japonica." He calls for Charity and herds the lot of us out to the limousine. "And don't worry about the guitar," he says as though certain words — and the pouch — have not passed between us. "You can surely get something from your music store man that will keep your chops up during the trip. And though I know he's not upscale enough to be carrying anything that will do for a professional, I'll get with him while you're gone and see what's on the market." A ghost of a smile. "Something that won't break the bank and that we don't have to wait two years for."

The pouch weighs heavily in my hand, but it is not only the pouch that concerns me. "Why are you doing all of this for me?"

The Boss's eyes are shadowed behind his dark glasses. Perhaps he can read me, but I cannot read him. "I'll tell you one of these days," he says. "But now isn't the time. I'm doing it. Let's just leave it at that."

All sorts of surprises from me, all sorts of conveniences lining up, all sorts of terrifying conclusions rushing to abut one another with horrific ease. And that night, when Charity has retired to her futon, I sit down at my computer and open the e-mail client:

Dear Uncle Seymour,

Might you find it at all convenient if I accepted your long-standing invitation for an extended visit to your ranch? As you know, I have a young ward now, Charity Monthage, and a trip to the north might well provide the emotional refreshment for which the two of us are longing.

Your devoted niece,
Echo

I read the missive over...and then over again. The right tone? The right turns of phrase? Too short? Too long? What is right anymore? What *could* be right, since despite Seymour's intimate familiarity with all the details of my childhood, adolescence, and adult life — details I myself do not recall — I have never met the man and have no memory of him?

The night is dark. It seems colder than it actually is. Outside, the Boss's men watch: invisible, vigilant. In the other room, Charity — dead — sleeps peacefully, visited by whatever dreams might come to those who have passed beyond this life and then returned.

I finally put my apprehensions aside and click *send*, wishing all the while that I could concentrate more fully on the e-mail, that my thoughts and attention were not so occupied and distracted by the Boss's padded bag and the semiautomatic pistol it contains.

CHAPTER TEN
(*pifa*)

The plains of Judith Gap stretch to either side of the highway, broken in the distance, east and west, by the Big Snowy Mountains and the rolling, pine-clad folds of the Little Belt. Wheat here, wheat and hay, wheat and hay undulating in the wind that sweeps down from the north, wheat and hay baking gray-gold in the heat of the summer sun, wheat and hay cupping in great flat hands the two-lane, north-south ribbon of asphalt laid down between the mountain ranges as though in accordance with the uncompromising severity of a gunsight...and the blue, blue sky arching above all.

In the passenger seat of the rental car, Charity watches the monotonous yet infinitely varied scenery flit past the window. Together, we have seen Cheyenne and overnighted in Sheridan, eaten lunch at a steak house in Billings, and stretched our legs in Harlowton, both of us sufficiently mundane in our appearance to have excited little interest on the part of the local residents, not even the Hutterites, who offered us no more than a glance: neither friendly nor hostile, but perhaps a bit curious. But nowhere have we stayed long enough to satisfy anyone's curiosity as to whence we come, why we travel, or whither we are bound.

My hands on the wheel, with little traffic to occupy my attention, I cannot but think of all three questions — whence, why, and whither — and of the small apartment we have left behind, the apartment where I first awoke into the Snow City of my dreams, the apartment now in the process of being abandoned, all traces of my presence there being steadily erased as the Boss's men transfer our belongings to our new home. I think of the nylon pouch the Boss gave me, currently tucked under my seat as innocuously as a bag of cosmetics. I think of Charity, who, I am certain, sees our departure from Snow City as nothing more than a welcome vacation after final exams and a police investigation that eventually led nowhere, an opportunity to leave behind for a time all reminders of her parents' rejection and her sister's ambivalence.

I steal a glance at her as she stares in wonder at the wind farm near the small town that took its name from this wide break between the mountain ranges. The white pinwheels spin high atop their pylons — now lazily, now briskly — their presence lending a sense of comfort and reassurance to an otherwise featureless, almost disquietingly empty landscape.

And then, as though feeling my gaze, she turns to me, evaluating me with her large green eyes, taking my measure. And at last the silence, strained to the point of fracture like a guitar string cranked beyond its tolerance, gives way with her simple question:

"We're running away, aren't we, Echo?"

I put my attention back on the road, suddenly seeing nothing save the ruler-straight highway. Another mile. Another two miles. The wind farm is behind us now. The town passed by in a twinkling. Charity is waiting. How did I ever think I could deceive one such as she?

Finally: "Yes, Charity. Indeed, we are running away."

"Because you got shot at. Because of me."

Dissemblance is beyond me. Not in the face of those eyes and their harrowingly intense gaze. But I try nonetheless. "Because of you? Really, my dear, I cannot see —"

"Oh, come on, Echo." Her tone is more of resignation than anger. "I can figure it out. My parents give me the high kickoff, my sister won't talk to me, you take me in, and then you nearly soak up a bullet. You're forgetting I was in my folks' house when I stole my stuff. I saw the tracts and the books and the website printouts. They were all over the place. Cripes, I think they were even in the bathroom. And then when you asked me about Brother John..." Her voice trails off. Somewhere in the distance, well out of physical sight, is the intersection of our road with the east-west stretch of highway that will take us to Uncle Seymour's ranch, and she stares ahead as though she can already see it. Perhaps she can. "They can't get at me because I'm already dead, so now they want you out of the picture. They want me back on the street, out of school, out of sight. They want to be able to pretend that I'm really gone. Forever. They want to forget I ever existed. If I'd stayed dead, they'd have my picture on the mantel and a lock of my hair in a box on the bedroom dresser. But since I was stupid enough to come back..."

She has wept before, but now the wound has worked itself too deep for tears. It is — must be — a cold ache, one that runs to depths equal to and perhaps greater than those that lie behind her eyes, and she stares straight ahead, that awful resignation welling up, engulfing her, threatening to drown any trace of hope she might have preserved. But I, too, know that chill emotion, know it personally and intimately, know how it looks with despairing eyes toward tomorrow, and the next day, and the day after that, and so on and on, seeing no hope, seeing — worse than no hope — only an endless reiteration of *now*.

I cannot and will not leave her in its grasp, and I pull to the shoulder of the road and unbuckle my seatbelt so I can put my arms around her.

"...they couldn't take it," she goes on. "They gave up on the Church because the Church didn't have answers. So they went over to Brother John because he had lots of them. And when I showed up, it was, 'No, that's not Charity. Charity's dead. That's a demon, and it's all right to hate her and turn her out. In fact, you're being righteous and godly by hating her, because you always need to hate evil, and she's evil,' so...so...so..."

I hold her tightly. She buries her face in my shoulder.

"...so now they can feel all good and warm and gooey about it," comes her whisper, half angry, half grieving. "God knows, it's probably the first time they've ever felt warm and gooey in their whole lives."

"Charity..."

"But I...I still love them. I can't help it. I came back...for them. And then it all...it all went wrong. I thought there was a chance it might turn out right. Eventually. If I kept trying. But it didn't. And now..." I feel her hands clutch my arms. "Now somebody's shooting at you," she manages at last. "They can't get at me, so they want to kill you. Echo...I'm...I'm so sorry. I don't know how to make it up to you. I...I...I don't know what to say."

Gently, I lift her head until we are eye to eye. Her gaze, at once undead and profound, bores into and through me, but for now I can face it without flinching, any disquiet on my part utterly quenched, obliterated, swept away by the depth of her need and the bond that joins us.

"You need not do or say anything, my dear girl," I tell her softly. "Yes, you came back for them. But now..."

The depth of her need. The depth of our bond.

"...but now...come back for me. You turned away from the light to come back for them. But you found me. I appear to have been waiting for you. So, I pray you, come back now...for me."

"You were...waiting for me?"

Waiting for her. Yes. Awakening to a new life, a new identity, even a new face and body: awakening as Echo Japonica...to wait for Charity. And now the thought has come to me that perhaps it was not for myself that I created Snow City. Perhaps it was for her...and for the chance to redeem, through my redemption of a lost ghost, my old battered, lonely self.

A ghost sheltering a ghost: perhaps it makes perfect sense. Can I believe that?

I want to believe that.

"That's like..." Charity turns her head, considering. Her amber hair falls in a bright cascade over my arms, my shoulders. "That's like...family. Like really being family. Not just a guardian. Like... like for real."

I pass my hand over her head, pull her cheek to my shoulder. *Staying this side of trouble.* "Indeed. I have sheltered you, fed you, clothed you, and cherished you. I will not draw a line at facing bullets for you."

She stares, almost unbelieving. "You mean that?"

"My dear..." It was not so in my old world, where betrayal and abuse were as common as birdseed; but despite the failings, cracks, and crevasses that are appearing in Snow City — that I am determined to correct, mend, make level — it will be so, indeed, it *is* so, in this place. "...that is what family does."

Outside, the wind sweeps across undulating wheat and grass, carrying dust in tawny waves along the road, shaking our automobile with its passing as a cat might bat at a cardboard box. I hold Charity tightly against me, heedless of the comparative chill of her touch, discarding any thoughts save those of her and of the defense I must provide for this young life — this young death — that I have chosen to shelter from what is for her an intimate and heartbreaking reality.

Her murmur is soft, almost lost in the gusting of the wind. "If I had to die again...for you...I'd do it. I'd do it. Honest to God,

Echo. I swear, I'd do it. Even if that meant I could never come back."

For a long time we are silent in one another's arms, looking at the grass and the distant mountains.

"Christ, Echo," she whispers at last, "I wish you really were my mother."

※

It is a picture-postcard landscape into which we step upon alighting from our car at Uncle Seymour's ranch. Nothing glamorous, true, rather the homely and the wholesome: a simple house of log and whitewashed wood construction — no more than three or four rooms by the look of it — a few outbuildings, a broad yard with a barn and a corral for the horses that regard us with deep brown eyes. Tidy graveled paths, windmill and well; and down at the end of the long, winding driveway, standing hard by the slip of road that has conducted us here over hills and through acres of pastureland and spotted cattle, the small church: clapboard sides, louvered steeple, unadorned cross surmounting a modest spire.

I have always shied from personal contact. Perhaps only the dead are non-threatening enough for me to consider such intimacy. And therefore, when Uncle Seymour (I recognize him, even though by all rational logic, I should not) comes striding out of the house — blue-jeaned and flannel shirted, gray and stocky, his eyes bleached blue as glacial lakes by the Montana skies — and catches me up into his arms as though I am a six year old, I instinctively stiffen.

He laughs. "Never the one for hugs, are you, Echo?" His voice, apparently used to making itself heard across fields and above the roar of wind, booms out into the yard. "Been that way all your life. Don't worry, I'm used to it. But here's home for you and Charity for as long as you want to stay. Esmeralda's got the cabin all aired out and ready for you, so you'll have your privacy, but I warn you: breakfast comes early, so if you're late you get grass and rain water, and come Sundays, services start right after morning coffee."

His blue eyes hold me as much as do Charity's green. *Been that way all your life.* But what child did he know...twenty, thirty, thirty-five years ago? What child *could* he have known?

"I-I confess I am not of a particularly religious persuasion," I manage, my feet still a good six inches off the ground.

"Oh, don't you worry," he assures me with a squeeze that comes precariously close to renewing the damage left by my shattered Kohno. "God's not much of a one for nitpicking. Just come and set a spell. Nothing like a good set to brace you up." For a long moment, his eyes, narrowing almost to slits in the brilliant sunlight, rest on the small church. "Look at the woodwork if you want: mortise and tenon, tongue in groove, dovetail and wrought iron. Big beams from trees that must have been three, four hundred years old, brought in from the hills on wagons and sledges way back when this place didn't even have a name, and sawed and carved to fit right here on the spot. Long time ago. I'm the thirteenth minister of that church, and though I'm afraid I can't turn a nice phrase like I read in some of the books of sermons in the back room, I always feel inspired by thinking about them that came before us: building houses, raising children, trading with whoever'd trade, helping whoever needed it, and all the while not forgetting about God and making sure He got a few hours out of the week set aside for Him."

He finally releases me, and I slide gratefully and with only the slightest hint of an involuntary stagger to the ground. "I cannot thank you enough for allowing us to trouble you, Uncle Seymour."

"No trouble at all," he assures me. "I've been hoping you'd come pay us a visit." His gaze turns to Charity, who, springing out of the automobile the moment it stopped moving, raced away to see the horses and is even now stroking noses and cheeks and giggling at inquiring sniffs that are *sure* there is an apple about her somewhere. "That's Sugar and Shadow she's talking to." A sigh and a smile. "Girls and horses: an eternal constant."

Charity returns to introduce herself, and I notice Uncle Seymour's expression change when he takes her hand, his glacial blue almost faltering in the face of her abyssal green.

But, "You're both more than heartily welcome here," he tells us as he and one of his hired men, Jesse, helps us carry our luggage to the tidy cabin that stands a short distance from the main house. "Does city folk good to get out where they can see some open space, I think."

And, indeed, there is open space in abundance all about us, for the fields and pastureland seem to stretch off forever, their dominion bounded only by mountains made puny by distance and the sheer expanse of vacancy that surrounds them.

"Play guitar?" asks Jesse, whose time among the far-reaching plains has reduced his utterances to the bare minimum. He holds up the battered, oblong case he has brought from the car.

"Not as well as I might wish," I tell him. "But it allows me to earn a living. Of late though..."

I falter. Jesse's brown eyes consider me.

We have all paused just outside the door of the cabin. The wind sweeps across the fields and ruffles Charity's hair, flexes the brim of Jesse's hat, stirs Uncle Seymour's shirt. For the moment, the only sound is the rustle, the vast, roaring whisper, of wheat and grass blades bending, touching, rubbing.

"I suppose I ought to mention," Uncle Seymour says at last, "that we do have Internet out here. And I do check in on what's happening in my niece's home town now and again."

I nod.

"I won't pry," he says, "but if you need to talk, I'm here." He looks to Charity. "And that goes for you, too, young lady."

She bows: she must have picked up the habit from me. "Thank you, sir."

"You just go ahead and call me Uncle Seymour." A wink. "After all, you're family now."

He could not have known what passed between Charity and myself amid the sweeping isolation of Judith Gap, but his words could not have been more apropos...or welcome. Impulsively, she throws herself at him and hugs him, luggage and all. "Th-thank you, Uncle Seymour."

His laden arms wrapped clumsily — but, as I notice, a little gingerly — about her, he gives me a smile and a wink. "Better be careful, Echo. You just might lose your position as favorite niece."

Charity's expression is one of utter bliss.

⋈

And I see that same expression quite often as our stay lengthens, idyllic day blending seamlessly into idyllic day, the nights warm and cloudless and starry, the fields rippling with the ever present wind. Our routine is simple, and it could be simpler still, were we both not determined to play more of a role in the household than that of pampered and idle guests.

Esmeralda, the housekeeper, is a graying spinster (and I see in her a premonition of what I myself will more than likely become someday: growing thin and translucent with the years, indefatigably wielding my guitar as she wields her mop and broom and saucepans), and she welcomes my help and my unspoken assurance that "city folk" are not above peeling potatoes and sweeping floors.

Or, for that matter, driving farm equipment and forking hay. Uncle Seymour is a minister, true, but he, like his neighbors and congregation, is a working man as well: Sunday mornings might put him in his pulpit, but weekdays find him out in the pastures and the fields with Jesse and the other men, and Charity, too exuberant to stay cooped up in the house, joins them. It is a rare daylight hour that does not find her out on the tractor with Uncle Seymour or at the corral with Jesse, and Sugar and Shadow come to her call willingly, as though understanding how eagerly and longingly she fought to return to a life filled with love and friends, as though determined in their own whinnying way to fill whatever void might be left in her need for affection.

And yet there is no denying her strange existence, for no matter how hot the sun, how strong the wind, or how determined her labors, her pallor remains, and even the most determined dust mote cannot find it within its power to settle upon her. Uncle Seymour and his men may return to the house for dinner flushed and grimy with toil, but Charity might as well be a porcelain doll: unblemished, unsmeared.

"She ain't sick, is she?" Esmeralda asks me in low tones one afternoon after Charity, returning from the fields in jeans and T-shirt, slaps my waiting hand with a boisterous high-five and races out to the small apple orchard behind the house, her eyes, unearthly though they might be, shining, and trailing behind her an aura of happiness as perceptible as the headiest of perfumes.

"She is just that way, ma'am," I reply. "I confess I cannot think of her as anything but an angel come to dwell among us."

Esmeralda crosses herself silently, obviously unable to make sense out of the girl's heedless flouting of the laws of physiology. Nor do I ever mention Charity's true condition to anyone at the ranch, though I am convinced that, in the course of one of her excursions with Uncle Seymour, she must have made her confession to him, for when the two return, his blue eyes are hued with thoughtfulness.

They pause in the doorway, and I hear the soft whisper of confidences:

"It's OK? And you won't tell anyone?"

"It's OK. And I promise." I hear the smile in his voice. "Cross my heart."

And then he is roaring for dinner, his appetite whetted, I am sure, by the aroma of the pies Esmeralda and I have been baking, the fruit supplied courtesy of Charity herself, who spent the morning climbing, young and easy, among the apple boughs. But later, as night falls and Charity and I bid our good-nights and set off along the gravel path for our cabin, the smells of barn and stable drifting earthily through the air, my uncle stays me for a moment, laying a hand on my shoulder.

I turn. "Uncle?"

His face, still red with the sun and the day's work, hovers shadowy in the backlight from the doorway. "I believe with all my heart that my dear Echo is a saint," he says, and for a moment, he presses his lips to the top of my head. And strangely, I remember the gesture. He must have done it a thousand times when I was a girl... even though I cannot recall a girlhood in this world.

Charity is asleep in the big bed when I, driven by half-remembered nightmares, finally rise, don a robe, and fetch my travel guitar — the one that piqued Jesse's near-monosyllabic curiosity — seeking solace in some late-night music. The spill of moonlight from the window turns her amber hair to silvers and pale beiges, and though my girl knows nothing of temperature or discomfort, I pause on the way to the door to fuss momentarily over the arrangement of her blanket.

Out on the porch, I uncase the guitar, find a chair, and tune. This instrument will, I am sure, never really love me as did the Kohno, nor will it accept any affection from its player. Here is plywood and heavy-handed lacquering, unreliable tuning machines, a horror of a nut and a travesty of a saddle: no one cared about this instrument during its manufacture, and though I took pains to adjust the setup and the action before we left Snow City, the guitar accepted my attentions brusquely, like a stray dog too wild and too distrustful to take a proffered bone with anything save a growl and a snatch of bared teeth.

"Come now," I tell it softly. "Come now. Your life is music. Make some with me now. I cannot master you, and you will not deign to serve, having resigned yourself to a life of lonely unwantedness, but we two can at least find companionship and, if nothing else, a tentative alliance this moonlit night. Perhaps some Scarlatti? The D-minor sonata? Would you like that?"

The guitar submits to being played, and my fingers stray over the strings and the frets, first in a few scales to warm up, then on into the sonata, the notes and chords turning, again and again, percussive and dissonant in the manner of the street music that the old harpsichordist, exiled by circumstance and employment from his native Italy, heard drifting out of the plazas and squares of Seville, heard stamped out in the rhythms of folk dances, heard (perhaps at times) whistled by servants or soldiers in unguarded moments and empty corridors, thereafter taking it for his own idiom: his hands straying to the keys, picking out the tunes, allowing them to find their own way into the polyphony he desired, following their lean and hard-to-master twists and turns, and with intricate and subtle imagination, raising them to the celestial.

Over five hundred sonatas he wrote, all brilliant, all scintillating with the Phrygian fire of the Andalusian sun, fragrant with the subtle odors of sound, pungent with Moorish spices, dark eyes, and the hard-edged accents of Arabic. And of that five hundred and more, only a paltry handful are within my guitarist's grasp, but I play the D-minor, my instrument at first grudgingly, then, perhaps with a sense of curiosity, more freely, allowing the music to escape, loosing it to gambol and prance about the moonlit yard between the cabin and the big house.

A feral hound...and a ghost. A ghost with a ghost for a ward. A ghost with a ghost for a family. And when at last I reach the end of the sonata, the guitar singing sweetly (itself caught up in Scarlatti's web, perhaps), the almost-forgotten thought with which I began playing — the nightmare that brought me up from sleep — is still with me, sustaining like the deep rumble of an organ pedal tone... as it has been sustaining all along, running a dark wash of somber reflection beneath the sad but sunny sonata, unheard by the physical ear, but coloring the music nonetheless:

A ghost. Yes. A ghost dreaming a dream of a perfect world. A ghost living in that dream, finding within it friends, colleagues, family, attachments. But what might happen to that world and to all those ghostly loves should the sleeper suddenly awaken or the laser-sighted projectile find its mark?

⸻

It is perhaps not surprising that Uncle Seymour's sermon the next morning — Sunday — concerns angels. Angels walking among us. Angels teaching us and ministering to us without our knowledge or awareness. The possibility that we ourselves must play the part of angels for one another. Though I am not a churchgoer, and though Charity is nominally Catholic, we sit through the Methodist service, both of us appreciating it in our own way, Charity herself, I daresay, remaining completely unaware of the role she played in inspiring the words being preached to a thoughtful congregation.

Lunch, and then my uncle and Jesse take Charity off for horseback riding in her favorite field while I return to the cabin for my daily practice session with my semi-hostile guitar: a more urgent proposition now, since our vacation is almost at an end and, with or without a professional instrument, I will have to resume my schedule of performances.

But as I enter the cabin, I hear an odd musical melody — distressingly electronic in nature — that I finally recognize as the ringing of the smartphone Charity has inflicted upon me. With effort, I manage to answer the call before the other party has quite given up and resigned him or herself to voice mail (which, for the life of me, I would not know how to retrieve).

"Ms. Japonica!" The Boss. "I trust you've been having a fine time with your uncle up there in the vast wastes where all my maps tell me there be monsters."

"We live not at all in such threatening desolation as that, Boss." But I am suddenly apprehensive, and my chuckle sounds a little hollow even to my own ears. Into our pastoral interlude has come a reminder of our reason for flight, and of what might well await us upon our return.

"Well, I didn't call to throw cold water on your vacation," he says. "Actually, I've got what might be some good news. Depending on your point of view, of course."

"Ah...good news?"

"Yes, ma'am. Seems like Charity's folks have gone and taken a powder. Packed their bags and left the scene. Blown town, if you catch my drift. No forwarding address."

"Perchance a...holiday?" The thought that their idea of a suitable site for a recreational sojourn might correspond exactly to my own squirms unpleasantly in the back of my mind.

"I doubt it." The Boss's reassuring thrum is back. "But if it is, it's certainly quite the group package: Brother John's gone too, along with the rest of his merry band. Are you listening, Ms. Japonica? The whole congregation. All of them. Left town. Dunno if they bought a ticket for the west coast or are doin' stand-up routines somewhere...or however the song goes...but they're out of your hair."

"You are certain of this?"

"I've had the boys running down every single lead we could think of. Not a trace of them anywhere."

"And Charity's sister?"

"Tall girl? Dark hair? Looks like the fudge sundae version of your angel? Well now, that's another story. She's still living at the family house. Alone."

"Is she well?"

"Far as we can tell. Seems to have money for groceries and necessities, seems to be comfortable. Not going out much, though. Can't say I blame her."

"And Brother John and the congregation? If they are not in the city, where indeed did they go?"

"Now, *that's* the big question, isn't it? Fact is, I don't know, but if you remember your state history, Ms. Japonica" —

State history? I remember no such thing. I did not dream history. I dreamt yearnings.

— "then you must recall that there's lots of old abandoned towns up in the mountains. Left over from the mining days. More often than not, those places would have had something along the lines of a church...along with a bar and a general store. It's my guess our bro and his people have holed up in one of them."

I am growing more and more confused. "But...but what in heaven's name could they be doing up there? Exploring new frontiers in the cyanic adulteration of fruit drinks?"

I feel my face grow cold the moment the words are out of my mouth. Not that. Not here. Not even for such as Brother John. Not even for parents who would call a daughter a devil and turn her out of their lives.

"Fruit drinks, Ms. Japonica? Not sure what you're getting at there, but as for our Brother John and his people, I'm guessing they've got some reason in their heads. Maybe they're isolating themselves from all of us sinners. Maybe waiting for the end of the world. Now, the way I figure it, after the world ends two or three times without anything in particular happening, Brother John'll lose some of his shiny and his people will come to their right senses. By and by. Not immediately, you understand, but by and by."

"Might the attitudes of Charity's parents toward their daughter alter as a result, do you think?"

"Can't say. Can't say what drove them into Brother John's paws to begin with. But let's hope so."

"I do so hope." Hope. Yes...Hope.

I assure the Boss that, this being Sunday, we should be back in Snow City by mid-week, and so the call ends. But when I turn around, Charity is standing in the doorway.

"There's a thunderstorm coming in," she explains. "Horseback riding is out. Was that the Boss? What did he say?"

I inform her of her parents' disappearance. She takes the news stoically, but her thoughts turn immediately to Faith, and I tell her what I know.

"She's all alone?" she says, obviously dismayed. "I mean...she can take care of herself but..." She sits down on the bed. "Oh, man...that's harsh. I mean, I'd go and help her, but I don't think...I mean...it sure seemed like she didn't..."

Indeed, our quiet interlude in the country has drawn to an end, the Boss's phone call putting an unequivocal cadence to what has been a succession of flowing and lingeringly beautiful harmonies. The following Wednesday afternoon, in fact, finds the two of us traversing the last mountain pass above Snow City, the highway here broad and smooth, the pines pressing in on either side, the walls of rock all but sheer where the way was blasted through, and, in the meadows that upon occasion open up to right and to left, silver streams and a profusion of summer wildflowers.

"Elk," Charity points. "I wonder whether they'd take to me like Sugar and Shadow did."

"I cannot think of any reason why they would not. Indeed, I cannot think of a single reason why anybody with a shred of sanity would not take to you."

"My...my family didn't."

I glance at her. Her eyes are shadowed.

The summer days are long, and though evening is drawing on, the sky is still blue and bright when we pull up in front of the rented house. Within, all is orderly and tidy, our furniture arranged with near military precision, our bedrooms freshly swept and mopped (and I cannot help but smile at the thought of G-shot wielding a duster), and the dishes and pots all carefully put away in the spotless kitchen.

"You must be tired after all that driving," says Charity. "I'll make some tea."

I nod and wander into the living room, too weary of sitting in a driver's seat to consider plopping down on the sofa, so I simply stand and contemplate the view from the window. If the Boss's men are on guard out there, they have apparently furnished themselves with some variant of the Tarnhelm, for I see no trace of anyone, save our new neighbor across the street, who is puttering in his garden.

On the end table, though, a note from the Boss:

> *Ms. Japonica,*
> *I am hoping that you will be rested enough from your travels to perform at the club come tomorrow (Thursday). I would, however, appreciate it if you would visit me at my house earlier that day. At your convenience, of course. Sometime after you get up. Call me at my cell number and G-shot will come round with the car.*
> *Ever yours,*
> *MAXWELL*

I sigh. Back to my old life. My old life that has of late been the object of so many strange transformations. But my thoughts are interrupted — savagely broken, in fact — by Charity's screams.

With any number of horrific scenarios flashing through my mind, I bolt for the dining room, and from thence to the kitchen, where Charity, standing on tiptoe, is staring and pointing out the window that gives a view of the backyard.

I wrap a protective arm about her shoulders as I lean forward to see, but it is dawning upon me that her cries stem not from terror, but rather from surprise and joy.

"It's Faith," she manages at last. "It's gotta be Faith!"

And then I see what was not there when we rented the house, not there when we left for Montana...and more than likely not there when the Boss and his men finished transporting and setting up our belongings. Centered in the backyard, sturdily though somewhat inexpertly planted, is a stout cedar post, atop which is fastened the copper-roofed shrine to Saint Francis that once graced the front garden at the Monthage house, the metal freshly polished and twinkling in the sunlight, the figure of the benevolent saint lifting its hands in benediction over the songbirds that are, even now, scrambling among the overflowing feeders that surround it.

CHAPTER ELEVEN

But I am not the only member of my strange little family — ghost and ghost — who, having returned home to a mixture of elation and apprehension, is called upon to plunge directly into the affairs of daily life, for Charity's summer school begins the next morning, and therefore, just as I must be playing at Club Pizzazz that evening, so she will be in classes during the day.

Owing to my impending change of schedule — from diurnal back to nocturnal — my sleep that night is rather broken, and I find it easy to be awake when Charity explodes from her bedroom, backpack in hand and clad in her favorite top and shorts, easier still to have the morning meal waiting for her...though it was somewhat difficult to locate all the necessary utensils, G-shot's idea of tableware and cookware storage being based, so far as I can tell, not so much upon function as on size and color.

No matter: Charity and I breakfast together, and she is as blithe as I have ever seen her. Faith's gracious gesture has raised her hopes, and attending summer school possesses no stigma for her: it is merely another chance to be with her friends while at the same time affording her further opportunities to prepare for her second year of high school.

"Will not many of your regular classmates be absent?" I ask. "I have never known summer sessions to be anything in which students willingly enroll."

"Hey, what about me? I signed up first chance I got!"

"You have other priorities, my dear. I am thinking of your friends. Vacations? Recreation? Summer jobs?"

Charity lifts her head and looks toward the kitchen windows. Outside, the bird feeder sparkles in the morning sunlight, its clientele already squabbling over a fresh batch of sunflower seeds. "They're my buds. The ones that didn't have something already planned, like jobs or trips with the family or stuff like that...they signed up with me. Rebekah was first in line, in fact."

I say nothing. It is so different here.

We finish our oatmeal and eggs, and then Charity insists upon clearing the table herself. "You go back to bed, Echo. You've got a performance coming up, and I know you always save the chaconne for last, so you've got to be all sharp and pointy for it. And...oh, jeez, I almost forgot: you've got that meeting with the Boss this afternoon. So you want to be all sharp and pointy for *that*, too. So you go catch some more Z's and I'll get the coffeemaker ready and set the timer for noon: there'll be something waiting for you to pry your eyes open with."

I smile. A return to bed sounds very good indeed. "Thank you, Charity."

She has already whisked off with the dishes, her manner so exactly like that of any other sixteen year old that I find it difficult to remember that she is not at all what she seems to be. "You're weeeelcome!" she calls from the kitchen. "I'll give you a jingle on your cell after school to let you know where I am. But I'll probably just be coming home to zone out for a while because it was a long drive..." A pause. "...and...I wonder." Her head comes around the corner, her pale brow furrowed. "Do you think someone like me could get a driver's license? I mean, like, the Boss pulled a bunch of strings to get me back into school and get you appointed my guardian, but driver's licenses start accessing state records and stuff and...well..." She sighs. "It would have been nice to be able to help you out on the long haul to Montana and back. But..." A shrug, and then she starts in with the dishes, her voice drifting to me above the sound of scrubbing and running water. "...I guess there'll just be some things I won't ever be able to do."

A long silence. The water shuts off.

"Oh, gosh." There is a terrible hauntedness to her tone. "Maybe a whole *bunch* of things I won't ever be able to do."

When she finishes up and returns to the dining room to pick up her backpack, I intend to ask her what she meant, but her breeziness is back now, firmly in place, and I am reminded of my own words about there always being a tomorrow.

One more look through the back windows, then. The bird feeder's copper roof is an effulgent blaze in the warming sunlight. "You know," she says, "with my friends back, and Faith looking like she's coming around...maybe...maybe everything will work out with my parents, too." A sigh. "It sort of gives me hope."

And then with a hug and a wave and an "I'm off!", she is out the door, bounding down the walkway, her amber hair bright in the morning sun.

I watch her through the window. So beautiful. So fragile. An angel walking among us.

But her last words have set my thoughts wandering:

Hope.

⇒⇐

A few hours of additional sleep allow me to feel quite capable of resuming my nocturnal existence as early as this evening, particularly since I have no wish to disappoint someone who has proven himself to be both benefactor and friend; and I shower and dress and call the by now familiar phone number. In a few minutes, the limousine pulls up in front of the house and I lock up and climb in...noticing as I do so that a number of my neighbors are staring, wide-eyed, from their front windows.

I make a mental note to assure them all that there will be no throwdowns in the foreseeable future.

In fact, as G-shot gives me a familiar nod and pulls away from the curb, I am beginning to believe that *nothing* of any uncertainty or disastrous nature will present itself. Charity's parents have taken themselves to the hills in the company of their like-minded believers, Faith appears to be inching toward a rapprochement with her sister, and my employment situation and living arrangements are steadily improving.

Perhaps the only clouds on the horizon are the question of how to earn a musical living with a half-starved wolf on my knee and — potentially more worrisome — Charity's haunted pronouncement about things she might never be able to do.

I come out of my thoughts to realize that the limousine has taken the winding highway up into the mountains and is traveling farther and farther into regions of spruce and lodgepole pine, the green needles dark in the sunlight, darker still when shaded by deep gorges and canyons and the rocky peaks that seem to grow taller even as I watch. But there comes a turnoff, and the car rolls evenly along a gated, graveled road sheltered by overhanging branches until at last we break free of the trees and pull into a wide, circular driveway fronting a large mansion.

There we stop, and G-shot politely hands me out as I stare at the grand house. Three, perhaps four floors, a multitude of windows, a broad flight of stone steps leading up to an enormous double door. Flowers everywhere: beds, pots, urns, trellises...even a rambling pair of English country roses that have twined themselves up the facade to the left and right of the door, the afternoon air heady with their deep, sweet fragrance.

"Not what you expected, huh?" G-shot observes.

I blush, for indeed, I expected something more vulgar, more fortified...and perhaps tricked out with a few half-clad women: something more in keeping with the tawdry glitter of Club Pizzazz than with the dignified austerity of an English manor.

"The Boss," I manage, "never fails to surprise me."

G-shot escorts me up the steps as though he were clad in doublet and breeches. "Club's always bouncing," he says. "We got rockers, punkers, youngsters who love a mosh pit, bands with horn-blowers who want bebop, bebop, and more bebop. Boss... he just want to get away from it all when he's done with business. Somebody who made a bundle in gold mines built this house maybe a hundred and fifty years ago, then went bust. Place sold for peanuts. It was in pretty sad shape when the Boss found it — there's still rooms ain't worth goin' into — but he set to fixin' it up and givin' it back its pride." He eyes me sidelong. "Boss try to do that with most people, you know, but he try to do it right. Some folks can't see being happy without drugs, for instance. Well, Boss can't abide drugs, so he does what he can to get 'em clean and on track to something better. Some folks are happy living on the edge, or girls wanna take a chance with the life. That's fine with the Boss so's long as that's what they want. And maybe they know it an' maybe they don't, but he always right there for 'em, holding out his arms to catch 'em when they fall. 'Cause they usually do. And when they get tired of living that way, he's there to give 'em a hand up."

"Keeping them all this side of trouble," I murmur.

"You got it exactly, girl-child," he says...then catches himself: "I mean...Ms. Japonica."

"I confess I find it difficult to imagine that he can make a living that way."

G-shot regards me soberly. "Oh, Ms. Japonica, you'd be surprised at the number of people think they can't be happy without takin' the kinds of chances that make the Boss money. But he keeps 'em safe — ain't no sense in not protectin' your investments, after all — and if they want out, there's always more on their way in. It's the kind that want to make their money *and* bleed their folks dry at the same time that's the problem, and they the ones the Boss keeps away."

At the big front door, I pull on his arm enough to stay his hand from the latch. "So I must therefore ask: why is he doing this all for me? I was a hermit, living solitary and without any trouble from which to be kept. And yet the Boss has lavished care and consideration upon me, not to mention my ward, to a degree such that I cannot possibly repay him."

"He tol' you himself, girl—...Ms. Japonica: it's him owing *you*."
"But *how?*"

"That's for him t' be tellin', I think. 'Sides, I don't know more'n half the story, so I couldn't do it justice by a long shot. But you shouldn't be keepin' him. He's a punctual man, after all."

Perhaps the mansion is a mansion — stately and grave — but inside, though the restrained furnishings and decor are much in keeping with the exterior, there are a few concessions to the Boss's...irregular...business dealings. Young men, black-clad and buffed out, are stationed here and there — at the foot of the broad stairs, on the landings, in strategic doorways — and though they seem at first glance unconcerned about what might be going on about them, I sense that, behind their dark glasses, their eyes are canny and vigilant, and that brutality is, for them, simply one among many necessary tools.

There are all sorts of happiness, I remind myself. *Some people want to live on the edge. And the Boss is there for them then, and still there when they get tired of it.*

But why me?

Together, G-shot and I climb the stairs leading up from the wide entry hall to the second floor. There, on the landing, a youngish man, whip-thin, awaits us. Dark glasses again, but with the addition of a pencil thin mustache and a matching goatee... these last perhaps something of a wink and a mischievous grin for those who might make too much of his all but girlish face. He is not overly dark — café au lait — but though he carries himself more like a dancer than a gangster, I recognize the telltale bulge of a shoulder holster under an otherwise impeccably tailored suit.

"Wassup, G?" he asks.

"Lady t' see the Boss," says G-shot. "His invite. This here's Ms. Japonica."

The young man beams at me. "Why, Ms. Japonica, I remember you. You played us some awful pretty music at the Blue Rose."

"She workin' at the club now, too."

"Like I ain't heard that, G? Cuts a fine figure, too, I been told."

"You watch your hands, Chaku."

"I will if you will." Chaku eyes me. "I'm figuring you got some surprises in you, ma'am. I will be sure not to be taking any liberties, you can bet top dollar on that."

G-shot tramps back down the stairs and vanishes into what, from the brief glimpse of TV monitors, chairs, and telephones I catch through the open door, must be the security center for the house, and Chaku gallantly and rather effervescently escorts me down a hall to a dark door. "I'm the Boss's personal secretary when he's playing the business man," he explains. "I can type, and they tell me I got nice legs, too. And I'm probably the only person left on the planet knows how to take shorthand...not that it's much use anymore."

Three quiet raps on a polished wooden door elicit a response in the Boss's measured voice: "Come."

Chaku swings the door wide. "You got to walk into the lion's den alone, Ms. Japonica." He says with a wink.

The Boss's office at Club Pizzazz was lavish and comfortable... and big. This, however, is restrained and simple...but, if anything, even bigger. A patterned sea of thick, Persian carpets covers the floor. A Hofmann and a Varo and a scroll with a Chinese mist landscape present themselves demurely on a seemingly infinite expanse of dark wood paneling. A simple, Shaker-style desk supports the sine qua non computer display and keyboard. Chairs, of course, and side tables; lamps and a filing cabinet of dark oak; a fireplace and a full-size wet bar. But nothing gaudy or extreme: only a quiet dignity that encompasses even the large, flatscreen television — currently dark — on one of the side walls. And at the far end of the room, wide pairs of mullioned windows, open to the summer air, look out on a rear garden that blends seamlessly from nearby formal English into, farther away, austere Japanese, and then, in the distance, untouched stands of mountain forest and meadow.

It is very quiet in here.

Smooth and polished in his gray suit as usual, the Boss politely asks Chaku to close the door and wait outside, then rises from behind his desk and steers me gently to a long table below the flatscreen. Upon it rests a large, teardrop-shaped object made of thick, pale-colored fiberglass. There is something familiar about it, but given its size and substantial nature, I wonder whether that familiarity actually stems from its resemblance to a small coffin.

But I finally notice the handle. And the clasps that hold the lid shut. Not a coffin at all. Rather —

"I must say, Ms. Japonica, you are one tough customer to shop for," the Boss intones from behind me. "You sent me and your Mr. Anthony on quite a globe-trotting adventure."

I blink. "Certainly, Boss, you could not have —"

"Via the Internet, to be sure," he continues. "I imagine we searched every good old nook and cranny in this good old world before we found what we were looking for...which was, of course, something suitable for a performing musician of no mean talent and with no lack of skill."

My eyes are fixed on the case. So sturdy it might easily be construed to be bulletproof, its lid displays, blended into its tracery of laminated and plexed fiberglass, the faint image of a leaf. I have heard of these cases before. And yes, they are indeed all but bulletproof. But they are used to cradle and protect only the most precious of instruments.

"Go ahead," the Boss prompts.

My hands are shaking as I release the three clasps and, almost fearfully, lift the lid. There, cradled in maroon velvet, its finish gleaming, its frets and ebony fingerboard polished to a fine sheen, its tuners ruddy with gold and its rosette an intricate, mosaiced lattice of leaves and flowers, its whole being shouting joyously of the music that it craves to make, that it *must* make, lest the very fabric of its existence be rent asunder by its own innate, irresistible desire, is what can only be named *guitar*, were such a simple word — a mere two syllables — adequate to the task of describing the instrument, its origins, its fashioning, and its potential future.

I lean closer. Within the body, the label:

José Ramirez
Clase 1a

And the signature below, its star-shaped, initial capital strikingly prominent, is that of Amelia Ramirez herself.

One hundred and twenty-five years of guitar building, research, experimentation, and craftsmanship lies before me, glowing like a drop of honey on the purest of summer days.

"H-how...?" I manage.

Hands in his pockets, the Boss strolls to the window, letting his eye fall on the gardens below — rosebushes, flowerbeds, trellises, fountains — and then beyond to the artfully artless assemblage of mossy rocks, streams, pools, and raked sand that separates rigid formality from untouched wilderness. "Hard to find something like that on short notice," he says. "Even with your Mr. Anthony helping me, I'd just get long silences on the telephone and lots of e-mailed apologies when I'd ask after top-notch affairs. Seems the waiting list for Ramirez 1a's — which is what your man seemed to think would be the best fit for you — stretches out a ways, and folks who got them won't part with them, when they part with them at all, for anything less than five figures. Now, I run a nightclub, Ms. Japonica, and yes I do a bit of business on the side, but coin like that is beyond me on short notice. Still, I *will* have my chaconne. Played on a fine instrument.

"So I took to doing some trolling on the Internet, poking my nose into things, looking for something that would ring that little bell inside me, and I found that online auction place. Something there caught my eye. It was what I was looking for, but it seemed to have had something of an unusual history."

He gives me a brief glance over his shoulder, a half smile on his face.

"Now, I'm sure you appreciate unusual histories, Ms. Japonica, being currently up to your neck in one...and I wonder sometimes whether you've got one of your own. But here I am blowing gas when I ought to be talking about guitars. Anyhow, I puttered and did some backtracking on the site, and I found that guitar had been listed over and over again. Poor fella trying to sell it must have been tearing his hair out. He tried everything. Started with a high price. Started with a low price. Offered an immediate purchase for next to nothing. But nobody bit. And why was that, you ask? It was because the guitar was one the poor fella'd ordered a few years before, only sometime in the middle of its being shipped to him, somebody took it into their head to drive a forklift through the packing crate."

I instinctively look to the guitar. There seems to be not a mark on it.

"Fella was heartbroken, 'course, but that's what insurance is for, and he got a nice settlement, along with a new guitar to boot. But that's where this gets interesting, because he must have been a musician like you, Ms. Japonica, someone who feels there's a spirit in instruments like there is in human beings, and so he wasn't about to toss the broken guitar in the trash. No, sirree. He sent it to a luthier in Chicago who knew his stuff, and that luthier put that guitar back together again: straightened it out, patched it up, splined the soundboard, refinished it, made it pretty much like new. And then the owner started looking for a home for it. But all those people who visited the auction site passed it by. Why? Because it'd been damaged. And they didn't want damaged goods. They read the description of the guitar — the owner was honest, and he told them the whole story — and they turned up their noses. So there you are: an orphaned, unwanted guitar. A beautiful instrument offered for a song, but passed by and left on the corner like an abandoned child."

His voice softens, and there is a hint of tears in it.

"But you see, Ms. Japonica, I'm a lot like you: I have a soft spot in my heart for orphans and abandoned children. And so after some e-mails between Mr. Anthony and the luthier who did the repairs, the instrument found its way here. But that's the thing with people a lot of times. They look, and they only see the damage. They should just listen. Just like with your girl: everybody, even her parents, looked, and saw a ghost. Or a demon. But you *listened*. Maybe not with your ears, but with your heart. You heard Charity's music: what she was, what she could be. And because you heard it, others started to hear it too. But there are still some who only see the damage. They forget that we're all damaged in one way or another, and that the point of being a person is to hear the music."

Almost timorously, I reach out and uncradle the guitar from its case, check the tuning briefly and softly, and then allow my right hand nails to dig into the strings. The sound is pure Ramirez: firm, tight, resonant. The action is superb, the instrument responsive...and it nestles against my chest and under my arm the way Charity did that first night, when I brought her home out of the rain-swept streets of Snow City.

Play me. Play me...please. Dear God...play me.

The Boss at last turns around, the afternoon light silhouetting his gray-clad form against the greens and browns of the distant mountains and the wide blue of the sky, touching his temples and jawline, outlining the curves and depressions of his skull. "And so," he says. "There's your instrument."

The guitar clings to me. "I can never repay you for this, Boss."

"I told you already: I'm still in your debt. And every time you play the chaconne, I go deeper into the red. Sakes alive, Ms. Japonica, I'm good and thoroughly overdrawn on my gratitude account because of you."

"Because...because of the chaconne?"

"Because of you and the chaconne both." He steps away from the window then, joining me at the table, laying a hand lightly upon my shoulder as though afraid that I might, like a morning frost, melt suddenly away, leaving him in a world unadorned with the diamond white glitter of those infinitely pure crystals.

"I got to tell you," he says. "I lied when I said I got into classical music when I was in college. Leastwise, I bent the truth a bit. Fact is, that was the time I finally came *back* to classical, when I finally heard someone who loved music just for the sheer wonder of making it playing his heart out on that piano in the lounge. It brought me back. But even so, it still wasn't the same as when my mother played the violin."

The light has shifted, and I can finally see his face. Sometime, perhaps when he was standing by the window, he removed his dark glasses, and now I am looking into black eyes aswim with memory and sorrow both.

"I was just a tot. But she'd grown up playing. Even had a job with the symphony. Played all sorts of stuff, did studio gigs with bluegrass bands, wound up on a couple recordings with jazzers. But it was Bach she loved, and the chaconne more than anything. And all through that part of my life I heard her play it. It was... everything. It was the world all boiled down and concentrated into fifteen minutes of music. It was her love for me, and mine for her and my father, and our lives together, and it said *family* and *belonging*...and I do believe that most of all it said *hope*."

Hope...

The name briefly turns my thoughts to Charity's parents, and from thence to Charity herself; and my gaze flicks to the window. The position of the sun tells me the afternoon is getting along.

Was not Charity supposed to have called by now?

"But things change like they always do," the Boss continues. "Times got bad, and there didn't seem to be much call for violinists...or for symphonies. My dad lost his job, and we started scrimping, pinching pennies every which way. Then my dad died. I suspect a broken heart, because he loved what he did: humping crates, driving truck, delivering. I guess he just sort of lost hope when the warehouse closed. Kind of shriveled up inside. Maybe you know what I mean."

I do know, indeed. Shriveled...and cold. And, in my case, beginning to live in an unreal world of perfected dream.

His voice grows heavy now, the comforting thrum sifting dustlike into a gray, grieving whisper. "Momma did what she could. Took odd jobs. Played in bars and dives. Zydeco and even some klezmer and rock and roll. But she still kept coming back to the chaconne, and I'd lie in bed, hearing her playing in the other room, hearing her trying to hide in the world that piece would make every time she played it, with everything in its place and fire so bright it just didn't leave room for anything that trucked with sorrow.

"It was the bars that undid her. Playing in them. First it was one drink. Then a couple. After a while she was bringing bottles home. It was rotgut bourbon and even worse wine, and I knew exactly what was going down."

His hand leaves my shoulder and he returns to his chair behind the desk, propping one elbow on the wood and laying his palm against the side of his face, his expression that of a castaway watching a sail disappear over the rim of the sea.

"The chaconne kind of got lost in there somewhere. I don't think I knew it until it was gone forever, because one day I realized I hadn't heard it in quite a while, and then I found the violin was gone. Sold for debt or for whiskey, I guess. Momma kept working, cleaning houses, doing the best she could, but..." He lifts his eyes to me. "...you understand what I'm telling you when I say that the music was gone, don't you, Ms. Japonica?"

I nod silently.

"Good and gone. Gone forever."

"What happened to your mother?"

"She died. Broken heart, like my papa. That left me on my own, and I tried college, and I tried this, and I tried that. Eventually I wound up where I am now."

Far off, doubtless from the distant highway, I hear a siren rising, falling. Police? Ambulance? Doubtless some emergency somewhere. But so far from the city? Silently, I breathe a prayer that my well-intentioned dreams have not succeeded in adding further misery to this world.

"Oh, I tried to find the chaconne again. I got records and CD's, tried everything. Szeryng, Stern, Perlman...I listened to them all. But they just didn't have what momma had. I dunno...maybe it takes a woman's hand to bring out what she did. I'd pretty much given up trying when I heard about this guitarist over at the Blue Rose who was of a decided enough opinion about the chaconne to end every performance with it. Now, I didn't think for one second that a guitar could do what momma's fiddle could do, but I decided to come have a listen. And that's when I found you, Ms. Japonica. Because even though a guitar is nothing like a violin, you make the chaconne sound like I used to hear it when I was just a tot lying in bed, hearing family and togetherness and hope drifting in from the other room."

I open my mouth to speak, but find no words. None that fit. None that are appropriate. None that are a match for the burden of responsibility the Boss has at last revealed to be mine.

And, like the needy guitar, like the needy child I took in from the streets, this needy child — left alone and orphaned to find his parentless way through life — makes of me a simple request:

"Please play it now, Ms. Japonica."

There is nothing to do but play.

A chair. A few books for a footrest. And with the Boss sitting back behind his desk, his eyes tightly shut as if, by sheer, determined will, he can himself remake his personal history and bring back not only his mother but the security of his family that a mixture of chance and bad luck — and perhaps the unforgivable ineptitude of the maker of his world — shattered into fragments, the opening chords roll out of the Ramirez with a sweetness that comes close to reducing me to helpless tears.

But I persevere. The music flows, the Ramirez — broken and restored, abandoned and taken in, lost and redeemed — responding eagerly, joyfully to my touch, tripping through the quick runs and scales, rolling massive chords out in waves of laving harmony, shifting through accidentals and through the pointillistic chromaticisms of the master's polyphony.

And when the last octave unison roars out of the Ramirez, the joy of the guitar is one with my own and, eyes closed, I cannot but cuddle the instrument to me as though Charity has once again come into my life. But with the thought of Charity, I realize that she still has not called me as she promised, and I open my eyes to see the Boss settled deep into his memories...and to see, at that moment — in his expression, in his posture — perhaps a little more:

The Boss's mother is not dead.

My realization is interrupted by a tap on the door, and without waiting for either permission or acknowledgement, G-shot opens it and sticks his head into the room. "Sorry to interrupt, Boss, but there's something on the news I think you an' Ms. Japonica ought to see."

The strangeness of G-shot's uninvited intrusion has not been lost on the Boss, and instead of a reprimand, he gives his associate a nod and goes so far as to wave both him and Chaku into the room as he picks up the remote control from his desk and switches on the big flatscreen.

Within moments, the display is filled with police cruisers and flashing light bars. Ambulances are waiting to one side, doors wide and paramedics running. At the top of the screen a red banner screams *BREAKING NEWS*, and a local newswoman is standing front and center.

"...with no motive apparent for the sudden attack which has left a teacher and six students wounded, several with critical injuries, police are still interviewing witnesses" —

Teacher? Students?

— *"and are reluctant to comment on the rumors circulating with regards to a possible kidnapping. One witness was overheard saying that a student was forcibly removed from a classroom, and that an attempted intervention by her teacher and classmates resulted in shots being fired by the assailants..."*

And with the brutality of a hammer blow, the scene — at first a mishmash of lights, vehicles, and milling people — resolves itself. There is Charity's high school. Off to one side, unmoving forms with respirators are being loaded into the waiting ambulances. The camera pans to one side and zooms in on Rebekah as she is settled inside a waiting Flight for Life helicopter, her face almost unrecognizable under a layer of blood, more blood seeping through the dressings wrapped about her body and limbs, and then, as the aircraft rises in a blast of downwash and dust, pans back to the newswoman, who has somehow managed to circumvent the police cordon and is in the process of interviewing a dark-haired, blood-spattered girl.

"*Charity is my sister, and I love her very much,*" the girl is saying, her voice blank with shock. "*Please...please bring her back safe. Please tell her that I love her.*"

I am on my feet, the Ramirez all but slipping from my hand, my mind balled into a fist about the name that my mouth, frozen at the sight of the nightmarish scene unfolding before me, cannot be made to utter, but which rings, screaming, within me, fit to deafen me with its soundlessness.

CHAPTER TWELVE

Night. Awake. Alone.
Charity is gone.

Of that there is no doubt. The news reports confirm it. Her classmates — those able to talk after the sudden, brutal assault by Brother John and his congregation — confirm it, but even more than that, her very *absence* confirms it.

And I am alone.

Once, I would have relished this isolation. Once, I watched Snow City as though from afar, taking from my separateness and hermitlike existence a kind of painful pleasure, all the while pretending that I played no part in the lives about me. But all that is gone now, and I am left empty, hollow, bereft, worried to the point of hysterical tears.

Having arrived at the high school after an insanely reckless drive down the mountain roads with the Boss beside me and G-shot drifting our relatively inconspicuous dark sedan through the winding turns and flooring the accelerator through the straight sections of asphalt, I gave my information and made my statement to a police detective in rational, measured terms...all the while fighting rebellious surges of emotion that persisted in bringing me near to screaming with anger, frustration, and fear, my self-control successful only because of the Boss's rock-steady sense of presence and G-shot's heavy and comforting grip on my arm.

But beyond that — words, information, claims of legal guardianship — I could do no more. Now the police must take up the challenge: examining a crime scene bathed in the blood of adult and child alike; discovering a motive...with which I am already altogether too familiar; inferring Charity's possible location...of which I remain terribly, terribly ignorant.

Though the Boss all but insisted upon a dispensation, I nonetheless played that evening at Club Pizzazz, donning my ridiculous stage clothes and bringing the gleaming Ramirez into its true element. But I did not play for the soft-skinned girls and their muscled companions, nor for the trendy and the intoxicated, nor even for those few who drew close to the stage as the magic of Dowland's artistry and Bach's chaconne unfolded before them. No: I played for Charity. She was — and still is (I know it, know it as I know my own breath) — somewhere, at the mercy of those who do not wish her well, and from my spotlighted stage I raised to her the most potent yet ephemeral of offerings — my music and my spirit — in the hope that by doing so I might, in some small way, comfort and sustain her.

And though the Boss looked on worriedly from the back of the room, obviously concerned that his musician might suddenly collapse into blubbering tears, why should my frail efforts be deemed mere vanity? Dream and longing created Snow City in the first place: there can be no reason at all that, binding myself to the notes and chords of my music, I might not reach out to, ally myself with, and aid one whom I have come to consider my friend, my family, even (dare I say it?) my daughter.

I returned to the house in the wee hours, but even a half-glass of rum and warm milk did not admit sleep, and I lie awake in my bed, hearing the rustle of summer leaves against the eaves, smelling the fragrance of night-blooming flowers, seeing, faintly, though my open bedroom window, stars twinkling peacefully in a sky left the darkest of velvet blacks by a moon now waned to a slim, late-rising crescent.

Sleep? Pshaw. I cannot sleep. I do not, in fact, think that I want to sleep ever again. Instead, I as much as cling to my wakefulness, waiting for Charity's key in the lock, her footstep in the entryway, her soft call of "I'm home!" But I know I wait without hope. She will not return. Not without the kind of intervention I fear lies beyond my powers, and perhaps even beyond the powers of the Boss, whose man, overwhelmed by numbers, was unable to prevent the disaster at the school, whose men — more numerous now, better armed, and knowing what stakes are at risk — are even now watching over me.

Charity...gone. I weep, drunkenly and near-deranged with my loss, incoherent with my fears regarding what might happen to one who so blithely insisted she was beyond all concerns of physical safety because she existed in the safest condition of all. Yet, though haunted by the persistent terror that, in a world created of dream, even so incontrovertible a fact as death might not be a bulwark against the unthinkable, I nonetheless fall into a fitful slumber as morning brightens the windows and the sound of birdsong, incongruous in the midst of such tragedy, begins to fill the air.

The electronic warble of my cell phone brings me out of my nightmares. It might...it *could*...be Charity. Everything that happened might be, yes, but the stuff of dreams.

But instead I hear the perfunctory voice of the detective who interviewed me at the high school. "Ms....Japonica?"

A flash of hope. "Yes...yes...have you found her, then?"

But even before the man replies, I feel the wrongness. His tone. Something about his tone.

Something is not right.

"You say your ward's name is Charity Monthage?"

"Yes," I tell him. "Sixteen. Amber hair. Green eyes. Five foot two."

A long silence.

"Sir?"

"Charity Monthage. That's weird. We just keep on getting that name. Everybody keeps saying Charity Monthage. Even her sister. Worst case of mass hysteria I've ever seen. The force's shrinks can't make sense of it. They say it's probably shock of some sort."

"My good man, please explain yourself. What does mass hysteria have to do with it? Charity has been abducted, and her friends have been brutally and grievously wounded. What more is there to say? Have you issued an AMBER alert?"

The voice on the other end of the line is matter-of-fact. This telephone call is just a job. An unpleasant one, doubtless, but a job. "Ma'am, we ran the numbers on Charity Monthage. She's been dead since January. We can't issue an AMBER alert or a missing persons bulletin for a dead girl. I sympathize with your situation, but you're going to have to deal with the fact that she's gone."

"Yes, she is indeed gone! She has been kidnapped!"

"I suggest you see a grief counselor, ma'am. And I have to remind you that giving false information to the police is a serious crime. I'm not going to report this, because everybody seems to having the same delusion. But now we're not even sure there *has* been a kidnapping. FBI's jumped in, and they're figuring it might have been some kind of terrorist attack."

Terrorist attack? In Snow City? Have I indeed brought it all here with me? Am I continuing to trowel, putty, and impasto into place such frightful possibilities? "That..." So bewildered am I that I actually splutter. "That is impossible. There are no terrorist attacks in Snow City...there are no —"

I stop my wayward mouth just in time, force myself to speak clearly and distinctly. "My ward is Charity Monthage. She is a student at the high school. I assure you that, despite your records and your reports, she is quite —"

But what shall I say? That she is alive? I cannot. Though the Boss could prevail upon friends and favors to return Charity to her school and her friends, he cannot alter reality, and the whole terrible weight of her predicament falls on me as, I am sure, it so often fell upon her: dead, but not dead. Water does not touch her. Dust will not settle on her. Sweat and even breath know nothing of her.

Petrified perfection. No change. Ever. No...

...no future?

I thrust the thoughts aside. "Charity has been in school," I tell the detective. "You may check the attendance records if you wish. Her schoolmates saw her abducted."

"They saw *someone* abducted, ma'am. Maybe. But since you've interfered, you and everyone else, we don't have a correct name or a correct description. We don't even know whether there's a little girl out there at all."

"Her name is Charity Monthage! She —!"

"Goodbye, Ms. Japonica. Be glad I've got better things to do than bring this up with the DA."

And the connection is broken, leaving me dizzy with helplessness. True, the possibility of an abduction still lies within the scope of the incident, and the police may well continue to look for someone. But they will not be doing so with any great surety, and they certainly will not be looking for Charity, and therefore precious hours, days, perhaps weeks will pass while they attempt to put a name to the missing first-year student.

And while they are doing that, something will be happening.

It might already be happening. It might be happening now, at this very moment. *This is a dream, molded by fantasy, so malleable as to easily be remolded by hate and insanity.*

Charity...

The police will be no help. The FBI, constrained by the same reality as the detective who called me, will be equally useless. Charity's rescue will, in the end, depend on Charity's friends, the friends for whom she returned, the friends she has made since her reappearance, the wake of light and love that she has, like a boat sailing on bright waters, trailed behind her since I took her in and gave her all that was in my power to give.

I am still staring at my cell phone. My *smartphone*. The one I barely understand. But it reminds me of the tracking program against which Charity argued so stubbornly.

She promised she would leave it on. If I did not snoop.

This is certainly *not* snooping.

I am already at the computer, waiting impatiently while the operating system loads, and when at last I have a desktop, I am on the Internet, searching for the correct program.

Though smartphones may be beyond my comprehension, computers are not, and in a few minutes I am downloading and installing the software. A reboot, a few clicks, and before me appears a map of Snow City and the surrounding mountains. But there is no sign of Charity's whereabouts: the program is instead asking me to create a user profile. Minutes, precious minutes, go by as I paw through cardboard boxes full of as-yet unpacked documents, bills, and records until I find the necessary information, and then my trembling fingers are again tapping away at the keys, entering my provider account number and Charity's phone number. At last, the map returns, loading slowly, displaying my girl's movements throughout the previous day. But though the line it traces shows her route away from our house and along several blocks and turnings to the high school, it thereupon terminates — just at the time of the attack — with the uncompromising finality of a severed limb.

Not a trace. Not a trace of anything else anywhere on the map. They must have destroyed her phone.

I hang my head. First the police, and now technology. Both have failed me. And what new horror awaits me this morning?

The answer comes almost immediately: the telephone in the kitchen rings. I run, stumbling, to answer, hoping once again that something is turning out right. Perhaps the detective has called back to admit being overhasty in his casual dismissal of Charity Monthage's abduction. But no, it is instead Father Hal, to whom, true to my word, I gave our new telephone number before leaving for Montana.

Tentatively, almost hoarsely, he first apologizes for calling me so early, but then plunges on to ask whether I can meet him at Our Lady of Comfort Cemetery.

"It's about Charity," he says. "I heard the news, and I went out to her grave to pray for her after early mass, and I found...well...I'm afraid it might be best if you came and looked yourself. Please, Echo: this is urgent."

<hr />

I linger at the house only long enough to shower and dress...and to call the Boss and inform him of what the detective said and of my failure with regards to the smartphone. In response, a long silence. I feel the storm brewing: black clouds, hidden bursts of lightless incandescence, a dark determination backed with a distinct propensity toward violence.

"So we're on our own," he says.

"It does indeed appear so. And I have just received a call from Father Hal, Charity's priest. He intimates that something is wrong with Charity's grave and wants me to meet him at the cemetery."

Another long pause, then: "OK, Ms. Japonica, I want you to listen. I'm going to have some men shadowing you, and they're the kind who aren't going to be gentle if anybody tries to give you grief. They'll stay out of sight, so you just go ahead and forget that they're there if it makes you more comfortable. And then you need to remember that folks like Brother John don't just spring up like weeds out of cracks in the sidewalk. They walk through the same world that we do, and they leave footprints. Things they do. Things they say. Sometimes things they're not happy about other people knowing. I know people who can find those footprints, read them, and come up with some pretty good guesses about where they lead. We'll start pulling in some information, one way or another, even if it means breaking some heads, and we *will* get your girl out of whatever Brother John's crazies have gotten her into."

My throat has turned tight. "Thank you," I manage.

"Third thing, woman. You remember that little present I gave you 'fore you went up north?"

"Yes."

"You said you know how to use it, so take it with you. Stop by someplace and get a holster. Something you can get to fast. There'll be a CCW waiting for you at the sheriff's office by this afternoon."

I have not carried a firearm on my person since...before. "Is that really necessary?"

"I'm thinking it is. These people we're dealing with: they're willing to use hard calibers on high school kids. That takes a special kind of nut job. So you get yourself ready to up the ante if need be." A moment's silence, the storm roiling dark and incandescent. "Now, you go see what Father Hal wants, and I'll get the ball rolling on this end."

"Thank you, Boss."

I hear a smile in his voice of a sudden, like a ray of sunlight fighting its way out of hurricane-driven clouds. "Call me Maxwell, Echo."

⇥┼⇤

I still have the rental car from the trip to Montana, and so it is but a matter of minutes and a brief stop at a firearms dealer before I meet Father Hal at the cemetery gates, the weight of the semiautomatic in a shoulder holster beneath my light summer jacket a mixture of alien, horrifying, and comforting.

"It's shocking," the priest says as he guides me through the gates and along the gently curving paths. About us, elder constructions from the time of grand memorials and statuary give way to the restraint (and practicality...at least where lawnmowers are concerned) of flat headstones, and then, with just a turn of a corner, the antique monuments take the field once more, thrusting up from the green grass like a sprawling Stonehenge. "Particularly shocking in light of what happened yesterday."

It is warm out here in the open, the few trees clumped and scattered too sparsely to provide anything resembling adequate shade. Father Hal produces a handkerchief and mops his brow.

"In all my time as a priest, I've always thought of evil as an abstract," he admits. "Something that went wrong somewhere, but something that's nonetheless fixable, given prayer and humane concern. But this..." He shakes his head, mops his brow again. "I don't understand this at all."

We round yet another turning. Given his manner and his words, I am expecting far worse, but what I see is bad enough: standing on the slope of a carefully landscaped hill is an upright block of granite bearing the name *Monthage*. Graven upon it, inscriptions tell of grandfathers and grandmothers, of parents and uncles and aunts. One gives Charity's name and the legend *Beloved Daughter*, but fronting those kindly words lies not the patch of peaceful and carefully trimmed grass that is the deserved lot of an eternal sleeper, but rather a gaping hole, torn out of the earth as though with a giant fist.

I stand at the edge of the pit, staring down.

Empty.

"Everything's gone," Father Hal murmurs. "The casket, the vault, everything. I've had the manager and the groundskeeper out here, and as best as they can figure, someone broke into the cemetery with a backhoe sometime last night." He points. "See there? Those are the tracks where the equipment crossed from the road to the grave and back again, and we found a torn out section of fence beyond that hill. There was no formal order for disinterment, of course, but the police are treating this as a separate incident from the attack at the school, so they've given it a rather low priority."

I feel my mouth tighten. Perhaps the Boss was perfectly justified in ordering me to carry lethal hardware. Perhaps I might well feel myself perfectly justified in using it. "And as far as the police are concerned, Charity has been dead since January. She therefore holds no priority whatsoever in their investigations."

Father Hal lifts his head. He seems suddenly gray and old. "But that doesn't make sense. Charity has been in school. There are witnesses. You can vouch for her yourself, Echo."

"I did so. And was accused in so many words of interfering with a criminal investigation because of my insistence that Charity Monthage, officially dead these seven months, was abducted from her classroom. Mercifully, the detective in charge of the case gave me to understand that charges will not be filed against me, since mine appears to be a widespread delusion."

"But how is that possible? How can they say that?"

"Papers. Records. All the databases indicate that she is dead. The police will do nothing for her."

"Dear God." Father Hal is all but wringing his hands. "But what then? Living or dead doesn't matter: a girl has been kidnapped, and we do *nothing*?"

I turn away from the gaping defilement of hallowed ground, turn to face him. "No. The *police* do nothing, but *we* — Charity's friends, those who wish her good will and good fortune and safe journey no matter how strange her path — *we* will most indubitably work for her safe return."

He nods, his expression turning serious, set, determined. "What can I do to help?"

"The Monthage family has been part of Saint Ignatius for many years?"

"Yes, yes. A couple of decades, at least. In fact, I recall hearing that Charity's father and mother were among the first to be married in the parish church shortly after it was renovated, which was about twenty-five years back."

"May I then impose upon you so much as to be allowed to examine the parish baptismal records? Those pertaining to the period lying between...say...eighteen and twenty-five years ago?"

Considering the gravity of the situation, Father Hal is more than happy to bend a few rules for me, but though I am half expecting to be led, flickering candelabra in hand, to some dark vault protected by an ancient, ironbound door, the records room proves to be no more than an office in the basement of the church, the documents themselves contained in an assortment of filing cabinets, many of which have seen better days.

"We've been trying to update as much as possible," the priest explains as he turns on the lights and bends to read the labels on the drawers, "but there's a huge backlog. The most recent records have been digitized: scans of the certificates converted to PDF files and the like. But we're working our way backwards..." He ponders, opens a drawer, removes several thick folders. "...as the Church often does, I have to admit. Twenty years ago, everything was paper. Nice paper, good thick stuff with seals and signatures and the whole nine yards, but paper nonetheless. Now it's all just magnetic fields on hard drives." He lays the bulky folders on a table. "I'd be happy to help you, Echo, but you'd have to tell me what you're looking for."

"I think it might be best if I disordered them myself, my dear friend," I reply, still not certain enough of my theory to burden my personal appraisal of a distraught and nearly incoherent mother's words with the weight of an explanation.

I drag up a chair and begin working my way through yellowing papers, white papers, thick cream stock and almost transparent vellum. Baptisms, godparents, officiating priests and, yes, seals and signatures and dates: all the minutiae that go into the beginning of a spiritual life.

An hour goes by with nothing more than the whisper of turning pages, my fingertips growing dry with the passing of paper after paper. And then, between one yellowing document and another, I find what I am looking for.

Nineteen years ago.

Hope Monthage.

I stare at the paper. "Death records?" I ask Father Hal. "Funerals, perchance?"

"What date?"

"A-about..."

I swallow. I am beginning to understand. Charity's return. Long buried secrets. The chink in the parents' otherwise impenetrable Catholic armor against misfortune and tragedy.

"About nineteen years ago."

Without further comment, he lays another folder before me.

Hope Monthage. Aged six months. The signatures of the parents are blurred and shaky, uneven.

There is nothing more to be gleaned from the church records beyond the existence of Hope and the dates of her birth and death. But I already know that she, like both her sisters, has been abandoned.

Hope was erased. She never existed. Not even a marker at the family plot.

It takes me but thirty minutes at the public library and only a little help from the librarian to find the pertinent obituary notice among the microfilm newspaper records. And only a little longer than that to locate the news story that intimates — nothing overt, certainly nothing sufficient to warrant an investigation — a slight irregularity in the circumstances of the death.

Mr. O'Dally is adamant: I should take a leave of absence from the Blue Rose until the situation with Charity is resolved. But he has not taken into account the stubbornness of a musician determined to make music. And not just for the sake of a half-listening audience: no, we are far beyond simple matters of entertainment here. Tonight, just as was the case at Club Pizzazz, there is a more urgent purpose to my performance, and I inform Mr. O'Dally that music *will* be made tonight.

And I play. I play for Charity.

Here at the Blue Rose I do not have to worry about glamour and flash. Here I can be the simple, black-garbed and blonde-braided guitarist I was months ago, before gangsters and lost ghosts entered my life. But gangsters and lost ghosts *have* entered my life: the Boss's shadowy form at his usual table in the back is enough to remind me of that. But though he appears relaxed, concerned solely with the evening's performance — the Giulini, the pop and rock, the Dowland, the Bach...and especially the chaconne — I know he has men guarding me, and that he has other men methodically working to find Charity: men exploiting the dark connections of the underworld and the shadowy lives of those he keeps just this side of trouble, men ferreting out word of Brother John and his strange followers, men asking, listening, tracking down the leads the police refuse to pursue.

He keeps, however, a respectful distance both during and after my performance, allowing me to concentrate fully on my music. Even after I return to my house I hear nothing from him: though my cell phone vibrates silently in my coat pocket as I close the front door behind me, it is not the Boss who is calling.

"'Sup, sister?" comes the unfamiliar voice the moment I answer.
"This is Echo."
"Tha's right. Sho' 'nuff. And we be the homies keeping an eye on you from 'cross the street. Ain't nothin' gonna happen to you, so you can sleep tight tonight. But I gots t' warn ya: they's company coming."
"Is he...ah...safe?"
"*She*, love child. And she check out OK. So don't you be throwin' lead at her with that mouse gun the Boss gave you."

I set down my guitar case, nettled. "With all due respect, sir, it is a nine millimeter with 115 grain, plus-P hollowpoints."
"Oho! The Boss be right: all *sorts* o' surprises out o' you, Ms. Japonica. Well, she be comin' up your walk right" —
My doorbell rings.
— "now, and she look like she be dragged through the ol' rat hole backwards. So you be nice t' her, hear?"

The doorbell rings a second time, as though with a sense of urgency. A quick glance out the front windows shows me a familiar sedan across the street. An unfamiliar face is behind the wheel... along with the presence of night vision goggles and what I suspect is a scoped, semiautomatic rifle.

And I open my front door to find a girl standing there, her face pale and drawn, her eyes red as though with hours of crying. Her dress is careless, but her hair is long and dark, her brown eyes, for all their puffiness, large, her resemblance to Charity unmistakable.

Faith Monthage.

"You're Echo Japonica, aren't you?" she says, shivering not with cold but with emotion and fear. "You've been taking care of Charity, right?"

She is near to fainting. I suspect she has run all the way from her house to my door, but — tall, slender, fine-boned, and of delicate constitution — she in no way shares Charity's preternatural endurance, and I do not hesitate to bring her inside, sit her on the sofa, and put a cup of tea into her hands.

"I was hoping to meet with you eventually," I tell her. "I wanted to tell you that Charity has never lost belief in you, even for the merest instant, and that you may be assured of her love."

"It's for Ch-Ch...Charity that I came," she stammers. "The police called. They told me she's dead, and that they won't help. They won't do *anything*."

I nod. "It is up to us to help her. I have a...friend...with connections. He is looking into it."

"Boss Maxwell?"

"Just so."

"Then you have to...have to...have to..." She is still winded from her run, sipping her tea between ragged breaths. "...give him this..." She rummages in her oversized purse and comes up with a manila folder. "I went home from the school and cried," she explains, putting it into my hands, "and then I decided that I couldn't just sit there. So I started going through all the stuff my parents left lying around the house. All the tracts and the pamphlets and the weird hymns, and...honestly, that Brother John...he's crazy. He can look right through you and see what makes you tick. Mom and dad had him over for dinner a couple of nights back in February, and I think that's when he started really coming down on them, because he'd guessed something. About their past. And he seemed to get a big charge out of putting me on the spot and telling me all the things about myself that I thought nobody could know. But mom and dad just hung on everything he said. But..."

I am alternating my gaze between her pale, ravaged face and the folder she has given me.

"...but I'm getting all messed up." The words, halting, tumble out of her. "I *am* all messed up, Ms. Japonica. It's all gone wrong. Everything's gone wrong. I should have hung with Charity from the beginning, but I kept doing what mom and dad said to do because I thought they knew best. But they *didn't* know best. That day...when it happened...I'd gone to the school to try to make up with Charity. You know, like, catch her afterward or something so I could say I was sorry. And then they showed up...along with those other people...and...and they acted like they didn't even recognize me. They were like robots. Even when they started shooting. But..."

I am still peering at the folder, opening it, puzzling over the photographs it contains.

"...but like I said, I went through everything, thinking I might be able to help find Charity, so I could maybe still make it up to her even though it's all gone to hell. So I could do *something*, you know? And I found some stuff that maybe will help put you guys on the right track. I...I hope it does, Ms. Japonica."

And with that, all her words said, all her emotions exhausted, she collapses into herself, shuddering with tears.

"Please call me Echo," I tell her quietly as I leaf through the photos. Here is a dilapidated church with a range of mountains in the background. Here is a group shot of what I can only assume to be at least a portion of Brother John's congregation. Another mountain view in the background, with the ruinous church to one side. And here is a —

I blink...stare. My hand is already clawing at my pocket, bringing out my smartphone, and it is fortunate that I have had the foresight to put the Boss's number on speed dial, for my hands are shaking to the extent that I can hardly input my unlock code, much less dial a ten-digit number.

"Maxwell," comes the familiar voice after but one ring.

"Boss...I mean, Maxwell," I say, my voice trembling. "I am honored to have Faith Monthage here at my house. She is doing her best to help with our investigations, and she has conveyed to me some photographs of what I think is Brother John's church. It indeed appears to be up in the mountains, and..."

"If we can get some decent bearings from the scenery, we might be able to triangulate it with satellite views."

"...and there is also a map."

CHAPTER THIRTEEN

Any attempt at stealth would only burden our urgent mission with unconscionable delay, and so it is the limousine, accompanied by several of the Boss's other automobiles, that brazenly shoulders its way up the winding mountain highway into the heart of the high country surrounding Snow City, the night sky, seemingly oblivious to the approaching dawn, growing darker with each passing mile.

Faith's map has given us directions, and the photographs have confirmed the map: we know the location of Brother John's church, and we are gambling that both Charity and her exhumed body are being held there...for reasons I begin, haltingly, to put into words as clouds crawl oppressively across the stars and crooked branches press close against the narrowing road. Faith herself is at my house with half a dozen men protecting her. The rest of the Boss's associates are crammed into the automobiles, armed and in some cases armored: I saw not a few Kevlar vests being donned as we prepared for action.

"You say they're going to do what?" In the seat beside me, the Boss is quietly checking his pistol: magazine full, one in the pipe, hammer back, safety engaged.

"I believe they wish to entirely negate Charity's existence," I tell him. "The vanished daughter Hope was the guilty secret that put a permanent chill on the family — Charity herself intimated that her parents demonstrated little if any emotional warmth — and Hope's somewhat suspicious death, along with Charity's posthumous reappearance, provided just the sort of leverage needed for a clever manipulator to bring the parents under his sway."

"I never hear o' anybody bein' *that* clever," says G-shot from the front seat. "Or any reason a body'd *want* to be."

I know too much. Criminals these men may be, but the real abysses of depraved behavior into which human beings can fall are beyond their comprehension. But I have myself seen those abysses, and much to my shame have, in a previous life, plumbed some of their depths.

Outside, the pine trees have grown gnarled and withered with the approach of the timberline, their branches turning twisted and deformed like so many hands reaching up from my past, daring me to come within their grasp. "Insanity is the gate," I whisper, keeping my gaze averted. "And insanity is itself the key to that gate: the gate leading to the complete abnegation of self-awareness. After that, there remains but the base, holistic processing of the preconscious brain. From thence come leaps of intuition and flashes of inspiration, true, but both, lacking the governance of humanity and humane considerations, can turn selfish, controlling, even demonic. Charity said that the man outside our apartment had strange eyes. Faith told me that Brother John could read one's inner thoughts and secrets. I doubt neither of them."

The pines fall away. On one side, sheer rock wall; on the other, sheer drop. The sky is a mad confluence of clouds: light and shadow writhing, savagely contending.

"And so," I continue, my voice hardly audible above the limousine's engine, "Charity's parents fell in with Brother John's adamant certainty, took him for their savior and their conscience, and repudiated their guilt and shame by convincing themselves that Charity is not their daughter, but rather a hellish visitant come to torment them."

"But then why dig up her body?" asks G-shot. "They gonna bring 'em together and make 'em both vanish like...like...oh, I dunno. Just *poof!*...and that's that?"

"Perhaps. Or perhaps forcibly confine Charity to the casket and bury the corpse and her living spirit together in some secret place."

"But if she's dead, and the girl we know is a demon...even though we all know she anything but...what good's that? It just don't make sense!"

The Boss lifts his head. "It doesn't have to make sense, G. It's like Echo says: they've gone beyond sense. The only thing that matters is that they *believe* it makes sense."

With hands I deeply wish were not so practiced, I draw my own weapon, drop the magazine, inspect it, smack it home and chamber a round. But as I thumb the decocking lever, readying the weapon for that first long, double-action pull just before the sharp crack as a trans-sonic hollowpoint leaves the muzzle and the slide slaps the hammer back in preparation for the comparative lightness of single-action discharges, a dark hand descends gently upon my own.

"Not unless you have to," says the Boss. "Leave the bad stuff to us." I am staring at his knuckles: scarred and callused with a thousand expressions of the unspeakable and unthinkable. "Something tells me you've seen and done a bit more than you've really wanted to, Echo. You might be seeing some more tonight, but unless push comes to shove, you surely don't need to be *doing* any of it."

His eyes, hidden by his dark glasses, nonetheless hold my own for a long minute, but at last I nod my acquiescence and holster the pistol. "As you wish, Boss."

A thin smile. "Please: Maxwell."

When I look outside again, the sky is turgid, roiling: a tempestuous mélange of shadow and fire. The landscape is a mazed confusion of twisted rock dotted with corpses of trees so dry and parched they know not the faintest touch of rot. Into this seemingly half-real world roll the limousine and the other automobiles, but now G-shot is conferring with Chaku, who occupies the front passenger seat. A red-lensed flashlight illuminates both a USGS map and Faith's hand-drawn affair, and the men's voices are muffled, concerned.

"Something wrong here, Boss," G-shot says at last. "This road don't match at all with the map."

But why should it? Everything about this place tells me that we have passed beyond the borders of my world. Here, what was once my life and what is now my life meet, mingle, and spawn the very stuff of the nightmares that so often visit me during my hours of restless sleep.

The Boss leans forward. "Are we still going in the right direction?"

"I think so, Boss. There ain't been no turnoffs. But the curves and such don't match up with either the girl's map or the government's. We were right on the money till 'bout ten minutes ago, but then..." G-shot gives a frustrated snort. "Hell, even the scenery don't look right no more."

But this is my nightmare, my incompetent creation, my potential abomination, and therefore...instinctively...I know this place. I feel it. "Straight ahead, if you please, G-shot," I tell him. "There will be..." My mind races ahead. Am I making this up even now? Creating road, rocks, trees, and landmarks only seconds ahead of conscious thought? "...two very large trees on the left. Dead trees. Pray, take the graveled road that leads between them."

The Boss turns his face toward me. "You *know*?"

"I have never been here before. But I confess I know. I know altogether too well."

"Then I won't ask any questions. G-shot: you heard the lady. And once we're on that road, take it slow and easy. Parking lights only."

A grunt of confirmation. In the passenger seat, Chaku relays the instructions to the other cars via handheld radio.

The pavement seems to buck and writhe as we approach the two trees. The road to the left bears the automobiles along with a brittle crunch of gravel and scree, and in another minute we roll into a rough widening of the way, one filled with a haphazard collection of automobiles: new, old, sedans, trucks...and one flatbed with a backhoe lashed firmly to the cargo deck. And all, all surrounded by a sea of contorted rock and desiccated wood, gnarled, dead roots boring still into stony interstices, as determined to maintain their lifeless grip as a vengeful wraith to strangle a faithless lover.

G-shot stops the limousine. The other drivers follow suit. Lights and engines shut down. The Boss's men swing open the doors, begin to form up, checking weapons, settling body armor.

"Maxwell..." I say, my voice quiet but urgent, "you must know this...what lies ahead —"

"Is hell. I know. I guessed already. You don't have to see this, Echo. We can get your girl out of there on our own."

I am already flinging my door wide. "No. This is my responsibility."

"Echo, how —?"

My words come out in a hiss. "Maxwell, my presence is the whole *point* of this."

The air is frigid. The dry wind cuts through jagged ravines and angled apertures, whines through dust-dry branches, and I am already shivering as, together, with G-shot at point, we set off along a worn defile. Above us, the lambent sky seethes in a horizon-spanning delirium. But ahead there is firelight, flickering, almost homely...and all the more disturbing for that:

what place have warmth and comfort in such a pestilent netherworld as this?

And then we hear the sounds.

Were they blasphemous chants or unclean prayers to demonic powers, they might actually be reassuring, their goal obscure, perhaps, but at least their utterance the work of rational beings. But language, seemingly, has no place here, and these vocalizations are a meaningless cacophony of random syllables and rhythmically conjoined phonemes. Yet, rising above their turgid Babel is a single, intelligible voice, one hoarse and half-strangled with what I can only suppose to be hours of screaming its exhortations to surrender, to destroy, to submit...and to unmake that which has so comparatively recently been made, found, sheltered, and loved.

Ahead, around a bend in our path, is the edge of what appears to be a large clearing. From thence comes the firelight and the voices, the latter now rising into a shrill crescendo. No time now for the niceties of careful reconnaissance and detailed planning: the Boss pauses only briefly to give instructions with gestures and pointed fingers, and his men nod their silent comprehension and disperse rapidly into the shadows, making for the perimeter of the open space. A minute goes by, the time dribbled out in seconds and deranged yells...and then, together, breasting the torrent of lunacy, the Boss, G-shot and I charge around the final turn to confront what I have already intuited.

It *is* hell.

It is *worse* than hell.

Swaying, wailing, a milling circle of what once were people, individuals, surrounds a heaped bonfire, the eager flames reflected in the blankness of insentient eyes. Here are businessmen and women, housewives, tradesmen, working people, blue-collar and white-collar, all together, all submerged in the non-identity to which they have been brought by their addiction to the most rarified and pernicious of drugs.

I see *him*, then, and I know him. The man who so frightened Charity. The man who, having once stood outside my apartment, now stands upon the broken remnants of an ancient church rebuilt into a wooden platform thrown up before a spectral crisscross of long-dead trees. The man who bored into Faith Monthage with his strange eyes and read her thoughts and secrets. The man who with wiles and insightful cunning turned her parents into something that would participate in a bloody assault upon high school teachers and students.

And those parents are here, one on either side of an open casket containing the corpse of what was once Charity Monthage, their eyes lifted ecstatically not only to the madness bestriding the platform directly before them, but beyond: to the figure tied high up on that dead and twisted cross.

Charity. Charity...naked. Bruised. Bleeding. Her long hair shorn, scraped down to bare, pale scalp. They must have whipped her. Cut her. Her wrists and ankles are chafed with her struggles against her bonds, but she is not struggling now. No, now she hangs, inert — as inert as the body in the casket — head slumped, mouth slack, eyes glazed.

I am already starting forward, but the Boss grabs my arms. "You can't do anything by yourself, Echo."

My rage is such that I cannot even begin to form words.

His voice is low, almost a whisper, but all the more intense for that. "Listen, Echo, we got men out there going to take care of this. Those people already tried to kill you once. Don't give them a second chance."

I find my tongue at last. "Release me, I pray you."

"You stay put. Trust me." I feel him lift his head toward the still figure on the crisscrossed trees. "You think she's still alive?"

The thrum of violence beneath his words is rising ever more clearly.

"She was never alive," I reply, "and therefore killing her is well beyond their power." I note, however, the row of plastic buckets at the side of the platform, catch, just then, the unmistakable odor of gasoline. "But they will burn her."

Burning, however, is the least of the threats that confront Charity, for if I, in my delirium, can make a world, then what has been raised, concentrated, and roused in this clearing tonight — these voices, this whirling din urged on to greater and greater enormities by a confluence of sublimated lust and gratuitous power — can surely annihilate a single human soul.

But the Boss hears only my words, not my unspoken fear. "In a pig's eye they will."

I struggle...in vain. "Let me go, please."

As though I am a piece of luggage, he passes me to G-shot. The big man's grip is easily double that of the Boss, and I am helpless. "In case you hadn't noticed, woman, I've grown rather fond of you. Sit tight now."

Muted flashlights flicker from the dark perimeter of the clearing. All is ready. Pistol in hand, the Boss strides forward, arm lifted in the prearranged signal.

His men appear from the shadows, guns drawn, surrounding the crowd, tightening like a black noose. But the meaningless chant continues, rising, growing, Brother John and his acolytes alike too caught up in their frenzy to take cognizance of the intruders.

Until the Boss fires a shot into the air.

Dead silence.

The clouds whip and whirl in frenzied chiaroscuro. The flames of the bonfire crackle through ancient wood. Brother John's voice has been stilled by the crack of the Boss's pistol, snuffed out along with the asemic vocalizations of the mindless gathering, and now it is his chest rather than mine that displays the shimmering ruby dot of a laser, a crimson thread of light tracing its diaphanous way back to the man with the scoped rifle on the far side of the clearing.

"Y'all just stay right where you are," comes the Boss's voice. "Nobody moves, nobody gets hurt. We've come to take our little girl home, and God help you if you get in our way."

The bonfire leaps. The sky swirls. Bereft of the constant flow of exhortation from the platform, the gathering stands motionless, stunned, unsure of what to do, but though insane Brother John may be, he is not so mad nor so possessed as to challenge that single, red dot on his chest.

"Ripper, Wrench," calls the Boss, "get up there and get her down. You be gentle now. And if you need help, you sing out. Don't play macho man with this: you treat that little girl like she's made of eggshells."

On the platform, Brother John struggles with two equally paralyzing, equally compelling impulses: the fear of the targeted round aimed squarely for his heart, and his need — I can feel it even from across the clearing: a burning, spastic, convulsive passion — to satisfy his acolytes in return for their craven servility.

The people around the bonfire waver, but having abandoned personal will and volition, they make no move either to confront or to escape as Ripper and Wrench climb the few steps to the platform, holster their weapons, and begin to clamber up the crisscrossed trees, one on each side.

Their body weight, however, causes the trees, stout though they are, to bend and wave, and the movement brings Charity out of her trance. Her eyes open wide as she sees the two climbers, and grow wider still when she catches sight of the Boss, G-shot, the armed men surrounding the crowd...

...and me.

She struggles, mumbling and whining. Perhaps they have broken her jaw. Perhaps they have cut out her tongue. With such inchoate madness, anything is possible. But when her struggles have so distracted G-shot that he unconsciously loosens his grip on my arms, I straighten my elbows and, with a determined jerk, pull free.

And then I am running toward the platform, hardly conscious of anything save the girl hanging suspended and in agony. The Boss is calling me back, but after a glance at Charity's physical corpse — waxen with the embalmer's art — another at the buckets of gasoline standing at the ready, and a fleeting urge to kick the girl's parents into bloody pulp, I close with Brother John himself, smashing an elbow into the side of his head with a gratifying crack and sending him toppling to the platform's rough-hewn planks.

I am on him then, in mount, my hands about his throat, leaning my entire weight on his carotid arteries, wishing that, through the same process by which I created this world and the means by which I seem, with each passing day, to be increasingly desecrating it, I could simply will him dead.

Despite imminent unconsciousness and death, he nonetheless turns his eyes — burning, filled with his insightful madness — to meet mine. I sense their probing, their inquiries, the steady and remorseless ferreting out of everything that I am.

And he sees.

And he gasps.

My hands, strengthened by their days and months of manipulating guitar strings, drive deeper into his neck. "What is it that so distresses you?" I whisper, leaning close so that only he can hear. "Allow me, please, to clarify. Everything that you are, everything that you think, all your actions, your very existence —"

With a gurgle and a spasmodic heave, he bucks me to the side, breaking my grip. Tangled in my skirt, I cannot get to my feet before he kicks me away. I see the targeting laser sweep toward him, but he throws himself clear of the shot, and I have barely gained my knees before he has grabbed the nearest bucket of gasoline.

I launch myself as best I can, hands reaching to stop him, but Brother John spins, his mad eyes fixed on the hanging form of my girl, and his face is narrowed and lined with both hatred of what he cannot control and rejection of what he now knows is the truth as he hurls the bucket's volatile contents straight at her.

But Charity is not alive. Nor is she really dead. She exists in a half-substantial, quasi-reified form that is neither of this world nor the next, and therefore, as I noticed the first time I saw her sitting alone at the pedestrian mall, the early summer shower falling all about and yet she remaining preternaturally dry, she remains unaffected and untouched by such externals as water or rain...

...or gasoline.

Though the lethal stream strikes full upon her naked chest, it is instantly scattered back along its own track, spraying, raining down, saturating Brother John, the platform, Charity's parents, and the still form in the casket. For a handful of heartbeats, everything is frozen in startled immobility.

And then the fumes, driven by the wind, reach the bonfire.

The concussion of the fuel-air explosion tumbles me from the platform, but it sledgehammers into the congregation, incinerating them as it propels the Boss's men back into the shelter of the surrounding rocks. Closer, though, is Brother John: burning, screaming, spinning as the gyre of flame devours him.

Charity's parents, too, are ablaze, as is the casket and the body that lies within it. But as though in acceptance — or perhaps despair — mother and father merely bow slowly to the smoldering ground, a slow whine of prolonged agony wheezing from their scorched, smoke-filled lungs as Brother John continues to jerk and spin, a mad marionette, a flaming scarecrow reeling back and forth across the burning platform, his cries growing fainter as the flesh melts from his limbs and his vocal chords turn to ash. And with a last, convulsive lurch as the marksman's bullet, now rendered superfluous, finds its mark, he falls and moves no more.

Beating out sparks and smoldering patches of my clothing, I drag myself to my feet. I do not see Ripper and Wrench: doubtless they were blown clear by the blast. But although Charity hangs well above the reach of the flames, the bases of the trees that support her are perilously close to taking light, and I kick away more than a few embers as I catch hold of one of the seamed trunks and begin climbing.

My skirt snags on a broken branch. I rip it free. My jacket loses buttons and most of its side seams. My braid, singed, unravels and half blinds me with windblown hair. But ahead, above, swaying with struggles and panic, my girl forces out random words, delirious sentences, and I am guessing that, though she doubtless saw the fire, she remains ignorant both of its consequences and her current peril.

Ten feet up. Now fifteen. Twenty. The wind shrieks. The trees are swaying horribly, and yet I persist, struggling, ignoring the drop below me. I will not fall. Charity needs me. I took her in. I sheltered her. I cared for her then, and I will care for her now.

The last few feet are a horror of pitching treetops and bitter wind, but at last Charity is before me, and she seems to come to herself, pulled away from delirium by my presence as I brace myself on a stub of branch and work feverishly and one-handed to free her.

Her bonds loosen, and now she has wrapped her arms about me, her pale face, bruised and wounded, pressed against mine, her hands clutching at my torn jacket and twining in the leather straps of my shoulder holster, her mouth yawning wide in a panicked, despairing scream: a single word ripped from deepest fear, deepest instinct, deepest and most primordial need:

"*MOMMY!*"

Swaying, fighting to retain both my grip upon Charity and my hold upon the tree as the Boss and the other men come running to help, I cradle her, my cheek pressed against her shorn head.

"It's all right now," I murmur over and over, as though by such repetition I can convince even myself. "You're safe. We're going to be all right."

Hands reach to us now: two of the Boss's men have swarmed up the bent trunks and are helping us descend, foot by foot, easing us gently to the platform beyond the reach of the flames. The wall of fire is still eating steadily away at the planks, and therefore Charity and I are carefully handed down from the back of the structure, where more hands — the Boss, the men from the perimeter, even Ripper and Wrench — are waiting.

Minutes later, we are in the limousine, and Charity is being carefully examined by Chaku, who, it turns out, is not only the Boss's personal assistant but his battlefield medic as well. But Chaku's advice and treatment are simple and obvious. Get Charity away from this place. Get her home. Get her someplace quiet.

And even more important are his unspoken instructions: Shelter her. Love her.

Beyond that, he can offer nothing useful, for Charity, undead, is beyond all medical science...as far beyond medical science as she is beyond anything I might possibly do to help her forget what she has experienced.

"M-mom?" she says, her eyes clearing slowly as, with gentle prompting, she begins to make inroads on a carafe of hot chocolate produced from the limousine's bar.

I hug her close in an instinctive attempt to warm her. "I'm right here, Charity. I'll always be here."

"Y-you're OK with b-being my mom?"

G-shot is behind the wheel, retracing the road toward the highway. Again, gravel and scree crunch beneath our tires, and when the dried corpses of the two gigantic trees appear in the headlights' beams, I feel something slowly loosening in my chest.

Shelter her. Love her.

Perhaps...somehow...I can make all of this right. It began with perfection. Perhaps...perhaps in some way...

Charity's eyes — losing their terror, turning fathomless once more — are on me, waiting for an answer.

I cradle her chill cheek with my palm. "Perfectly OK. If that's what you want, Charity, then that's what I want."

She gives a half-laugh, half-sob that shakes her thin shoulders beneath the blanket with which she has been covered. "You know...Mom...you're talking to me like a real person all of a sudden. You're not holding me away."

We pass the trees, and gravel gives way to weathered asphalt. No, I will not hold this girl away. Not ever again. Not for so long as the power is mine to hold anything. But even after we are well on our way back to Snow City, even after Charity has fallen asleep with her head on my shoulder, even after, beside me, the Boss has settled in, slouched back into his seat, ruminating on his inner world of strange justice and stranger violence, with the sky above us clearing, lightening into a tranquil summer dawn, my thoughts persist in straying back to the clearing, back to the bonfire, back to the madness, the mindless chanting, the insane flames of Brother John's eyes.

The others do not know it, but I, nearly last in the group as we bore Charity along the defile and away from the scene of death and immolation, was rash enough to look behind as we took the first turning. And when I did, I saw nothing but trees and rock vying with one another in an otherwise featureless landscape. The fire was gone. The clearing was gone. The incinerated corpses, the casket, the shattered bodies...gone, all gone, vanished like vapor, like so much shadow and fog.

⇒⊱ ⊰⇐

The sky has assumed its comforting and brilliant azure when we pull up to the house. Chaku used the radio to warn of our approach, and the guards are waiting for us. Their faces go drawn and grim at the sight of Charity, but after awakening with a small cry, she regains her composure and assures them all that she is fine.

"I'll need a nursemaid for a while," she says, "but I'll get over it." A smile for me, then: deep, luminous, and infinitely gratifying.

But as I am helping her out of the limousine, taking her weight to aid her still wobbly legs, I cannot but reflect that although the first part of her statement is indubitably true, the second is, I am quite sure, patently false.

Her eyes flick to mine, and (the old abyssal insight now returned, returned perhaps redoubled by her ordeal) she sees my thoughts. "I've got a fighting chance at least. You need to get over it, too, Mom. All that stuff is gone. We can start again."

Faith is waiting timorously on the porch, but she totters forward and puts her hands to her sister's smeared cheeks. "Char..." she stammers, "I'm...I'm so sorry."

They are in one another's arms then, and, surprisingly, it is Charity who is murmuring the words of comfort and reassurance.

The morning light grows around us. My neighbor comes out to attend to his rosebushes...and stares at the strange tableau in front of my house. A hum of traffic arises as Snow City begins to attend to its daily tasks. A twinkle in the blue, blue sky as a jetliner makes its way westward, crossing mountains far removed, infinitely removed, from the peaks of evanescent nightmare among which we traveled last night.

Faith opens her brown eyes, lifts her tear-streaked face to me. "Aren't you going to take her to the ER or something?"

"Faith..." Charity's voice is soft, soothing. "Don't get down on mom. She went through a lot to save me. Everyone here did. And the ER can't do anything for me. I'm dead. They wouldn't know where to begin."

Faith's eyes shift from me to Charity. "M-mom?"

Snow City

Charity nods. "Echo's mom now."

Something about her words and her tone appears to tell Faith everything, and the dark-haired girl nods, straightens, and overcomes her innate diffidence enough to ask the question, addressing me simply and directly, her words nonetheless hesitant, redolent of loss and sadness:

"Do you...maybe...have room for one more?"

Very different she is from Charity. Shy rather than brash. Alive rather than dead. But to such ends my life in Snow City — my created life, my dreamed life — has brought me.

I free an arm and wrap it about Faith's shoulders. "Sure," I say. "Welcome home."

CHAPTER FOURTEEN

We do not sleep that day. Rather, while a few of the Boss's men remain outside, unobtrusively on watch, we talk: Charity, Faith, and myself. Just the three of us; my strange little family grown now even stranger.

Mostly, we speak of commonplaces — grades, hopes, dreams, breakfast, lunch — but now and again, recollections of what occurred over the course of the last few days briefly surface, and I learn how, while being dragged away amidst the brutal carnage at the school, Charity screamed at Faith to save herself, and how Faith responded by smashing her way out through a window with a folding chair...thus remaining alive and able to provide me with map and photographs. How Mrs. Thornton, the teacher, and Rebekah, Charity's friend, deliberately took bullets meant for others. How Charity's hands were indeed broken by her captors, how her tongue was indeed cut out...and how somehow, while hanging on her twisted cross above that babbling mob, between one blessed lapse into unconsciousness and another, my girl — daughter now — found her flesh miraculously knit, the wounds and damage evaporated as though her strange unliving preservation remained insistent upon keeping her ever as she was the day the automobile ended her young life: ever whole, ever perfect.

Just how insistent, just how whole, just how perfect, I find out only a little later, for after night falls and fatigue at last forces us into slumber as we are and where we are — fully clothed, huddled together, clinging to one another on the sofa as a summer rain patters softly on the roof and windows — I awaken suddenly from dreams of my old world, the terror of the visions driving me back to the present...to hear, in the dark, quiet house, the sound of weeping.

The faint light shows me that Faith still sleeps, but Charity is missing, and I disentangle myself from my elder daughter's arms and pad down the hallway to find, in the brightly lit bathroom, a girl standing before the mirror. She is naked, and her waist-length hair falls down her back like an amber river, her unmarked skin flawless as fine porcelain.

Charity. As she was. Not a trace of a wound. Not a cut. Not a blemish. Not a bruise.

In the mirror, I see her green eyes lift, notice me. And then she turns, wrapping her arms about me as she continues her quiet lament.

"I...I got up to pee," she says at last. "And something wasn't the same. And then I noticed my hair...and...I turned on the light. And I'm just like I was. I stripped to be sure. Everything they did to me...everything's gone away. It's like I can't change. I can't get wet. I can't get dirty. I can't sweat. I just...stay the same."

She lifts her head.

"It's like I said before, Mom. Remember? There are so many things I'm never going to be able to do. I don't think I'm ever going to grow up. I'm never going to be any different than I am. I'm just going to be this way. Forever. That's not what people do. Not real people, at least." Eyes cast down again, she presses her forehead against my chest. Her tears soak through the front of my blouse. "I'm...I'm not real."

I grope out to the bathrobe that hangs on the back of the door and cover her, and she huddles under the terrycloth as I hold her close. "Sweetheart...Charity...don't do this to yourself. You're as real as anything else in this world."

But my throat tightens even as I speak, and I wonder that her fathomless green eyes cannot detect my tacit duplicity.

Summer classes cannot but be canceled: not only are the memories of the attack too fresh in the collective mind of the community, but the fabric of the school building itself has suffered grievously — broken windows, bullet holes, shattered doors and furniture — and the terrible stains of blood prove difficult to eradicate, even for the most seasoned and strong-stomached among the janitorial staff.

Nevertheless, the students — those unhurt or with no more than minor injuries — rise to the occasion, banding together not only to study, in independent groups, the subjects for which they had initially enrolled, but to undertake as well a broader, more humane course of instruction, one based upon action and ministry; for with unspoken agreement and understanding they themselves aid in caring for those less fortunate: visiting the wounded in the hospital and in their homes, running errands for adults incapacitated by physical trauma or by grief, serving, in the purest sense, the community and spirit of Snow City.

The summer lengthens, and my world makes its slow progress toward healing: the prostrate regaining strength enough to sit up and walk, taking joy in the fresh air beyond their sick rooms, relishing their newfound freedom; the ambulatory watching their wounds fade...with rising hopes that their memories might, someday, take a similar course. Once Rebekah is discharged from hospital and left to the not-so-tender mercies of her physical therapist, Charity is more often than not seen pushing her wheelchair to the park, or to the museum, or even to no set destination at all, the two chattering to one another, incredibly, in the fashion of girls who have never seen the wrong end of violence. Faith sometimes joins them, but being somewhat less outgoing, and with her eye on her eventual graduation and college career, she usually remains at home, studying at her desk in the bedroom she and her sister insist upon sharing. I myself continue my performances at the Blue Rose and Club Pizzazz, altering my attire, my appearance, and my setlists as appropriate, but always, always ending the evening with the chaconne, the Boss invariably lurking at a back table or lounging at the side of the room, hearing in my music (as I now understand) the accents of his mother's violin, the reverberation of a more innocent and optimistic time.

The girls have sleepovers...and an occasional restrained celebration when one of their friends reaches a new milestone in his or her recovery, and at times it seems that Snow City is indeed returning to normal: bright colors, kind people, a sweet community of care and emotional sustenance for all. And yet I fear that perceived return might be illusory, even fleeting, for having once been so violated, this world cannot but be subject to future assaults, and my concern is compounded by the increasing frequency of my nightmares, the visions, growing more intense, returning with distressing regularity.

Often now, I find myself being awakened by Charity just as a scream prepares to erupt from my throat. Her touch, her eyes, the knowledge that, through my actions toward her, I myself, in a small way, manifest what it is that I find so precious in my created world... all these comfort me, and as Charity took refuge with me, so I take refuge with her: her arms about me, cradling me, her hand stroking my hair, reassuring me as best she can.

It is on one of those occasions, an hour or two before dawn, that we sit up together, drinking tea at the kitchen table so as not to disturb the still-slumbering Faith.
"Is that a Saint Christopher medal?" I ask her as the impure shades reluctantly release me from their grip.
She blushes, a barely discernable reddening of her pale features. "Father Hal gave it to me."
"I didn't know you'd seen him."
She bows her head. "I took the chance and went to confession. Though I didn't really know whether God wanted to hear confession from someone like me. I picked Father Hal because...well...like...he knew already, and he wouldn't give me this OMFG business when I told him who I was."
"Father Hal is a good man. I'd...I'd go so far as to think of him as a friend. He helped me track you down."
Charity blinks. "He did?"
I nod, but I have made it a point never to mention anything of the lost Hope to either Faith or Charity. And so, to change the subject: "But what I can't understand is why a saint like you" —
"Oh, pooh. I'm not a saint."
— "would need to confess."
Her eyes grow haunted, then. "I think that...maybe I need confess to you, too, Mom."
I stare at her, blank. "What on earth?"
She passes a hand over her face. "This gets kind of hairy, but I think you need to hear it. Mom...Mom, I gotta tell you this. When I was up on that cross in the mountains...I gave up. It had been...I guess it had been a couple of days...it seemed like forever...and I...I just gave up. I didn't think anybody was coming for me. I couldn't...couldn't get myself to believe that anyone cared enough. To come for me. After all, I'm just a dead girl. Use once and throw away. My par—" She catches herself. "The...bio-thing, you know...they threw me out and then they tried to kill me...which is kinda

funny, since I got killed months ago. But what I'm getting at is that they threw me out. They told me to go away. And I thought that maybe you, too..."

I reach across the table and take her cold hands. "Never."

"I know that," she says. "Now. A-and I guess I knew it then, but with everything that had happened, everything that they'd done to me, everything that I'd seen them do to my friends at the school...I couldn't *feel* it. And so I gave up. Nobody was coming. Nobody cared. I was all alone out there with all those people who wanted me...just...gone. A-and..."

She looks away. Her voice turns hoarse, choked.

"...I even gave up on God. He didn't care either. So I wound up doing what the Church calls despair. And that's a really awful thing to do. And then...then there was the other part..."

Interrupting would be sacrilege, and I remain holding her hands, feeling the cold, undead clasp of needy, undead fingers.

"...I mean...I can make up all the excuses I want, but that doesn't change anything: Brother John and...and *they*...came to school that day because they were after *me*. And so it's because of me that Rebekah's in a chair...and maybe won't walk again... and that Mrs. Thornton still has a bullet in her head, and that all those others got hurt. Some of them real bad. It's because of me."

Sacrilege? But I must nonetheless protest. "That's not true, Charity. You can't take that on yourself. Those people — Brother John and the rest — made their own choices and carried out their own actions. You didn't make them do what they did."

But the thoughts come to me, unbidden and unclean: I made this world and came to live in it, bringing with me my past, my nightmares, my unclean memories...and did *I* therefore make their choices for them? Did *I* make them do what they did?

My inner doubts cause me to fumble for a moment, but: "It's... it's just not your fault."

She keeps her eyes averted. "I feel...felt...like it is, though, and so that's another reason I went to Father Hal.

"And what did he tell you?"

She meets my eyes at last. "He thought about it for awhile, and then he told me I was a kind of a special case, but that I should remember that God forgives everything, and though despairing wasn't the best thing in the world to do, God doesn't expect us to hold up under more than we're designed for. So He understands if we break sometimes. That's why we've got stuff like confession and forgiveness. He..." Her voice drops to a murmuring whisper. "...Father Hal said it would be OK if I told you this, and in fact he said that I *should* tell you this, all of it, and that I should confess to you, too, because it wasn't fair to despair about you, either. So I need to. Confess, I mean. But, anyway...he said that he'd despaired, too. When he heard about what happened at the school. When he found that they'd dug up my grave and taken my body. When he heard about what they'd done to me. So we were both sort of in the same boat, and it wasn't just God that had to forgive, but you as well, and most important of all, we all had to forgive one another...and forgive ourselves, too."

She musters a smile: wan, but nonetheless affectionate.

"So after he gave me absolution, we went up into the sacristy, and we knelt down in front of the altar, and we said a rosary together, and Father Hal said that as far as he was concerned, me and God were even. And that's when he gave me the Saint Christopher medal, because...because he said we both knew pretty well that I'm on some kind of...like...strange journey, and that I can use all the help I can get."

Dawn is rising. Outside, rain patters away, the growing light gray and misty. We hold hands at the kitchen table, not speaking, just being together, and appreciating that being.

Charity despaired of me? How can I blame her? I myself, pushed to extremities that were doubtless not one tenth of hers, despaired of an entire world and so created another. And I cannot help but wonder how far beyond despair I might find myself should I watch my imperfect perfection slowly collapse under the weight of its miserable creatrix's past.

It has happened. It will, I fear, happen again. It quite possibly is happening even now.

My nightmares. What are they saying? What are they telling me. What are they *doing*?

Even now?

"Will you forgive me, Mom?" she asks softly.

Down the hall, the clock alarm in the bedroom Faith shares with Charity clicks on, and we hear, courtesy of an import CD, the opening bars of a Japanese pop song of which both my girls are inordinately fond.

The singer: Hatsune Miku. Herself an artificial creation — a vocaloid software program — with no substance or reality of her own. But Miku-chan is listened to — and even, in her animated form, watched — most affectionately, not only by her fans, but by her developers...and the latter are perfectly willing, should they discover some flaw in her fleshless perfection, to intervene, to correct, to gently guide her back to the ideal of which they first dreamed.

Here, then, is Snow City. *Enfleshed* perfection.

Can I do less?

"A thousand times over, Charity," I say.

⇌┼⇌

Come September, the high school is finally repaired, all evidence of the horrors removed, repainted, plastered over, washed away;

and an interfaith ceremony marks the rededication of the facility at the start of the fall term.

But a more important rededication occurs a week later, in my own living room, at one of the strangely solemn parties given by the students — in this case by Faith and my still somber Charity — to mark major steps in the recovery of their injured friends: with her parents and physical therapist and many of her classmates present, Rebekah, all but despaired of because of the bullets that grazed her spine, wheels her chair to the center of the room, moves her footrests out of the way, slowly rises...and haltingly walks.

Tears of joy flow freely that day, and in them I see the truest manifestation of all that is Snow City. That sympathy. Those feelings of kindness and compassion freely and unstintingly given and gratefully received. But even so, as the weather turns as it always does toward winter cold and the first light dustings of snow mark the mountains' dark pines, I continue to watch anxiously for signs that my corrosive past might be continuing its incursions upon my dream; and even were I able to convince myself that the grievous events that so frightfully blemished the summer were but the last, filthy dregs of another place, dregs now rinsed away, banished by the determination of unsullied minds and hearts, my concerns and worries cannot but be prolonged and heightened when I recall that the Boss's mother is (I am sure of it) still alive, still caught in her web of depression and alcoholism.

Since his initial revelation, the Boss has never again mentioned her. To him, so it seems, she is dead. Dead to the world. Dead to her music. Dead and gone. And therefore I must take it upon myself to correct what I have — unwittingly, ineptly — set amiss. And so, later in November, after Thanksgiving, with a sense of relief and even holiday cheer gradually beginning to take hold of the snowy city and my performances at the Blue Rose and Club Pizzazz falling into a predictable and tranquil pattern, I notice, one night, during my second set at the club, that the Boss has for some reason absented himself from the main room, leaving G-shot standing alone at the door to the stairs.

My chance. And I have no compunction about taking it.

"I am quite aware," I inform him during my break, "that it is the Boss's greatest desire to continue the pretense that his mother no longer numbers among the living, but I am quite sure, sure in fact to the point of certainty, that she has by no means departed this life, and I would be infinitely obliged to you for any assistance that might allow me to establish her whereabouts."

G-shot is understandably reluctant. "Oh, now, Ms. Japonica, I don't understand half the words you use, but...you askin' me quite a lot here. I think."

Feeling absurd as I totter before him on my high heels, my long hair coaxed into a superabundance of tendrils and curls and my eyes easily appearing twice their normal size by virtue of the makeup I am (much to my distress) becoming quite accustomed to applying, I nonetheless press my point. "G-shot, if there is any possibility at all that I might in some way aid and succor her even in her deepest distress, I must act upon it."

"Ma'am, I gotta tell you: the Boss, he's pretty definite 'bout what he wants. And he don't want her bothered. Because *she* don't want herself bothered."

"My understanding is that she is severely undermining if not outright destroying herself with drink. And you would therefore, by omission, become a party to condemning her to that fate?"

He is reluctant, yes, and even somewhat frightened (if such an emotion as fear could find any place in a man like G-shot), but though I regret abusing him in such a way, I press my moral advantage: without intervention, she may well die. And she might well die alone, despairing, and abandoned.

Abandoned. Like Charity. Like Faith.

Determined to make straight what I thought to be bent, I found Charity, brought her home, gave her a family. I took in Faith unquestioningly.

The Boss's mother? Can there be any doubt whatsoever about my course of action?

On my next day off, then, after calling at Mr. Anthony's music store to pick up a package, I navigate the ice-slick streets toward the address I have browbeaten out of G-shot...and find myself amid squalor. Here, then, is ample evidence of my abject failure and continuing incompetence: the down side of town. The forgotten side of Snow City. Crumbling buildings, ragged people in ragged clothes, undernourished faces and expressions ranging from vacant to furtive. Here are the lives my past has tarnished, the lives the Boss has sworn to keep this side of trouble. And, indeed, he might well be succeeding, but I cannot but wish he were succeeding better than he is...and that I myself had supplied him with more fortuitous raw materials.

I would not dare come here dressed as I would for Club Pizzazz, but even my customary attire — simple braid, modest skirt, blouse, coat, and hat — cannot but attract attention, and before I have reached the first turning, I am accosted.

A movement out of an alleyway, a gun in my face. He wants my purse and my package...and my memories leap back to a former existence in which he would have, without a second thought, wanted my life as well. Nevertheless, my hand remembers its former duties well, his gun is out of his possession and in mine in a moment, and the muzzle of the weapon thereupon cracks into his temple...and I all the while cursing myself inwardly for my knowledge and my ability.

Two more men are running up. His friends?

"What the hell you doin' here, Ms. Japonica?" demands one, and I recognize his as the voice that, months ago, alerted me to Faith's impending arrival. "Here we be tryin' to keep the homies out o' trouble, and you be showin' up an' wavin' fresh meat aroun'." He regards the prostrate form sprawled in a pile of muddy snow. "And turnin' into a one-girl army, too, looks like. *Lots* of surprises from you. Remin' me not to go up 'gainst those pretty little guns you got there."

"I confess I did not know you were here, sir," I tell him as I safety the gun and put it into his hand. "I would have been more than happy to allow you and your colleague to handle matters according to your own customs. But I am presently on an urgent errand. Would you do me the kindness of attending to this gentleman and disposing of his weapon appropriately?"

"We on it, Li'l Miss SEAL Team. I'd tell you to be careful in these parts, but it looks like you got those bases covered."

I bob my head thankfully and continue on my way, trying to ignore the sound upbraiding now in progress behind me:

"*What* the *hell* you be *thinkin'* of, Homes? You go pickin' on some blonde chicky-poo jus' because you think she an easy mark? Sho' as God's britches you got what was comin' to you. Jeezus Kay Raist, I got half a mind to finish up what she start."

A street, a corner, a turning...and the cold afternoon abruptly turns dim, as though an early evening has come to Snow City. But a glance at the sky tells me that the sun remains bright: it is the street itself that is shadowy, forlorn, the daylight seemingly repelled by the concrete and brickwork, broken hopes settling like so much soot in the heaped and half-melted snow, falling dark upon overhanging roofs and besmearing puddles of dirty water that seem as immobile and unchangeable as the mountains that surround the town. And deeper into the shadows I go, following G-shot's reluctant directions, finding a set of concrete stairs, climbing first up, then down, then stepping into a stagnant hallway lined with worn, battered doors: a nadir of human habitation existing at the heart of what I once hoped would be my refuge and my solace.

No refuge here. No solace. Only the bitter dregs of my imaginings trickled with dismaying inevitability to this center of heartbreak, leading me at last to a sagging door so neglected that it seems hardly more than a collection of splinters held together by peeling paint. Shifting my package to free a hand, half-afraid that even the politest tap of my knuckles might well reduce frame and panels alike to dust and slivers, I realize that I do not even know her name.

But I knock. "Ma'am?"

The door holds together...and swings inward on creaking hinges to reveal a bare room: clean enough, and warm, but ragged, worn, run-down. Facing me, a window, its curtains thin and yellowed with years of sun. To one side, a bed with a threadbare counterpane. Beside the bed, a dresser whose missing foot cants the top such that the dried remnants of ancient corsages and the dusty, framed photographs of a young woman with a violin are perilously close to slipping off. And near the center of the room, on a half-shredded rag rug, a low table, seated at which is an old woman, slumped forward, her head on the tabletop, a bottle in her hand.

"Ma'am?"

A presence behind me. A hand on my shoulder. "She's dead, Echo."

The Boss.

I glance back. His dark glasses mask his expression, but I see that his cheeks are damp.

"G-shot knows his buttered side from the dry," he says, his voice all but toneless. "He told me you were coming, and why, and I do appreciate the thought." He is speaking to me, but I know that his gaze is fixed on the solitary figure in the room beyond the door. "She died about an hour ago. I came here to check on her, just like I always do, and so I was there at the very end. She just kind of let go...finally. It was the drink. And grief. And all those other things that you just can't seem to pry away from someone once they get their hooks sunk in deep enough."

I glance down at the package in my hands, feeling the depth of my failure. "You informed me previously that she was dead —"

"Yeah." We are still standing in the hallway, looking through the open door as though viewing a scene in a shadowbox: the remnants and mementos of a woman's life compressed into a ten by twelve foot room, lit by a frost-patterned window and a bare electric fixture in the ceiling, the whole tale told with one sweep of the eye.

It is all here. The corsages, the photographs, the liquor bottle, the room itself: bare walls and cracked plaster. Here is a life begun bravely, then slowly eaten away by misfortune and by a perfectly understandable failure of spirit.

"Yeah, I did," he says. "And that was the truth. Just like what you're seeing now is the truth, and just like my telling you she died about an hour ago is the truth, too. That first death...well, that came with the drink. I saw it in her face. Something just went out of it. Oh, she smiled and all, but it wasn't *her* anymore. And then when she sold her fiddle, something else went out of her. Something big. She just started looking straight ahead, as though if she kept her eyes focused hard enough, she wouldn't see what she'd lost."

His mother's head, resting on the table, is turned away from me, and I am glad that I cannot see her face. "A sad end. To die in such unhappiness."

I feel the Boss's hand tighten briefly on my shoulder, and then he sighs. "That's the thing," he says softly. "I'm not sure she was all that unhappy toward the end. Sakes...people can find happiness in the damnedest things. Told you that before. I think that, maybe, she might have found her own happiness. Mind you, it wasn't anything like what you and I'd call happiness, but she made as if it suited her. She had a place to live, a nice warm room, and when it'd get hot, I'd come put an air conditioner in the window so she'd be comfortable. Every day I'd be by to tell her that I loved her, and I'd bring food and make her eat. And I'd throw out that damned squeeze the boys at the liquor store kept trying to fob off on her when they thought she was too far gone to notice. I'd get her good stuff. So she'd feel warm inside...in that cold place where her heart used to be...and not be sick come the next day."

He glances at the package in my hands.

"I tried that too. When things got better for me. I tried, but she'd given up by then. And I suppose that was a kind of freedom for her. A weight off her soul...so that it wouldn't crumble so fast. And maybe that made her happy, too."

I clutch the package to myself. Failure.

"But I think maybe she'd forgotten all about music," the Boss continues. "By the time I tried, I mean. She was just looking ahead, like I said, not seeing anything else."

"And you were present when she passed on."

"I wouldn't have had it any way else. I reckon I just knew, because I showed up early today."

A long breath. The long, whispering breath of a man faced with what he cannot change, what he must endure with the stoic courage that custom and the societal contract force upon him.

"I'm going to have to call the police, Echo," he says at last. "The coroner and his boys will want to come have a look at her, and I'll be having to make a statement. Best you go home: there's no reason you need to be associated with the likes of me beyond our professional relationship."

I turn my face from the scene beyond the door and meet the eyes behind the dark glasses. "And since when," I ask, "did abandoning a friend in time of need become appropriate behavior?"

He bows his head. Quietly then: "Thank you."

Silence, then. Silence in the hall. Silence in the room beyond. The hush of the dead. The deep, deep well of quietude left behind when the music has come to an end and the vast space once filled by such tenuous and fleeting things as notes, durations, pitches, harmony — or heartbeats, voices, loves, and loyalties — manifests in all its terrible emptiness and potential. And finally, as though stepping into a sanctuary, I enter the room and tread softly to the still form. Kneeling beside what was once a woman and is now dust, I unwrap my package and gently place a violin and a bow on the table, lifting her cold hand to settle it upon the instrument as though the two had never been parted.

CHAPTER FIFTEEN

The snows come heavy then, stacking drift upon drift, muffling sounds, frosting windows, confining pedestrians to narrow, shuffling pathways where once wide sidewalks beckoned, making even the simplest of automobile excursions a study in frictionless motility, and Faith and Charity and I must all take turns shoveling our driveway and front walk out from under what seems a near-daily accumulation of several inches of fresh powder. We therefore gratefully accept an offer of aid when, after one particularly heavy snowfall, our rosebush-tending neighbor produces from his amply furnished garage — *voilà!* — a snow blower...and proves quite willing to lend us his services *gratis*.

But he is happy to accept a cup of hot chocolate — one of Charity's specialties — in recompense for his time and his efforts, though he insists that, he being retired and a widower, both are his in abundance and are, as a result, of no consequence at all. We therefore, the four of us, spend a pleasant hour in the living room, sipping our chocolate, chatting, and watching even more snow being deposited outside by the latest in a series of storms that is demonstrating itself to be of more than passing persistence.

But I notice that Charity is falling increasingly silent, and by the time our neighbor leaves, she has withdrawn into nods and whispered monosyllables...which I can, upon reflection, understand.

"I really can't fathom the man at all," I say as, from the front window, I watch him pick his way across the slurry of snow and ice that hides our street.

"He seems pretty OK." But Charity's voice is barely audible above the sound of water and the clatter of cups and spoons that Faith is washing up in the kitchen.

I see our neighbor safely gain his front door, and I let the curtains fall back. "Charity...he hardly said a word to you. In fact, I don't think he said anything to you all the time he was here. He didn't even thank you for your chocolate. And he gave me *such* a look when I introduced you. As though I were some kind of madwoman."

She turns away from me — so unlike her — and I know that something is wrong. But I have known that something has been wrong all along, have I not? With Snow City? With my world? Now, however, it is manifesting not at the pedestrian mall or in the down side of town, much less in some half-real and fantastic *Grand Guignol* of a mountain clearing...but rather in my own living room, among the commonplaces of sofa, chairs, and area rugs.

My hands come to rest on her shoulders. "Charity...tell me. Please."

"It's OK, Mom. Really."

"Someone treating my daughter as though she doesn't exist is certainly *not* OK."

She shakes her head. "Mom...that's happening a lot now. People not seeing me, I mean."

I stare. Not seeing her? "Wh-what?"

"It's like I said. I'm not real. These days, I don't know whether I've *ever* been real. But it's like...like it's catching up with me now. People who already know me...they see me just fine. People who've never met me before..." She shrugs. "Well...they don't. I'm just not there."

"Perhaps they are afraid?"

"Mom..." Her voice is patient: the precocious adolescent educating the overly obtuse adult. "...people don't know I'm a ghost unless I tell them. It's always been that way. And, in any case, before, after I first came back, everyone could see me. You saw me on the bench at the mall, remember?"

I fold my arms about her. "I could never forget."

"But they're not seeing me now. If...like...we go to a new store or something, Faith has to do the checkout. Because the clerks don't see me. And..." She shrugs resignedly. "...the first-years at school don't see me. Same with the new teachers. They grade my homework and tests, sure, but they're always asking why Charity Monthage isn't in the classroom."

Still encircled by my arms, she turns to face me. Her eyes, though sad, are nonetheless brave, determined. As brave and determined, I am sure, as they were when she faced down the beckoning light and refused whatever afterlife might have been awaiting her.

"I don't know where this is going, Mom. Maybe I'm not supposed to be here anymore. Like...like maybe I've finished what I came back to do, whatever it was, and now that it's done, I'm...just not needed."

I grasp for words. "Please don't say that, Charity. You're needed. Everybody needs you. *I* need you. This whole world —"

I slam my mouth shut against the termination of the sentence and the hint of revelation it might contain. Yes, I need Charity. And since I need her, then this world, still changing with each passing day, growing (I dearly wish) larger and more wonderful but nevertheless (I deeply fear) more terrible, needs her even more, for what nightmares might be unleashed should its maker succumb to despair?

Her eyes again. Large. Green. Fathomless. Insightful. She looks...and she sees. Not the final secret, perhaps, but the fact that my own despair has begun. The Boss's mother. The man with the gun. The beggars, the destitute, the homeless wandering among the run-down and dirty buildings that grow colder with each passing day of shroud-like snow and ice...

...and...up in the mountains...

...and at the school.

She sees it. She has, I realize, been seeing it...hearing it...for some time now.

"Do you want to talk about it, Mom?"

"Talk..." Our roles have abruptly reversed. I, the comforter, have become the comforted. Yet despite her canniness, despite her ability, poised as she is on the cusp between adolescence and adulthood, to step without effort from one part to the other, I still attempt to shield her. "...about what?"

Another sigh. Precocious adolescent...or insightful adult? Obtuse adult...or shattered refugee from a horror-filled abyss? "C'mon, Mom," she says. "I've noticed. Remember that it's me who's sitting with you when you wake up from those nightmares. It's like you and me are two peas. We just come from different ends of the pod." Her green eyes lift to mine. "Sometimes I get the feeling you're just as much of a ghost here as me."

I feel my face go pale.

"So that puts us in the same boat," she continues as though she did not see...as though I do not know that she saw. "We need to hang together. Something's happening to me, and I'm pretty sure that something's happening to you. It's like...like something's just gone out of you. You smile and all, but it's not you anymore."

"Charity...Charity, I..."

"You're gonna have to 'fess up here, Mom. We can't have two out of three in the house going all achy-breaky. What's Faith gonna do if that happens? Where's she gonna live? The bio-things' estate is screwed up to the nines, the Boss is having trouble twisting enough arms about the formal adoption even though Faith's *not* dead, and she's still kicking herself for avoiding me for so long." Her eyes are tragic, yet sympathetic. "You don't hear her at night, Mom. She cries about it. In her sleep."

My hands are starting to my face — to hide my tears, to hide my shame — when a footstep comes to the kitchen doorway. Faith is standing there, dishtowel in hand, drying what I assume to be the last cup from our cocoa klatch. Her eyes, frank and brown, are on us. "Uh...am I interrupting something?"

Charity's voice turns light and breezy in an instant. "Not a bit, Sis. Mom's just mauling me a little. I think it's called 'bonding'."

Faith looks more than a little doubtful. "Uh...OK. I guess."

Faith cries at night. About Charity. I did not know.

But Charity turns back to me with the same impish grin I have seen in the past, and my heart lifts. Here are my daughters. Here is my family. Together. United. Safe. Maybe...maybe my dreams — my larger, wonderful dreams — *can* become true, all the nightmares swept away by something so simple as this mismatched and considerably more than outré household.

But I sense her lingering sadness. She has seen too much. Felt too much. Just like me. Except that her experiences are not threatening what she holds most dear. Except that my existence is not beginning to display signs of slow dissolution.

Charity motions for Faith to come join the group hug — "C'mon, Sis: we're all in this together." — but in the brief interval given the two of us while the older girl sets aside her cup and towel, she takes the opportunity to give me a light poke. "Looks like you're off the hook, Mom," she whispers.

And then once again I am rooted by those eyes. Can she see? Does she *know*?

"For now."

※

Though Charity does not press me further, my respite proves illusory, for as the snows continue into the new year, so do my nightmares, the latter steadily increasing in virulence until I am forced to close my bedroom door and put a pillow over my head when I retire lest my groans and cries awaken not only Charity but Faith as well. Come evenings, I crawl through my performances, determined to disgrace neither myself nor the composers whose works I play, but the pit of sorrow yawning widely beneath the flow of notes from the Ramirez frequently moves my listeners not to applause — whether perfunctory or enthusiastic — but to stunned silence, and I lift my tear-streaked, sweat-spangled face to a roomful of reactions ranging from imminent weeping to outright shock.

Clearly, this is no way for a musician of any sort to treat an audience, but though I see quite plainly the doubtful, worried expressions worn by Mr. O'Dally and Luigi (not to mention the Boss's reserved but deep concern), I can say nothing to them by way of explanation. I therefore do my best to fight my growing despair, hiding in the works of the masters, wrapping myself in their protection, taking courage from melody, harmony, and rhythm, burying myself in the purity of music.

But that is the waking world. My dreams provide, unfortunately, no such defenses or havens, and the nightmares continue...as do my increasingly inadequate and futile attempts to hide them. But strangely enough, with the approach of the spring holidays, it is Faith who finally comes to awaken me. And not because of my nightmares.

"M-mom," she says, "something's wrong with Charity. It's scaring me."

I rise and pull on a robe. "What is it, Faith?"

"I'm not sure. It's hard to describe. She's like...ice. Colder than usual, but there's more. A-and she won't wake up."

Her last statement sends me pelting down the hall to the girls' bedroom, where I find Charity in bed, her form, strangely transparent, illuminated by moonlight alone, her outlines delineated only by what seems to be the barest touch of twinkling starlight.

Her face is calm in repose, her hands, tranquilly folded on the thick comforter, might well be made of glass, the purest crystal. I can see the pillow and the fabric through them, and though the sight of my girl so bizarrely transformed terrifies me, I am nonetheless reassured by the utter serenity of her expression. For her — so says her face — care is gone, and she walks in profound bliss...somewhere.

"What do we do?" Faith whispers.

"I think..." I do not want to think. Thinking drags me toward the unthinkable. But Faith is my daughter, too, and I will not add to her fright. "...that she's all right. This is just...something that's happening to her." I put an arm about Faith's shoulders. "Part of what's been happening to her for a while." My elder daughter looks apprehensive, and I do my best to reassure her. "She told me about how some people aren't seeing her anymore, Faith. And maybe Father Hal said it best: she's on some kind of journey. I don't know what it is, but...but it can't but be for the best."

Faith's face is pale in the moonlight. "But you don't know for sure."

"No, I don't. But look at Charity's expression. If she accepts this with such equanimity, then shouldn't we try to accept it as well?"

Snow City

A long moment, and then the determination I see so often in Charity finds its way to her sister. "I'll stick with her no matter what. I'm not leaving her again."

But it is, I know, not a question of Faith leaving Charity, or, for that matter, of myself leaving Charity. Now it seems to be a matter of Charity leaving *us*.

I look at her Saint Christopher medal, strangely solid against her transparency.

A strange journey indeed.

Stranger than that, even, for after Faith, desperate, turns on the room lights, Charity assumes once again her semblance of real flesh and blood, opens and blinks large eyes at us, and asks us what might be the matter.

"Char...you were hardly there!" Faith blurts out. "You looked like you were made of glass!"

Later, in a robe, sitting in the living room with a cup of herb tea warming hands that will never again be warm of themselves, Charity ponders her sister's words. "Yeah...yeah...I guess I was in some weird places." For an instant, I see her eyes drift in my direction, but then, almost embarrassedly, she turns them back toward Faith. "I'm sorry I scared you, Sis. But...it's, like, all starting to make sense now." Incredibly, she smiles at both of us, radiant, pure as the angelic presence with which I have always compared her. "It'll be all right," she tells us. I'm sorry if I freaked you out." Once more that wry grin, that impish smile. "Hey...for crying out loud, you both gotta get used to stuff like this if you're gonna be living with a ghost!"

Though her humor strikes me as forced, Faith takes it as genuine, and for the first time since she awakened me, I see her relax. A ghost, perhaps, but her sister nonetheless. And if Charity can smile about it, then it must indeed be all right. And therefore she allows herself to be persuaded back to bed, Charity herself guiding her down the hall, pausing only briefly at the bedroom door to give me a wink and thumbs-up.

Which leaves me to the night, the memories that haunt me, and the terrors that make darkness anything but my friend. Unlike Faith, I cannot be so sanguine about Charity's reassurances. Something happened this cold, March night, something that reaches back to the time I saw Charity flitting, wraith-like and lost, through the cold pools of light beneath the streetlamps outside my apartment window. But after playing three exhausting sets, I arrived home not more than two hours ago, and fatigue is pulling me to my bed...no matter that that particular article of furniture has, to my eyes, begun to assume, increasingly, the characteristics of an Inquisitorial rack.

I fall asleep without knowing it, and I am again enmeshed in the terrors of a world in which I witnessed the torments of a thousand Charitys — strung up on scaffolds, hung from gibbets, beheaded, dismembered, shot, raped — where my hand was often upon the grip of a handgun or a carbine, where, daily, the newscasts showed entire cities dissolving under the withering plague of deliberately spread pathogens, and where the madness of Brother John and his congregation was reflected again and again in the eyes of fanatics, believers, patriots...

...but this time, all, everything, is tactile, immediate, *present*. I see and feel more than I ever have before, more in the duration of a single breath than I have in all my previous visions. Plexed, re-plexed, enfolded and re-enfolded, layers of war, wounds, empty eye sockets, burnt flesh, bubo-riddled torsos, the bewildered faces of mutilated children, the withered and stumpy revenants of weaponized leprosy, the distant flash of retina-searing nuclear fire expanding tremendously, hugely, infinitely fast, ever-growing, laying its incinerating hand on continent and sea alike, stretching out to seize the entire globe, turning the vast, gray, and polluted sphere to a seething pool of liquid fire —

The scream is out of my throat before I can stop it.

But there is a cool hand on my mouth, muffling the sound, and another hand on my shoulder, holding me gently but firmly down lest I fling myself out of the sheets and onto the floor, senseless of bedroom, house, city, world...trapped still in that crashing hell of gouting steam and molten rock.

"There, there," Charity is saying as she moves her hand from my mouth to my forehead. "There, there...it was a dream. It's OK, Mom. You'll be fine."

Still in the grip of what I have seen, heard, and felt, I struggle against her, "It's real. I saw. It was real...and it's all gone..."

"Shh..."

"Oh, dear God...it's all gone...and it's gone for real. I *saw* it..."

"Shh, now, Mom. Shh." Charity's hand is cool on my brow, her eyes, serene and deep, comforting, and they draw me gently from the coils of the dream and back to reality.

Reality?

"There's nothing left!"

"I know," she says simply. "I saw."

My fevered head cradled by the sweat-soaked pillow, I look up at her. Again, she is transparent, limned in a starlit haze. Her eyes are perhaps the most solid thing about her, but I can make out, even in the darkened room, her expression, one compounded equally of infinite peace, infinite sympathy, infinite...

...shall I call it sadness? Loss? Grief? But if I do, then surely those painful emotions have somehow expanded to so extraordinary an extent as to transcend themselves, transmuting spontaneously from sorrow to mystery, and from mystery to infinite, infinite joy.

I cannot fathom Charity's expression. I can no longer fathom Charity herself. But:

"You...saw...?"

A slow nod. "That time before, when Faith came and got you, I was in your dreams, Mom. And I was in them again just now. It's like I said: we're two peas. Just different ends of the pod. And so we're like...simpatico. That's why you found me in the first place, I think. And that's why I wound up seeing your dream life." An automobile passing down the street outside flicks the window with its headlights, momentarily solidifying her where the streaks of illumination fall upon her transparency. "At first I wasn't quite sure what it was, and it was all 'OMFG, what the hell's this'? But then I felt that you were there too, and I managed to put it all together. I..." She sighs, turning her head away for a moment. "I'm sorry I pulled the third degree stuff back when we were having all the snow, but I just...well, like, I just wanted to know. I still do. And I think it's time you told me. Because I've been seeing stuff, and I think I'm supposed to do something about it. But I can't...until I know what it is I've been seeing."

I stare up at her, half afraid that I might fall into those abyssal green eyes, but she reaches out and switches on the bedside light, regaining her solidity.

"That's better," she says. "I'm a ghost, but I don't have to stuff it up your nose, do I?"

"Charity, I..."

She shakes her head, amber hair rustling. "No more fooling around, Mom. You gotta tell me."

"I don't want to hurt you."

She leans close. "Mom...I'm a ghost. It can't hurt me."

And so, in the hour just before dawn, with spring in the offing and the grip of the snow beginning to break, reluctantly relinquishing the frozen earth to the encroachments of crocuses and the first optimistic and probing leaves of tulips, with the arrival of morning advancing, daily, second by second, minute by minute, and the balance of dark hours and bright hours tipping steadily toward the light, I make my confession to Charity.

I tell her everything. About my former world. About what happened there. About how it might well be a mercy that the end for that world came quickly, all but instantly, in a burst of heaving, actinic fire. But, more grievously, I tell her about how Snow City came to be: from my dreams, from my denial of what *was* and my constant, unrelenting, internal affirmation of what *could be*. About my awakening one morning to that *could be* having been made *is*. About my first bewildered hours and days as I tried to fit together the pieces of my new life, poring over pay stubs, income tax returns, driver's license, computer files, address books, telephone caller IDs...

"I noticed my hands right away," I tell her. "They were so different. That was a shock." Though I do not explain why. "It must have taken me an hour to work up the nerve to look in the mirror."

"Were you scared when you did?"

Am I really telling her all this? "Yes and no. Yes, because it meant that I was really here. No, because I'd been seeing myself this way for a long time. In my dreams. When I created my life here. I was never what I was...before. I was always...what I am now."

She smiles. "Always *Echo*?"

"Yes. Always a reflection of someone else."

"You're not someone else. You're you. And you're my mom. And this is the world." She puts a cool hand to my cheek. "And I don't particularly care how it got here. It's my world. And it's your world. And I'd say you did a pretty good job."

I heave myself up then, wrap my arms around her, the hot tears stinging my eyes. "Charity...I'm so sorry...about all of it. I thought I'd made everything perfect here, but...but...it looks like some things followed me. Or maybe I was just so used to thinking of a horrible world that I wound up building some of it into this one. It wasn't supposed to be this way. You weren't supposed to come back only to be tossed out by your family. Brother John wasn't supposed to egg your parents on until they did...those things. There weren't supposed to be bad places here, or people having to give up what they loved, or —"

"Shh...shh..." Charity rocks me just as I so often in the past have rocked her. "It's going to be OK, Mom. Now I know. And now I think I know why I came back. The real reason. I mean...like...it was for my friends and all, but what I said before is true: I'll never grow up, get married, or have a family. And I can't die because I'm already dead. So all of that's out. My friends, and Faith: they're all going to be moving on. Next year'll be third year for me and Rebekah and the rest, and they're all planning for college — heck, Faith is going to be *in* college — and I'm still going to be hunking around, a sixteen-year-old ghost." A long sigh. A long, conscious sigh. "But now I think I've figured it out. Now I've got something to do."

My eyes are clenched so hard they ache. "What, Charity? What do you have to do?"

She takes hold of my arms and waits for me to look at her. And when I do, when we are face to face, my eyes pleading and hers fathomless, opening into mysteries and perhaps into solutions to the seemingly insoluble: "I'm going to fix it, Mom. You've done..." Another shake of her head, she herself seemingly baffled at the enormity of what she has to express in such paltry and limited things as words. "...everything for me. You took me in. You gave me a home. You didn't give a damn about death or ghosts. I needed someone, and you were there. You loved me...and I want you to know that...that I love you."

I nod, speechless, frightened at the thought of what might be coming.

"But my time here is running out. People are starting to not see me. I'm turning into a glass statue at night. I'm going to have to go where I was supposed to go in the first place. But you took care of me, so I'm gonna darn well take care of you. You made a beautiful world, Mom. But you brought some bad stuff with you — or it followed you or something — and there's more bad stuff eating at you every night. You know it, I know it...I think in some ways even Faith knows it. And the Boss has been calling me on my cell three and four times a week, asking whether there's anything he can do for you."

"There's nothing anybody can do."

"That's not true. Maybe normal people can't help you. But I can. I'll have to go eventually. OK, fine. But when I go, I'm going to grab hold of all the bad stuff that's hanging onto you...and I'm going to take it away. So you won't have to worry about..." Tears are streaking her face. "...about all that. You can just live here...and be happy...and have Faith for a daughter and have all the friends you've made...and you can play your music not because you have to so that you don't go crazy, but because music's a good thing. And that's gonna be my gift to you, Mom. My way of repaying you for everything you've done for me. My way of making up for all the bad things I kicked off when I came back."

"Charity, you didn't —"

She lays a chill finger on my lips. "If there's guilt going around, we've gotta share it. The two of us. I was selfish and wanted to come back. And maybe that was just enough to tip the balance and set loose what you always wanted to keep chained up. There's no way of telling. But since I have to go anyway, I've got a chance to settle everything once and for all. To set it right." She smiles. Again: that sorrow so transcendent that it mingles inextricably with utter joy. "And that's what I'm gonna do." For a moment, the spunky sixteen year old surfaces again. "I'm..." She laughs, and I seem to hear the bright sound coming from a distance, as though she is already standing in a separate place, one lying beyond Snow City, this world, the bournes of life itself. "...I'm just not sure how I'm supposed to do it." That wry smile. "God...you'd think there'd be a user's manual or something."

"I'll help, Charity. We'll all help. But I never thought of anything like this when I made Snow City. So I don't know what to do either."

She takes my hand, still smiling. "It's your world, Mom. And like I said, you did a good job. So something's gonna turn up. I just know it. We might not get a user's manual, but we'll get a...a signpost or something. And we can take it from there."

And something does indeed turn up, for the weeks pass, Faith graduates, Rebekah runs again. Charity sits nightly by my bed, guarding me from my nightmares, though I do not expect ever again to see that...other place. Spring gives way to summer, and our neighbor's roses bloom while he, determined to prolong the season of flowers — as I myself (though knowing full well that, just as with roses, her season will inevitably end) wish my own flower might linger as long as possible — determinedly prunes and deadheads.

I wonder often about the man with the gun, the down side of town, the hopeless faces I saw there, and though I am enough of a coward that I avoid revisiting the area, I find in myself, after my confession and my unspoken absolution, enough courage to perform again as I once performed: letting the masters speak for themselves without burdening their music with my despair.

And shortly after summer vacation begins, Charity brings me her cell phone, the screen displaying an e-mail message from Uncle Seymour.

My dear niece,
I don't think a day goes by that I don't think of you. I know there isn't a night when I don't talk to God and do my best to put in a good word for you. I hope you're getting along, and I hope what happened last year hasn't put scars into your heart that are too deep for you to handle. I talk to God about that, too. And I don't forget to mention your sister and all your friends. And of course, there's Echo. I imagine she's having a fine time managing a household with two daughters. Come to think of it, I seem to have picked up

a new niece along the way, and I haven't met her yet. Looks like you'll have to be paying me another visit.

And I think it ought to be soon, because there's that field up here where you used to go horseback riding. You always looked like you didn't have a care in the world when you were trotting Sugar or Shadow through all the tall grass and the flowers. Funny thing, though, everything else around the ranch has greened up real nice, and the black-eyed Susans and buttercups and bluebells are piling on like there's no tomorrow. Except in that one field. It's still bare and it's got nothing but old, dry stalks sticking out of the ground. And Sugar and Shadow won't go into it.

I think it's waiting for you to come set it right.
Your loving uncle,
Seymour

I finish reading, lift my eyes to Charity's.

"I think something else is waiting for me there too, Mom," she says.

CHAPTER SIXTEEN

Judith Gap again. Plains and mountains surround us, summer fields ripe with early wheat, hawks wheeling on high thermals, antelopes flashing into view and out again, our automobile rolling through the miles, past town and wind farm, pausing at rest stops and snack shops, then rolling on once more along the lonely asphalt with the wind sweeping evenly across all.

Faith has her driver's license, and would spell me at the wheel without complaint, but I know that her real desire, if not outright need, is to be with Charity, making up as best she can for the time during which the two were estranged, and so — without complaint — I handle the entire drive, leaving the girls to hold hands silently in the back seat, to share the quiet communion of affectionate siblings for as long as they can...before their inevitable parting.

And parting there will be without question, for Charity is indeed leaving us. A cursory look at her in daylight reveals nothing more than an amber-haired girl with large green eyes and an unusually pale complexion. Nights, however, return her to transparency, and when my sleep in our Sheridan hotel room was broken by Faith's quiet mumblings and sobs and I rose to make sure my daughters, living and dead, were safe and well, I found the older with her arms clasped about the almost invisible figure of the younger, unwilling to relinquish her grasp, even though the time for that embrace is limited.

And how limited it is, I can see perhaps better than Faith, for even now, with the road stretching north and the sun pouring down like honey, my glances in the rearview mirror will, upon occasion, reveal Faith, but not Charity, the undead sister already withdrawing her reflection from the world as she will soon withdraw her very existence.

What farewells she made to her friends and her teachers and to Father Hal and even the Boss himself I do not know, but I do know that she made them, for she came home late one afternoon very solemn and quiet — quiet compared even to the stillness that had been surrounding her since my confession to her and her subsequent absolution and decision — and simply asked me, "Will we be leaving soon, Mom?"

"Tomorrow morning," was my reply, and she looked relieved: no lingering afterthoughts, no turning back, no uncomfortable chance meetings. All was in order, in place, finished, done... put away. In the future there would be other lives to be lived in Snow City, colleges to attend, marriages to be celebrated, children, relationships, friendships. But they would not include her. That door was closed to her. Indeed, she had closed it herself, with her own hand, her own decision, her own determination — spunky and forthright to the last! — to lay to rest that which my inadequacies had marred from, perhaps, the very beginning.

And perhaps it is that decision and determination that lends to her such grace as I from time to time see when her visibility allows it. She knows where she is going. She knows what she must do. There is no fear in her, not the slightest hesitation, and she steps from the car to the ground in front of the modest house, corral and barn and runs to greet Uncle Seymour, Jesse, and Esmeralda with an expression of unalloyed bliss, as though whatever might lie before her, whatever task must be done, whatever barrier must be surmounted, whatever border must be passed, she cannot but, with such friends and such a family to support her, transcend all, doing and surmounting and surpassing with the same stubborn grit as that which remade her physical body and brought her back from the dead.

I lead Faith to her new relatives, introduce her, and coax her past her innate shyness, and then the girls go to meet the horses — Sugar and Shadow — who have been at the rails of the corral, waiting patiently ever since our automobile appeared in the distance, and when Jesse (in his monosyllabic way) and Esmeralda (wiping her perfectly clean hands on her apron) take their leave and return to their chores, Uncle Seymour and I are left alone in the yard, the sigh of the wind interspersed with the light voices of the girls at the corral and the occasional squawk of a chicken from the coops around the corner of the house.

"You've raised them well," says Uncle Seymour. "You should be proud of them."

"Nay, I must protest: I cannot take any credit whatsoever for their virtues."

"Oh, yes you can." And with that he guides me around the house to the field on the eastern side of the barn, the field in which Charity discovered her love of horseback riding and her fondness for Sugar and Shadow...and theirs for her.

It is indeed a striking scene. The rest of the land belonging to the ranch shows a vigorous growth of wheat and hay, clover and wildflowers, vegetables and the generous apple trees. This field, however, is desolate: brittle, leafless stems from last year's blooms, dry grass bent flat by the winter snows. All is brown and gray, as though the very earth is in mourning.

"Like I said in the e-mail, the horses won't go in," says Seymour as we contemplate the barrenness. "But it isn't like they're scared of the place. It's more like they're saving it. For Charity. Like they know she has something to do here, and they don't want to spoil it for her."

"She is going to leave the world, Uncle Seymour."

"I reckon I guessed that."

My eyes are on the field. Dry. Barren. "She cannot grow up. She cannot change. The world will move beyond her and leave her behind. Indeed, it is already doing so. And..." Is my wayward tongue threatening to betray me? I defy it. "...and I believe she has some private affairs to which to attend in the course of her passage. Some unfinished business."

Whose affairs, whose business, I do not say.

At my words, Seymour gives me a long, searching look. He speaks to God often. And God, I do not doubt, speaks to him.

What, I wonder, has God told him?

"I guess she does, Echo," he finally says.

※

Like the somber festivals that marked the progress of healing among the high school's wounded — the girls giggling in muted, almost reverential tones, the boys engaging in reserved, respectful banter — supper that evening is a strange mix of cheer and sorrow. Esmeralda provides a feast of main courses and side dishes, with no less than three pies for dessert, and all of us, from Uncle Seymour presiding at the head of the table, to Jesse, to the workmen and the ranch hands and even Esmeralda herself (coaxed out of her kitchen and into the place of honor opposite the master of the house by my courteous insistence and the girls' laughing tugs at her apron), do our best to pretend that this meal does not presage a departure no less painful than eternal.

Only Charity herself seems unaffected by the ambivalent and uncertain mood. Hers, instead, is the quiet assurance of a steady heart that has at last realized its purpose and its goal. Lit by lamplight and candlelight and, from the open window, the last touches of a rosy sunset that together conspire to give a deceptive vigor to her unnatural pallor, she passes dishes, plates, and helps the gnarled ranch hands about her to meat and drink with smiles and a glow of sanctity, as if by her simple and common actions she could (if only she knew, if only we all could comprehend, interpret) demonstrate the profound sacredness of every action and every moment of this world, the world of Snow City. But even her seeming impotence — she unknowing, we oblivious — is, by her own existence, transmuted into profundity, and in so being, strengthened into puissance, for the sacramental nature of Snow City can in truth only be grasped (and watching her, I begin to understand darkly, obscurely) when it passes unnoticed, unthought-of, without comment. Its true nature is that of unselfconscious kindness, of axiomatic virtue, of harmony so innate as to be self-evident.

And there is my lesson. And there is my loss. I am creatrix and dreamer, and I am — and have been — all too aware of the origins and meaning of Snow City. And like the musician, painter, or sculptor who begins to consider obsessively each motion of each finger, each stroke of the brush, each placement of the chisel and tap of the mallet, the conscious mind intruding into the creative flow of muscle and instinctive reflex until art disintegrates into a morass of failure, I have introduced into this world my own awareness, my own conscious meddling, and thus have endangered — outright broken — the very perfection and harmony I so wished to preserve.

Can Charity take that with her as well? Make the dreamer unconscious of the dream? Even when the dream itself depends upon a conscious determination to reject horror and embrace the artless kindness of an impossible world made real? I wanted...so much...for Snow City. I wanted the immense, perhaps impossible, remaking and refocusing of everything I knew about human nature. Can one girl correct what took years of yearning and nightly wishes both to perfect and to indelibly mar?

There she is: young but unliving, fresh but destined for an ending that knows nothing of decay, fragile yet possessed of an unbending will and an unflinching courage

And therefore she can. And she will.

And when, at the end of the meal, Uncle Seymour rises and lifts his glass with, "To journeys, and to their endings. To final rests in safe havens," and we join him in his toast, I hear Charity's murmured addition: "And to happiness for all," and I find my throat so tight with tears — joyful or sorrowful, I cannot tell — that I am all but unable to echo the words.

What sleeping the three of us — Charity, Faith, and myself — manage that night, we manage together, as if by sharing a bed in the small guest house, hands clasped, arms about one another, we can...perhaps not prolong (for prolongation is impossible, the dawn rolling toward us inexorably), but rather intensify our remaining time, even though that time might be spent as dreamers dreaming amid a larger, vastly encompassing dream. And though the world, the universe, is now poised upon the brink of a cataclysmic metamorphosis at once far larger and more profound even than the effort of will and frantic passion that created it, I remain unvisited by so much as a hint of nightmare. Instead, I dream of the world — this world — as it should be, as it (so I hope) can be, as perhaps it actually is, the accretions of violence and madness I have witnessed proving in the end to be no more than a brittle and crumbling facade that has obscured only briefly my intended perfection, an encrustation now about to be scrubbed and chipped away, revealing once again hope, love, and affirmation.

Can it be?

I hope so.

But I open my eyes in the darkness to find that (almost as I expected) Charity is not with us. But it is not her time yet, and I find her at the window, looking out at the full moon, the study in silver and sable that is the yard, the prairies stretching on and on, and in the distance, the dark hints of mountains.

And above all, stars. Stars and more stars. The Milky Way arches over us, reminding me of galactic distances beyond any human contemplation, the infinity of space and the time that binds it into existence, wholeness, and the toils of birth and death.

"It's beautiful, Mom," she says when she feels me standing behind her.

"It's lovely indeed."

She turns to me, and her transparency is only heightened by the slant of moonlight falling through the glass. Only her eyes are firm, definite...and perhaps it is only their definiteness that is visible, her gradual slipping away rendering all other manifestations inconsequential. "And you gotta remember that, Mom. You just gotta. It *is* a pretty world. It's a good world. And the people here are all good people. Look at the Boss: he's a crime lord, but he helps people out all the time, and he doesn't do that whole exploitation thing. And, yeah, I know he's got girls on the streets, but he protects them, and he gives them their fair share, and, heck, I found out from G-shot before we left that he's got medical insurance for them and even money socked away for their college tuition if they ever want to go that route. And G-shot: yeah, he pounds people every now and then, but he pounds them for a reason."

"Only when they deserve to get hurt," I murmur, remembering words spoken to me a bare year ago.

"Yeah. You got it. But the Boss is, like, the safety net. For everyone. He's there for when people get to their lowest. And most of them don't get to their lowest in any case. They're just at the club for some fun and maybe to snatch a piece, but deep down they're all good...a-and you gotta remember that, Mom. Because you made them that way. And you made a whole lot of people who are...just great. I mean, look at the girls in my class: they're all cute as buttons, with personalities to match. And the boys...darn it, every one of them wouldn't say a harsh thing if his life depended on it, and they'd all give up everything for each other if the stuff ever hit the fan."

I look out at the moonlit world, wondering. Did I really do all that?

"So it's not your fault some things went wrong. It's like you said: people make their own choices. And you've been..." She clings to me as though the reality of her departure has suddenly made itself real enough that her fear is overcoming her hopes. "...you've been wonderful. You're the best mom a girl could have. A-and...I want you to know that even when I'm gone, you'll still be my mom. And I might not know where I'm gonna be, but if being there means that I'm not going to be able to see you now and then, or at least stay close to you somehow, then whoever's in charge is going to have some problems."

I have no doubt of the victor in such a confrontation. "What future journeys we might have together," I tell her, "or where they might take us should they come, I don't know, but there will always be a room in my house and a place at my table for you. I don't think I need mention my heart."

She hugs me, unabashed, without a trace of the shyness of a sixteen year old uncomfortable with expressions of affection toward a parent. "I know."

Outside, a mockingbird begins its song, echoed a moment later by a territorial robin bent upon reaffirming its claim upon its range, its nest, and its mate. Some moment, some cusp between one time and another has passed — perhaps the faint breeze has freshened as if in prophecy of a coming day, perhaps it is simply instinct built up over millions of years of imagined evolution — and I know what Charity's next words will be.

"Time for me to get ready," she says.

⊷╂╂⊶

The full moon rides low in the west, casting shadows at once slanting and profound, and the field is dark, but its rough landscape of downed grass and broken stems makes itself evident nonetheless: subtle variations in the play of light, the rustle of meadow mice amid dry stalks, a rattle of old weeds in the tireless wind.

It is not dawn yet, but the chill in the air tells of the light to come, and our small group at the western end of the field — Faith, myself, Seymour, Jesse, and Esmeralda — zips jackets and buttons coats, speaking to one another of commonplaces, and of summer's height and the eventual harvest...neither of which Charity will see.

Charity herself is off at the stables. It was her request that one of the horses might accompany her. "It's just borrowing, Uncle Seymour," she said. "I promise."

"Borrowing is fine," he replied. "And even if you need someone to go with you all the way, that's perfectly all right, too. I'm sure Sugar or Shadow will be happy to stay in the company of such a fine girl."

The lantern he held let us see her, and Charity blushed as much as her condition would allow, but she assured him that borrowing would be enough; and then she took the lantern and vanished into the darkling pre-dawn, and we heard the sound of the stable door.

"Will she be all right?" Uncle Seymour asks as the minutes lengthen. Jesse and Esmeralda plainly do not know, though their understanding of what is about to take place is more than evident in their expressions. Faith knows, but is too close to tears to utter anything coherent. I take it upon myself to answer.

"She is an angel," I say, praying that I am speaking the truth, that despite her human — but imagined — girlhood and her all-too-real trials and sorrows, she nonetheless possesses something of the celestial, some rarified and precious distillation of all that is good about this world. "She is doing what we all wish to do someday. She is returning home."

"Home." Uncle Seymour sighs. "Home's a good place to go. You're always welcome at home." His hand descends upon my head like a benediction. "A comforting thought, Echo. Thank you."

The sound of horse hooves accompanied by a softer, human tread in the darkness that is now lightening imperceptibly, the distant, eastern mountains beginning to exhibit, at their topmost peaks, a faint but distinct presence, and Charity appears, leading the saddled and bridled Sugar. She is, to my surprise, dressed in her winter coat and snow boots...in fact, she is clad exactly as she was when she wandered homeless and unwanted among the streets of Snow City, when a blonde musician first saw her, worried about her, obsessed about her, and at last took her in.

"Sugar said she'd take me," she explains. "Shadow was crying too hard." She sees my eyes searching her garments, and she shrugs. "What happened up in the mountains...and then afterward...it told me that I'm supposed to go out as I came in." She musters a wan smile. "Remember: these clothes came back with me. They don't belong here any more than I do."

"Dear girl, you always belong here."

"Not anymore, Mom. Besides..." She hands me the lantern and turns eastward, toward the imminent dawn. "...I've got a job to do." A pause, a moment of rest wherein even the wind temporarily ceases, falls silent, holds itself bated, waiting, and then: "It's time."

Solemnly, then, she hugs us all. Uncle Seymour. Esmeralda. Jesse. Faith...lingering in the embrace as though that will allow her to recall throughout whatever eternity awaits her the feel, scent, shape, heartbeat...everything about her older sister. Faith, half a head taller, bends to rest her cheek on Charity's shoulder.

But the dawn is still growing, and Charity finally turns to me, and for the last time I — once the stranger, now the full participant — can fill my arms with my daughter, trying in my own way to imprint every detail of her existence into my memory.

"Take care of my sister, Mom," she whispers.

"There's no doubt of that," I reply. "Faith is my own flesh and blood." And only Charity could know just how true that is, Faith and, indeed, everything, living and unliving — air, earth, seasons, fire, water, love — being of me and therefore one with me. A terrible burden, an infinite joy...and I wonder whether that knowledge will indeed be taken from me with Charity's passing. I suppose I will find out. But will I know that I know? I cannot say that I care anymore: all this, this sky, these fields and mountains, tiniest dust mote and remotest galaxy...all are no longer about me, but rather about Charity, completely about Charity, with no room, not the smallest interstice, for the entrance of any other concern.

One last tightening of her arms, then. "Remember, Mom," she whispers so that only I can hear. "You have to remember: it's not your world anymore. It's everybody's world. They all get to make their own decisions. They all get to choose their own lives. You can't take responsibility for what they all do. That's not your job." She pulls away just far enough for me to see her smile, half transparent in the faint light, but blindingly, tranquilly present. "Even moms have to let go eventually, right?"

With an ease she learned from Jesse and Uncle Seymour, then, she sets her foot to the stirrup and swings into the saddle. Starlight crowns her, blurring and haloing about the whisper of visibility that is her hair and face, but my eyes are not so filled with tears that I cannot see her pause thoughtfully...and reach to her collar.

Then she is bending down from the saddle, her hands going around my neck, fastening the chain of the Saint Christopher medal. "I have to go as I came," she whispers. "And I think it's your journey now. So you should have this."

A long look at all of us, then. A nod. And once again her eyes alight on me.

"'Bye, Mom," she says simply, and then, without waiting for a reply, she gently tugs at Sugar's reins and sets off into the field, into the growing light, her figure transparent at first, invisible in the darkness, but taking on a semblance of solidity as the sun gathers itself at the rim of the world and the horizon gains definition, broadens, and grows ever more brilliant.

The daystar is a ball of flame now, eclipsing the mountains, and Charity is still riding into the field, growing smaller with distance and with a remoteness that has nothing to do with yards or miles, but with a more transcendent breadth, one that spans life and death, that stretches between worlds. And still she rides, shrinking to a dark dot in the ever-growing light, finally vanishing into an incandescence that is more than any simple manifestation of solar fire, that cannot but stem and proceed eternally from that primordial blaze that dwells beyond the gates of the firmament whose portals are now swinging wide to admit a stray child, long lost, a child coming home at last. Nor is her arrival devoid of greeting, for just as my dazzled eyes tear beyond sight with both light and the pain of parting, I catch a glimpse of a young woman's form, flaxen hair streaming in the dawn light, standing infinitely far off yet immanently close, slender arms outstretched in welcome to one who was, for a handful of months and a few scattered weeks, mine, my own, my daughter, and though I know that, mortal as I am, I can demand no guarantees and no assurances, still I find all uncertainty banished from my heart, replete as that presence is with the very essence of hope.

Eyes streaming, blinded by the light, I lower my head at last, wondering, as murmurs from the others begin to surround me, how I can continue to live, to work, to exist in Snow City. But a clutch at my arm recalls me: Faith.

"Mom...look."

She is pointing at the field. The sun has risen, and a more homely light has taken the place of the divine fire of which we were allowed a brief glimpse. But the field that was, minutes before, a wasteland of wrack and drought, of withered grass still caught in the cold, dry clasp of winter, is now green, lush, alive with buttercups and black-eyed Susans and bluebells and sweet clover, the colors and the hues deepening, becoming ever more vibrant as, moment by moment, the sun climbs into the sky and the new day begins.

I look at Faith. Her eyes are brown and frank.

"She set it right," she says.

Minutes pass. Jesse at last gives us a nod and drifts off, called by the day's work. Esmeralda goes to start a belated breakfast for the ranch hands who are already up, gathered at the house, and hungry. Uncle Seymour plants his lips gently and momentarily atop my head and strides off to the church: no formal service, but rather a personal and very private conference with the One he serves.

Only Faith and I remain throughout the day, waiting and watching, wondering whether we might be vouchsafed some final reassurance, fleeting though it may be, of the safety and well-being of the one we love. But, really, we need no such thing. Her safety is without question. Her well-being is assured. Indeed, she has passed beyond any need for either.

Still, we wait. And at last, in the lengthening shadows of evening, with the field now as lush as any other on the ranch, flowers nodding and grass waving in the endless wind, Sugar comes back.

Charity does not.

EPILOGUE

Daughter Faith is away now, attending college in the state capital. I had hoped for a music major, but it seems that literature calls to her more strongly than notes and melody.

Having resumed my performances at my two venues, my life is once again full of the precision of the classical guitar, the Ramirez a demanding but sympathetic partner in my work, my audiences appreciative, my employers considerate and approving. I continue to play the chaconne for the Boss — some things do not change, will never change — but I am afraid that whether he knows it or not (and I suspect that he does indeed know it), he must share that intricate cathedral of sound with another, one who will live always in my music, one who graced my life and then moved on, gifting me not only with the Saint Christopher medal that I always wear but, selflessly, with a final, profound blessing...the nature of which, though I instinctively sense its monumental consequence, I do not, strangely enough, seem able to remember.

It is afternoon, and I am practicing for the evening's performance. The house is, aside from me, empty, but that does not matter anymore. There is emptiness, yes, but it is filled with a thousand memories...and if there is any regret mingled with that warm river of recollection, I cannot find it.

The telephone rings: Faith. Telling me that she will, as usual, be home for the weekend. I believe she worries about me being alone, but I am not alone. I have my music...and my many friends.

And more than friends, I sometimes think, for the telephone eventually rings again.

"Echo? Maxwell. I've been thinking about you today. Of course, I always think about you. But I wonder if you'd do me the honor of having dinner with me this evening...after your gig at the Blue Rose, of course. A late dinner? Someplace quiet?"

I smile. "That would be nice. I'd like that, Maxwell."

"Call me Max."

My name is Echo Japonica. I think sometimes that perhaps I had another name once, but I do not remember it now. And when I reflect on my life — my girlhood, the nervous way in which I first entered the Blue Rose coffee shop and asked (with ridiculous timidity) whether there might be any desire for a guitarist, the placid, peaceful years I have spent plying my art among the odors of coffeecake and steamed milk and lattes and espressos...and the strange way in which I managed to pick up a new and rather unusual gig, one night a week, at Club Pizzazz — questions about old names and even old existences evaporate, and then I am sure that, without question, I have always been nothing other than myself, and that I have always lived — lived, loved, made music — here in Snow City.

Made in the USA
San Bernardino, CA
13 March 2018